ATHLETES IN ACTION

ATHLETES IN ACTION

THE OFFICIAL INTERNATIONAL AMATEUR ATHLETIC FEDERATION BOOK ON TRACK AND FIELD TECHNIQUES

EDITED BY

HOWARD PAYNE

EDITORIAL BOARD
JIM ALFORD (IAAF) · FRANK DICK (BAAB AND ECA) · HELMAR HOMMEL (DLV)
PHOTO-SEQUENCES
HELMAR HOMMEL · HOWARD PAYNE
ADDITIONAL PHOTOGRAPHS · TONY DUFFY

IAAF DEVELOPMENT PROGRAMME BOOK NO.5

PELHAM BOOKS

First published in Great Britain by
Pelham Books Ltd
44 Bedford Square
London WC1B 3DU
1985

British Library Cataloguing in Publication Data

Athletes in action: the official International
    Amateur Athletic Federation (IAAF) book of
    track and field techniques.
    1. Track-athletics – Coaching
    I. Payne, Howard
    796.4′2′07   GV1060.5

ISBN 0 7207 1509 1

Filmset by Butler & Tanner Limited,
Frome and London
Printed by Mondadori, Italy

Frontispiece: Ulricke Meyfarth setting one of her many
world records in the high jump

Contents

Acknowledgements

This book is the result of a truly great team effort by people from many different countries. Dr Primo Nebiolo and the International Amateur Athletic Federation (IAAF) have been magnificent in their support. The authors have been hard-working and very patient in spite of my constant stream of 'slave-driving' letters to them! Also very patient, but always there with solid encouragement have been Dick Douglas-Boyd and his team at Pelham Books.

The Editorial Board of Jim Alford, Frank Dick and Helmar Hommel have worked hard to read the draft and prepare the final version, and the book is enhanced by the photography of Helmar Hommel and Tony Duffy. Many of the drawings are the work of Pauline Hill and Glenis Barry.

Special thanks go to John Holt and his staff at the IAAF headquarters in London, among them Jim Alford and Anne Foulkes who not only made most of the initial contacts with the authors but also ended up translating some of the text into English!

Meanwhile back in Birmingham it was Renate Cleaver who did the back-breaking work of typing and retyping drafts and kept smiling even when it seemed the book would never be complete.

Foreword

by IAAF President Dr Primo Nebiolo

The rapid expansion of track and field athletics during the last few years has been accompanied by a similar widening of the scope of the IAAF Development Programme. Nowhere is this better illustrated than in this latest addition to coaching literature, the fifth IAAF Development Book.

One of the most striking features of modern athletics has been the speed with which many developing nations have reached world standards in some of the running events, but invariably this success has been within a very narrow range and most of these countries are keen to widen their horizons and make a broader impression upon the athletics world. *Athletes in Action*, which, as its name implies, is much more lavishly illustrated than the average coaching manual, has been produced for the IAAF to create interest in a wide range of events, to help motivate young people to take them up and to guide them in the basic and advanced principles of technique.

The IAAF is grateful to photographer and editor Howard Payne, photographer and co-editor Helmar Hommel and co-editors Jim Alford and Frank Dick for their work in putting together this book. We are especially indebted to the contributors from all over the world, for their assistance in supplying the expertise and experience to make this a truly international coaching book.

Introduction

THE PROGRESS OF ATHLETICS

From earliest times people have enjoyed competing against each other at running, jumping, throwing and walking. With the development of track and field athletics and road racing during the last century or so, the rules, specifications and structure of the competitions have become formalized and performances have improved beyond the expectations of each preceding generation of athletes. For example, when I started my own hammer-throwing career in the early 1950s, the hammer was still being thrown from grass- or cinder-surfaced circles into 90-degree sectors and the world record was just over 60m. The film *Geordie* which was being shown in the cinemas at the time was considered to be a fantasy because the hammer-throwing hero was depicted winning the Olympic Games with a throw of 67m! If anyone had predicted then that I could throw over 67m myself I would have thought them mad, and yet years later I was to be disappointed when I could not surpass this with every competition throw.

When I retired in the early 1970s we hammer-throwers were just beginning to dream of the possibility of the 80m throw. Nowadays the USSR leave several 80m throwers at home when their team goes off to major games, and we must realistically expect the 90m barrier to be approached before the end of the century. The old grass circles have given way to carefully prepared concrete surfaces; the sector has come down to 40 degrees; laser beams have replaced the tape measure; and the concept of the ideal hammer-thrower has become a sprinter-type superbly conditioned motor genius rather than the big strong giant of the past.

TECHNIQUE

There is one aspect I have not mentioned in the above example of the meteoric rise in performance of hammer-throwing standards, and that is technique – which is the substance of this book. Changing techniques, or the rationalization of older techniques, of running, walking, hurdling, jumping and throwing have brought athletes nearer to the perfection they strive for.

Technique takes a back seat to conditioning in middle- and long-distance running, but in all the other events it is the thing that athletes and coaches live and breathe. It brings them absolute joy when it goes right, but plunges them into the depths of despair when it eludes them!

VISUAL AIDS

As well as supervising athletes' physical conditioning, coaches everywhere will be striving for their athletes to gain technical mastery of their events. In addition to direct coaching instructions they will use many different audio-visual methods to demonstrate the techniques of the world's best performers. These methods will probably include still photographs, movie film, video recordings and photo-sequences. Each has its own advantages and disadvantages.

In this book we are concerned with the use of the photo-sequence aid to coaching and teaching. Its main disadvantage, that of not clearly revealing the rhythm of movement, is outweighed by the immense advantages of portability and simplicity, which, in viewing, require no special expensive equipment, and its superiority over film and video in the clarity and sharpness of the 'frozen' image. Similar phases of a movement performed by different athletes can easily be compared: for example the differences in lower-arm action at take-off for the pole vault by various vaulters can be measured, and the positions of the discus noted as discus-throwers ground their lead legs at the start of the delivery. Comparisons of this kind are difficult and cumbersome with movie film and video, even though it cannot be denied that they are also invaluable aids in coaching and teaching.

In certain events, such as running, it is important to space the pictures in a sequence at equal time intervals, ie to 'sample' the movement at regular time intervals. But in other events, such as hammer-throwing, the photographer can 'take advantage of the disadvantage' of the photo-sequence not being able to depict rhythm, and select out his pictures to speed up the slow movement of the swings, gradually select his frames more frequently in the turns until he is sampling at a maximum during the delivery in order to slow that extremely fast movement to a point where the brain of the observer can resolve the movement more easily.

THE AUTHORS
So much for the photo-sequences. Much more important is the spirit in which the authors of the various chapters have come together from so many different countries of the world to share their expertise for the benefit of all coaches and all athletes of the world irrespective of nationality, race, colour, creed or sex. It seems to be the mark of great coaches that they are fiercely loyal to their own athletes, but nevertheless they feel 'driven' to share their knowledge and their skills to help the athletes of less fortunate nations. The International Amateur Athletic Federation (IAAF) is not simply an organization for administering international athletics, it is also the vehicle by which athletes and coaches exchange their ideas and help each other through the Development Programme. Athletics is all about competition and competition is all the more exciting when it is a close affair between many athletes of equal ability. Nothing is more boring than unequal competition in which, for example, runners are strung out all over the track. Thus it is important to improve the standards of performance of all athletes – which is the purpose of this book!

Purists of the English language may object to the style in which parts of this book are written,
but we have deliberately not interfered unduly with either the literal translation from other languages nor the attempts by some of the non-English-speaking authors to provide their own translations. Coaching is very much the art of expressing one's thoughts to the athlete, and sometimes attempting grammatical correctness and 'good' expression can be a limitation on the communication of ideas. Any athlete who has sought the advice of a good coach who doesn't speak his tongue, will know that 'incorrect' language is no barrier and that the coach will instinctively find words to convey his meaning, perhaps with even more clarity and inspiration than one who speaks that athlete's language.

THE PURPOSE OF THE BOOK
There are already many, many books for the would-be athlete just starting in the sport and there is a similar wealth of literature about training methods at all levels. However, there is a relative scarcity of material when it comes to the technical aspects of the events at the level of performance of the already established and the advanced athlete. So it is mainly this gap that is intended to be filled by this book. The authors were requested, in the guidelines sent to them with their invitations to participate in the book, to confine their writings to the techniques of the events at an *advanced* level of performance, using the sequence pictures and their own drawings and photographs to illustrate the points they were making. However, the following was also added: 'You may feel that aspects such as training methods, tactics, etc, are inseparable in importance from the actual technique of performing the event, also you may wish to emphasize certain elementary basics of the event, so the content of your chapter is left very much to your discretion.'

Maurice Houvion, especially, in the pole vault chapter took the last sentence seriously and included some excellent material on certain aspects of training and coaching, which although not technical, are very important for successful performance in competition. All readers, whether concerned with pole vaulting or not, are advised to study the philosophy of this great coach.

THE PERFECT TECHNIQUE
Coaches and athletes are forever arguing about the 'ideal technique'. Generally, this is a good-

natured debate and it is important that there should be open-mindedness about the sport – the only time to get worried is when the argument becomes dogmatic and some people think there is only one way to high jump or only one way to throw the discus. Jimmy Pedemonte, who wrote the hammer chapter of this book, puts it very plainly when he says (some changes by me to make it generally applicable):

> The technical foundation should take into account the fundamental elements of technique (ie those factors that, as far as we can possibly agree, really represent the 'framework' of the movement) and at the same time it should respect the characteristics of each single athlete, so that an individualized technique can be built. Too often we, as coaches, have made the mistake of forcing all our athletes to perform the movement in the same manner. The justification for this approach resides in deducing the ideal technical model from the style of renowned champions. In the majority of cases such a coaching system only sets limits on natural motor expression. Because of the great number of individual variables that exist, we should mould onto our athletes only those few elements that, because of their biomechanical characteristics, appear to be basics and not capable of being set aside.

Thus it is the hope that this book can help athletes and their coaches to discern the essential elements of technique in their events and to combine these with their own individual strong points to bring them nearer to their own 'perfect' techniques.

1 SPRINTS

Gerard Mach

Canada (Poland)

(Acknowledgements to the Canadian Track and Field Association)

From 1946 to 1958 Gerard Mach competed with distinction for Poland in the sprints (personal bests of 10.5, 21.4 and 47.4 sec in the days before rubberized tracks). He won more than thirty championships in Poland, in both individual and relay events and he held the national record in 400m. He competed in several World Student Games, winning the 400m in 1951.

Graduating in 1954 with a masters degree in Physical Education from the Sports Academy in Warsaw, Gerard continued the coaching he had started in 1952, and as Head Coach led the Legia Club of Warsaw to become the strongest club in Poland, strong enough to win against most national teams in Europe.

In 1964 Gerard Mach received the Specialist Coach Degree, the highest award in coaching in Poland. In 1965 he began a period as National Head Coach during which time he coached such international superstars as Irena Szewinska, Marian Foik, Wieslaw Maniak, Andrzej Badenski and Marian Duziak, all of whom were Olympic medallists, plus Stanislaw Gredzinski and Jan Werner, who were European Champions.

Gerard's methods gained recognition throughout the world and he was regularly asked to coach in the USSR, GDR, Czechoslovakia, Hungary, Romania, Bulgaria, Italy, Finland, Yugoslavia, Japan, etc. His successful tour of Canada in 1973 was particularly important as a month later he was appointed Canada's first National Coach. The Mach magic worked quickly in the new environment and he had all four relay squads through to the finals in the 1976 Olympics.

Gerard Mach is a member of the IAAF Development Programme coaching team, and as National Program Director and Head Coach of Canada, he has helped Canadian athletics to progress to seventh place in the world on the basis of the results of the 1983 World Championships.

The Individual Sprint Events

GENERAL

In order to describe the technical aspects of the sprinting events, the Olympic Games sprint events should be considered; in these Games the world's best athletes have competed against each other under the same conditions. Since the first modern Olympic Games in Athens in 1896, the following sprint events have been introduced:

MEN	WOMEN
100m in 1896	100m in 1928
200m in 1900	200m in 1948
400m in 1896	400m in 1964

Other events were staged in international competition such as: 100 yards, 220 yards and 440 yards. Indoors, because of the nature of the facilities, the 60m, 50m, 60 yds and 50 yds events are run. The large number of different sprinting events from 50m (50 yds) to 400m (440 yds) makes it possible for all kinds of talents to participate in competition. The very short and mostly very strong types take part mainly in the 50 to 100m events (Ira Murcheson, Enrique Figuerola, Wieslaw Maniak, Alexander Korneljuk, etc). Medium-built sprinters with well-developed muscles are very successful in all sprinting events. Most of the Olympic winners in the 100m and 200m, such as Jesse Owens, Bobby Morrow, Valeri Borzov (Fig 2) and Lee Evans (Fig 3), the world record holder in 400m, were in that group. Very tall athletes are more successful in the 200m and 400m, for example

Tommie Smith, Henry Carr, Arthur Wint, George Rhoden and Otis Davis. Tall world-class athletes are also seen in the 100m event, for example Bob Hayes, Steve Williams and Carl Lewis. A similar range of different types of talents have participated in the women's sprint events, eg Annegret Richter, Renate Stecher (Fig 4), Marlies Gohr, Marita Koch, Angela Taylor, Angela Bailey, Irena Szewinska, Wilma Rudolph, Jarmila Kratochvilova, etc.

The above-mentioned athletes, and many other successful competitors in the sprinting events in the past, have represented all different body types. All the world-class sprinters can be easily classified in one group where the running technique is concerned, with many small differences in their own individual styles.

The goal in each sprinting event, as in all other events and sports, is to win and become the best. To cover the distance in the shortest time is the objective.

Over the past fifty years (women's 200 and 400m introduced later) the improvement in the male events has been more significant with regard to the special speed endurance component than the technical aspect. In the sprinting events, the improvement of the special speed endurance component through the training process is illustrated in the table below:

		20m	40m	60m	100m	200m	400m
1936	start			6.5 sec	10.2 sec	20.7 sec	46.1 sec
1984	start			6.4 sec	9.9 sec	19.7 sec	43.8 sec
Improvement	0.012	0.022	0.032	0.1 sec	0.3 sec	1.0 sec	2.3 sec

There are many factors involved in the improvement of performance in the sprinting events. The most important ones are:

1. Reaction time
2. Starting position
3. Powerful muscles
4. Starting and acceleration technique
5. Maximum speed running technique (effective stride length)
6. Special speed endurance preparation to maintain speed
7. Curve-running technique (200m and 400m)
8. Technique at the finish line
9. The condition of the track surface
10. Wind and weather conditions

When track and field are compared, over the last 50 years, the field events have developed much more technically.

eg High Jump	MEN	WOMEN
	1936–2.03m	1936–1.60m
	1984–2.39m	1984–2.07m

Fig 1 The first starting blocks – an ancient reminder of the technical achievements of Greek civilization

SPRINT TECHNIQUE

Sprint technique has not changed in principle since the 1896 Athens Olympic Games where the winner of the 100m race, Thomas Burke of the USA, already made use of the crouch starting position, very similar to the currently used short start, which still remains the easiest and most effective starting technique.

There is not a remarkable difference in technique between top athletes but mainly between beginners and world-class athletes. Up to a certain level of performance a 'born talent' can be successful, but in order to win in the Olympic Games, to improve world records in the men's and women's sprint events, excellent preparation is required. In the past, 0.1 sec (manual timing) was a close win. Now the 0.01 sec difference (the automatic electronic timing picture is the automatic judge), which can separate runners, is the result of excellent preparation in all aspects, one of the most important of which is perfect technique. In the sprint events – 100m, 200m and 400m – the sprint technique can be divided into the following phases:

a) Starting technique (position)
b) Acceleration technique
c) Maximum speed and maintaining speed technique
d) Technique at the finish line
e) Curve-running technique

Starting Technique (position)
Since all sprinters, male and female, are different (morphological, psychological and level of training factors), starting positions adjusted to their individual needs should be worked out. Even athletes who have already become stronger and faster, following certain programmes, can and should try further corrections of the starting positions as well, since the starting position is important for the improvement of results. Although there are many different variations of the starting position, in general they can be divided into three groups: the short, the medium and the long start.

Fig 2 (*Right*) Valeri Borzov (USSR)
Fig 3 (*Below*) Lee Evans (USA)
Fig 4 (*Below right*) Renate Stecher (GDR)

The three starting positions are measured from the starting line to the front-leg starting block. The starting positions can also be classified in the following way: a) short – very easy to execute b) medium – intermediate difficulty c) long – the most difficult*.

For a long period of time (1896–1948) holes were made by most sprinters in cinder tracks in the starting position. Although Eddie Tolan won the 100m and 200m in 1932 in Los Angeles and improved the world record to 10.3 sec, the hero in the sprinting events was, and is, Jesse Owens (later also Armin Hary). Their starts and accelerations still are the models to follow for many young athletes and coaches.

THE SHORT STARTING POSITION (Fig 5a) In the short starting position the starting blocks are close to the starting line. The front starting block should be placed one foot length from the starting line. The rear starting block should be adjusted one foot further back.

The sprinter assumes the position 'on your marks' with his bodyweight resting comfortably on the legs in the crouch position. The hands, shoulder-width apart, touch the ground behind the starting line with fingers and thumb pointing away from each other. The arms can be lifted without causing the athlete to fall forward. The eyes are focussed downward and forward. At the command 'set' the athlete lifts the centre of gravity (hips). The rear-leg angle is about 170 degrees. In this position the arms can still be lifted without the athlete losing his balance. This position closely resembles the standing start position of the distance runners.

Next, a leaning position is taken, with shoulders and hips slightly forward. From the hips to the shoulders the body angle is steep. This is an excellent starting position for beginners and athletes who are not strong and powerful. Since the centre of gravity is located high, the first strides are shorter and less powerful. The short starting position is a very significant energy saver which is of utmost importance in the 400m and 200m events.

Irena Szewinska, the former world record holder in 100m, 200m and 400m and winner of seven Olympic medals, used the short starting

*The terms 'medium' and 'bunch' starts are more commonly used; front block 1½ to 2½ foot lengths behind the start line; distance between blocks ¾ to 1½ foot lengths. The most effective near-leg angle is accepted as 110–120°.

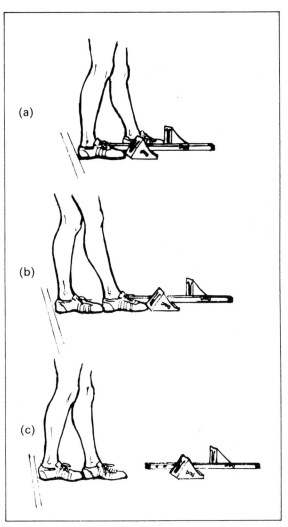

(a)

(b)

(c)

Fig 5 Block positions. (a) Short starting position (b) Medium starting position (c) Long starting position

position, as did Zenon Nowosz, one of the world record holders in 60m (6.4 sec). The start of Carl Lewis can be described as a short starting position with high hips.

THE MIDDLE STARTING POSITION (Fig 5b) The front starting block is located two foot lengths from the starting line and the rear starting block is one foot length further. The starting position should be taken in the following order: hands at shoulder width on the ground; rear (better skilled) leg in the rear block; and the other leg in the front block.

Fig 6 (*Overleaf*) Valeri Borzov (USSR), 1972 Olympic champion, uses a medium spacing in this sequence

Fig 6

In the set position, the angle of the rear leg is about 140 degrees. The slope of the body from the hips to the shoulders is not very steep. The body-weight is on the legs and arms. This is the position most frequently used by sprinters. Incidentally, Valeri Borzov had his starting blocks a little closer than a foot length together and his position in frame 2 of Fig 6 is exceptionally steep, but this is still considered to be a medium starting position.

The majority of champions in the 100m and 200m, like Borzov, had a medium or quite strong body build.

THE LONG STARTING POSITION (Fig 5c)   In the long starting position, the front starting block is situated three foot lengths from the starting line and there is one foot length between the starting blocks. While in the on your marks position a pressure on the arms occurs which will increase in the set position (Gohr in frame 2 of Fig 7) and become very pronounced after the forward lean. The hips are slightly higher than the shoulders. The angle of the rear leg is about 110 degrees.

In order to hold the proper forward-leaning position, the athlete brings the rear leg forward and maintains the forward lean in the first acceleration phase. The athlete must be very strong, powerful and fast. The athlete attempts to avoid:

a) arm shake in the set position (the starter may 'hold' for very long, 3–5 sec)
b) up and down movement of the hips and knees
c) suddenly assuming the upright position after the start
d) lifting the heels too high
e) stride too short (not effective and resulting in an early upright position and stumbling)
f) stride too long (too slow) which may cause a break in stride

The long starting position is certainly the most difficult one. It should be applied very carefully; many athletes find this particular position rather ineffective. It should not be used by beginners or by weaker or less prepared athletes. Since it is also energy-consuming, sprinters would be advised against using it in the 200m and 400m races.

The long starting position was advocated by many coaches in the period 1967 to 1969. Tommy Smith, Don Quarrie and Steven Riddick are the top athletes who used positions very similar to the long starting position.

All the three above-mentioned positions are good and 'work' – provided they are applied to suit specific needs of individual athletes. Further adjustments can, and should, be made in order to have a particular athlete effectively use the techniques to his best advantage. In the 60m race all the three types of starting positions were successfully used by world record holders.

Start into the Curve in 200m and 400m
The three starting positions (with individual adjustments) are also used in the 200m and 400m events. When starting on a bend, however, the blocks are placed near the outside of the lane and directed at a tangent to the inner line of the lane. The hands and the starting blocks do not touch the starting line or encroach on any other lane.

The athlete should be coached to run the curve close to the inside of his lane in order to run the shortest distance possible.

Acceleration Technique (Figs 6 and 7)
Through exercises and tests the best starting position (short, medium, long) has to be established so that the athlete is confident and feels comfortable in the starting blocks. Following the starter's command 'on your marks' the athlete takes the starting position. The arms are straight and shoulder-width apart. The hands with the fingers and thumb at a wide angle are on the ground behind the starting line. The neck and head are held naturally as an extension of the torso and the eyes are focussed on the track. After the command 'set' the athlete lifts the hips according to the chosen starting position. In the final phase, the shoulders will be pressed forward to a forward lean. In the forward-leaning position the athlete needs maximum concentration for the first action of the arms and legs. When the starting pistol fires a forward (and not an upright) movement should be executed. A forceful arm and leg action follows.

The arm opposite to the rear leg starts the forward action. The other arm swings vigorously backward. The arms are bent at a 90-degree angle. The arms play a dual role in sprinting: they help to balance the runner and also to set the pace of the legs. The feet are pressed against the starting blocks in the set position. The rear knee is pulled forward quickly and low. The front leg is fully extended. A straight line can be drawn from the toes of this extended driving leg to the athlete's head, emphasizing that the force of the driving leg is in the correct forward direction. Too long a stride, caused by an athlete's lack of strength in bringing the rear leg forward, can cause a break in rhythm.

During the acceleration phase (30–60m) the body will gradually rise from a pronounced to a slight forward lean. Also during the acceleration phase, the stride length will gradually increase. The start and acceleration phase is the most expensive part of a race, in terms of energy consumption. Therefore, in this phase there must be coordination without tension. The stride length and speed will increase, and the arms will work in harmony with the legs. The hands are lifted not much higher than shoulder level.

Maximum Speed, Maintaining Speed and Deceleration

Athletes after achieving their maximum speed in the 100m should try to stay fully concentrated in that phase. Almost all the world's best athletes demonstrate a perfect running technique with the most effective stride length and no tension.

Model – sprint running

HEAD AND NECK   Full extension of the body; no sideways or up and down head movements; eyes focussed forward. (See Quarrie sequence, Fig 8.)

SHOULDERS   Relaxed, no twisting movements. (See Lewis sequence, Fig 11.)

ARMS   Forward, backward swinging with 90 degrees at the elbow or less. Fingers slightly curled. (See Wells, frames 13 and 14 in Fig 10.)

BODY   Slight forward lean, running 'tall'. (See Smith sequence, Fig 9. His head position is unusually high.)

DRIVING LEG   Full extension right through to the toes. (See Smith No. 10.)

RECOVERY LEG
a) the heel moves to the buttocks. (See Lewis No. 12.)
b) the knee pulled forward – to a high knee position. (See Quarrie No. 3.)
c) Full leg extension. (See Quarrie Nos. 12 and 13.)

d) landing on the outside edge of the foot. (See Quarrie No. 7.)
e) supporting phase (heels touch the ground, however, not all athletes do so – Calvin Smith keeps high on his toes.)

Curve Running

The faster the sprinting speed in the curve, the greater the centrifugal force will be. In the acceleration, as well as in the speed phase, an inward body lean is required for balance. (See Lattany sequence, Fig 12.) The greater the centrifugal force, the greater the body lean necessary. The inside lanes are tighter and more difficult to run. Shorter athletes have an advantage over very tall athletes, especially on short indoor tracks. Since the outside part of the lane is a further distance away, an adjustment of the technique is required – the movement of the inside leg and arm (left) is shorter than that of the outside leg and arm (right).

Technique at the Finish Line (Figs 13, 14 and 15)

The reading of the photofinish picture becomes increasingly more important as sprinting standards improve throughout the world and finishes in important races become very close. Sometimes even the colour of the vest determines who is the winner (a contrast of the vest and background is necessary). A bad finish line position (Cook sequence) can mean a loss of up to half a second. A forward dip during the last stride before the finish line is the most commonly used technique. (See Crawford sequence.)
Athletes should avoid:

a) tension
b) a premature forward lean which causes slowing down (see Cook sequence)

Fig 7 (*Overleaf*) Maries Gohr (GDR), world champion in 1983, uses a long starting position but has a pronounced bent-over position as she leaves the blocks which results in very short strides over the first few metres
Fig 8 200m full stride in the straight: Don Quarrie (Jamaica), 1976 Olympic champion, has classic style
Fig 9 Running 'tall' is Calvin Smith (USA), 1983 world champion in 200m
Fig 10 1980 Olympic champion Allan Wells (GB) in 100m
Fig 11 Carl Lewis (USA), winner of four gold medals at the 1984 Olympics, showing relaxed and balanced technique
Fig 12 Mel Lattany (USA) leaning into the 200m bend

Fig 7

6

5

4

12

11

10

18

17

16

24

23

22

3

2

1

9

8

7

15

14

13

21

20

19

ig 8

Fig 9

4

5

6

10

11

12

16

17

18

Fig 10

4

5

6

10

11

12

16

17

18

Fig 11

Fig 12

Fig 13 The 'dip'. (a) The finish technique (b) The difference: with and without the lean at the finish

c) a jump, as this is slower than running
d) upright running which wastes time
e) a backward lean which is unacceptable

ELEMENTS OF RUNNING TECHNIQUE

There is a great range of training methods available designed to improve different aspects of sprinting. The most effective method is a natural repetition of coordinated movements, from ideal execution in slow motion to rhythm form and maximum speed. The following selected exercises include all the elements of the running technique (see diagrams on pages 33 and 34):

1 High-knee marching on toes (Fig 16a):
  a) the ideal is no head movement; no shoulder movement; arm action 90 degrees forward, backward; high knee action; full leg extension ('tall'); and staying on toes.
2 High-knee marching with extension (Fig 16c):
  a) all elements as above
  b) from the high knee action, extension of the leg prior to landing
3 Skipping:
  a) all elements as exercise 1
  b) soft and relaxed rhythm
4 Skipping with extension (Fig 16b):
  a) all elements as in exercises 1 and 2
  b) soft and relaxed rhythm
5 Bounding (Fig 16d):

  a) all technical elements as in exercise 1
  b) in bounding exercises full extension of the rear leg
  c) landing phase
6 Bounding with extension:
  a) all technical elements as in exercises 1, 2 and 5
7 High-knee running (Fig 16e):
  a) all technical elements as in exercises 1 and 3
  b) maximum speed
8 High-knee running with extension (Fig 16f):
  a) all technical elements as in exercises 1, 2, 3, 4 and 7

STRIDE LENGTH VERSUS FREQUENCY

Sprinters improve their speed in a most effective way when they simultaneously increase stride frequency and stride length. As previously mentioned, there is no ideal starting position that can be used by all types of sprinters; there is also no single formula for stride length. In most cases where beginner athletes are concerned, very short and strong athletes will win in 60m to 100m races against tall and skinny ones. Yet after proper training the situation can radically change (eg Irena Szewinska).

The coach should differentiate between various types of sprinting talents and should endeavour to develop the athletes accordingly. It seems that athletes using their optimum long stride are still more

Fig 14 (*Opposite*) Haseley Crawford (Trinidad), 1976 Olympic champion, leaning into a controlled but fast finish

Fig 14

Fig 15

1

2

3

4

5

6

7

8

9

Fig 15 (*Opposite*) The difficulty! Kathy Cook (GB), Olympic bronze medallist, mistiming the dip finish 2m from the line

effective in all sprinting events (one should not, however, take into consideration understriding or overstriding athletes).

Although European Championships have been won by very strong powerful athletes with a very high stride frequency (Heinz Fütterer 100m 1954 and Wieslaw Maniak 100m 1966), sprinting technique did not change accordingly since later on athletes using a different technique, such as Armin Hary and Valeri Borzov, were even more successful.

More sophisticated test equipment and scientific measurement programmes are now available to adjust stride length and stride frequency for optimum performance. For each athlete there is a given optimum in the length and frequency which will make him most successful.

Fig 16 Exercises for sprinters (indeed for all athletes). (a) High-knee marching on toes (b) High-knee skipping with both legs extending (c) High-knee marching on flat feet with leg extension

CONCLUSION

Every sprinter wishing to achieve maximum results should pass through the following three stages:

1 Be coached by a good coach in all necessary sprinting aspects and strive for perfection in sprinting technique.
2 Have his strong and weak components identified and worked upon through training tests and competition.
3 Have a long-term individual development programme which can be adjusted according to current needs.

Since at top world level technical elements are the same in principle, different style adjustments should not be copied mechanically without understanding why they are being made.

Olympic gold medals and world records are the rewards of a long-range individual programme with all the necessary support, eg coaching, programme support, living support, medical and paramedical, scientific, etc.

(a)

(b)

(c)

(d)

(e)

(f)

Fig 16 *continued* (d) Bounding (e) High-knee running
(f) High-knee running with extension

2 MIDDLE DISTANCE
Harry Wilson

England
(Acknowledgements to the British Amateur Athletic Board)

Harry Wilson represented Kent county at all distances from 100m to Marathon so it can truly be said that he has running in his bones! He was best at cross-country and ran in Welsh colours in five World Championships. On the 'slow' tracks of the 1950s his 10,000m time was a respectable 29 minutes 35 seconds.

Harry started coaching in 1958, gradually moving from sprinting to middle- and long-distance running. His results are world-famous and although he tries to confine his attention to eight or ten athletes at any one time he has helped over 50 internationals. Harry's most prominent athletes in recent years have included Olympic champion and world record holder Steve Ovett, as well as Julian Goater, Tony Simmons, Phil Norgate, Jo White, etc.

Harry Wilson leads a busy full life, working as a marketing manager for a large organization and spending every spare moment as national coach for middle distance. He was coach to the British team at the Moscow Olympics, several European Championships and the first World Championships. His expertise is in great demand throughout the world and he is a frequent lecturer/coach at conferences and training camps in many countries.

Middle Distance

TECHNIQUE

Seb Coe (Fig 1)

Frames 1 and 2 show the right foot coming to the ground during the recovery phase of the leg action. The foot moves back and the outer part of the ball of the foot strikes the ground first. The heel then drops lightly to the ground in the middle of the supporting phase so for a fraction of a second we see the runner in a 'flat-footed' position. As the only function of the right leg at this point is to support the bodyweight, this flat-footed position provides a solid base and at the same time allows the calf muscle to take a momentary rest*. This would not happen if the runner stayed high up on the ball of the foot as in the sprinting action. The arms are quite relaxed at this point and are in line with the body.

In frames 3 and 4 the bodyweight moves over and in front of the right foot and the right leg starts to begin its driving phase. While the right leg was carrying out its support function the left leg was folding up to swing through with the left foot tucked up closely underneath the buttock. Frames 3 and 4 show the start and completion of the right-leg driving phase and it is vital at this point that the athlete has a powerful thigh lift of the leading left leg in order to allow full extension of the driving leg. Coe shows a full extension of his right leg as he continues to drive right through the ball of the foot to the toes. Great strength is needed to apply force for a long time against the ground and mobility is required to apply the force over a long distance. Hip mobility allows him to

*It is debatable whether this is merely a supporting phase – F.D.

extend the leading leg well beyond the body and the driving leg well behind the body. Powerful calf muscles and ankle mobility enable him to use the feet fully as an extra lever.

Mobility and strength add distance to the stride length and enable the champion runner to cover the ground in a free and relaxed manner, whilst runners with less strength and mobility seem to be struggling with a shorter stride just to stay in touch. As the left thigh was driving forward and upwards, the right arm was reacting to the powerful thrust to the rear of the right leg by also driving forward and up. It is important that this reaction is taken up by a correct arm action which calls for the arm to be flexed at roughly 90 degrees and to swing slightly across the body. By flexing the arm the runner makes a short lever which is less energy-consuming than the long lever of a straight arm.

If the arms are not used correctly then the shoulders will provide the reaction, and shoulder movements are both wasteful and slow. The shoulder and upper part of the body will twist to provide the reaction and much more energy is required to move these large masses than is needed to swing the lighter arms. Twisting movements in the shoulder will encourage twisting reaction by the lower part of the body, which can lead to the feet not coming to the ground directly in line with the forward drive.

Frames 6, 7 and 8 show the runner in the ground-covering recovery phase and show again the advantages to be gained by having great mobility in the hips. Frame 8 shows more clearly the landing on the outer part of the foot. Coe keeps his feet and knees pointing straight to the front which means that all his drive is in a forward direction and not being wasted to the left and right which would be the result of feet and knees turning out. As runners tire and the thighs become fatigued there is a tendency for the knees to turn out which produces a shorter stride and a deviation of the forward drive. Frames 9 to 13 show the leg recovery and driving phase and 13 illustrates more clearly the suggested arm action. Coe's head remains steady, pointing to the front and there is no energy-wasting tension in the neck or shoulder muscles.

Other Sequences (Figs 2, 3 and 4)

The other sequences show equally efficient and economic runners, but one or two points are worthy of mention. Steve Ovett (Fig 2) shows a particularly fine rear leg extension and forward thigh lift but allows his arms to drop down a little during the support phase. Steve Cram (Fig 3) shows a similar tendency and one suspects that if we could have viewed this sequence from the front we would have seen a slight loss of forward drive due to his knees and feet turning out slightly.

Both Ovett and Cram display full rear leg extension and full drive through the feet and these two points are not so clearly seen in the action of Jarmila Kratochvilova (Fig 4). However, the world record holder still shows much more drive and range of movement than most women runners and clearly shows the value of being powerful. However, the techniques we show are only the tip of the iceberg and the ability to maintain the technique is the result of many years of hard and progressive training.

TRAINING

The hallmark of the good runner is not just that he has a good technique but that he is able to maintain this technique in high-quality races. He makes running fast look easy and this effect can only be produced if he is superbly conditioned by hard and thoughtful training. The runners featured in the photo-sequences are typical examples of what we discern if we start to examine the training methods of successful runners, ie the use of the same training ingredients, but with variations in the emphasis placed on the different ingredients.

The major improvements that are made as a result of training are an increase in the athlete's oxygen uptake (ie the amount of oxygen that he can utilize from the air he breathes in) and in his ability to tolerate a high oxygen debt (which is inevitable in fast races when the athlete's oxygen uptake cannot satisfy the oxygen requirements that the fast pace demands). Apart from these two main factors, the runner will also spend time on improving technique and his sprinting ability.

The ability to sprint is greatly influenced by leg strength, mobility in the lower limbs and the use of the correct technique, so most world-class runners now spend time on these three points. Some athletes use weight-training exercises to gain leg strength but many more prefer to use more natural methods such as sand-running, hill-running and such exercises as bounding and high knee-lifting. The runner who uses hill-running must attempt to maintain a normal length stride in his repetitions and as the legs tire towards the end of each run, he should resist the temptation to shorten his stride or to allow his knees to turn out.

Improving oxygen uptake is best achieved by running aerobically, ie by using steady-state rates of varying distances and intensities, where the phrase steady-state refers to the maintenance of a fairly even heartrate throughout the duration of a run.

The pace of these steady-state runs will depend upon an athlete's fitness at a particular time and upon the distance run (generally speaking the shorter the distance, the faster the pace) but there is a minimum pace that needs to be achieved if there is to be any training effect. This training threshold can be roughly calculated by the following method:

a) Record the heartrate at rest in beats per minute.

b) Count the heartrate in beats per minute immediately after an all-out effort over 300m or 400m.

c) The difference between a) and b) gives the athlete's pulse range. Add two-thirds of this figure to the resting rate counted at a) and the resulting figure is the heartrate that needs to be reached in order to achieve a training effect. Running at a rate of 10 or more beats per min-

Fig 1 (*Overleaf*) 4 × 800m relay. Seb Coe (GB) during the successful world record attempt. He is also individual world record holder and 1980 and 1984 Olympic 1500m champion

Fig 1

4

5

6

10

11

12

16

17

18

ute below this training threshold has very little effect. As an example a runner who has a resting rate of 60 beats per minute and a maximum rate of 180 beats per minute should be doing aerobic work at a pace that will produce a pulse-rate of approximately 140 beats per minute. Runners will train over a range of distances; the runner mentioned here would probably be practising steady-state runs such as:

(i) 5–10km runs at a pace that will produce a heartrate of approximately 165 beats per minute.

(ii) 10–15km runs at a pace that will produce a heartrate of approximately 155 beats per minute.

(iii) 15–20km runs at a pace that will produce a heartrate of approximately 145 beats per minute.

Although steady-state running will form the major part of a runner's aerobic work, variety can be introduced by running some fairly easy paced repetitions, interspersed with very short recovery periods. Two examples could be:

a) A 1500m runner – 12 × 200m at race pace with 30 seconds jog recovery between each 200m.

b) A 5000m runner – 6 × 1000m at race pace with 30 seconds jog recovery between each 1000m.

With this type of training the pace is not so intensive that the work becomes anaerobic and the recovery is so short that the pulse-rate drops very little below the training threshold. We can imagine a runner who uses the above sections recording pulse-rates of approximately 160/165 beats per minute after each fast run and pulse rates of approximately 125/130 beats per minute after the recovery periods.

The increase in oxygen uptake that comes about as a result of prolonged and gradually progressive aerobic training means that the athlete can negotiate longer distances or faster paces before going into oxygen debt. A good example would be Steve Ovett whose oxygen uptake has increased by nearly 20 per cent since he was 17 years old with the result that in a 1500m race he can now cruise at 58 seconds per lap then finish fast, whereas when he was younger 61 seconds per lap was his cruising pace.

In order to encourage the body to adapt to a condition of oxygen debt a runner will need to use the anaerobic energy process in many of his sessions. Training at a fast pace is necessary in order to ensure that oxygen requirements will exceed oxygen uptake. A runner will not be able to maintain a fast pace for very long before easing off and the whole concept of anaerobic training is based around the idea of periods of fast running interspersed with recovery periods. The faster the pace and the longer the length of a fast stretch then the higher the resulting pulse-rate and subsequently the longer time needed for the athlete to partially recover.

The most common forms of anaerobic training are interval running, repetition running and *fartlek*, and a brief description of each of these types of training follows.

*Interval Training**

The original form of interval training was to carry out a series of runs over a set distance in a fixed time with a set recovery jog between each run. Parameters of pulse-rates of 180 beats per minute at the end of each fast stretch and 120 beats per minute at the end of the recovery jog were set and as the athlete became fitter and was able to achieve target times with lower pulse-rates, the training could be intensified by increasing the pace of the fast runs, increasing the number of the fast runs, increasing the distance covered in the fast runs, or reducing the recovery time.

The original concept of repeating a fixed distance is still the one most commonly used, but nowadays many athletes also use varying distances in one session, eg 1 × 600m, 3 × 400m, 6 × 200m with appropriate recovery jogs between each effort. Although interval running was once regarded as being essentially a track session, there are now many runners who use the same principles on circuits over grassland or in woods. I personally prefer to see athletes who are running distances of more than 400m use circuits away from the track and preferably circuits that include some gentle slopes. To be successful interval training must be progressive to a point where an athlete can run several repetitions of a certain distance in a time much faster than he covers that distance in a race eg I would expect a man hoping to run 3 min

---

* This is a form of aerobic training developed by Gerschler, so there is a confusion of terminology here, ie 'interval training' versus 'interval running' – F.D.

42 sec for 1500m to be able to run 8 × 400m in 56/57 sec with a 300m jog between each repetition.

I have found it valuable for experienced runners to include some extremely intensive interval training in their programmes and have used fairly short but very fast repetitions interspersed with very short recoveries. This means that athletes can only run a small quantity of fast runs so they then have a longer rest before attempting another set of repetitions. An example of a good-class 1500m runner using this sort of session would be 5 sets of 3 × 200m in 25/26 sec with a jog of 30 sec between each 200m and rest of 4/6 min between each set. This particular type of session is extremely exhausting both physically and mentally and I would not suggest using such a session within five days of a major race.

Repetition Running
Here the athlete uses longer distances than in interval training and as the pace is still fast it follows that a longer period of recovery is required. Because of the quality and the distance covered it is unreasonable to expect an athlete to perform many repetitions and a typical session for a good-class 5000m runner would be 6 × 1000m at approximately 5/6 sec faster than race pace for the distance, with 4/5 min jog recovery between each repetition.

I would suggest that repetition running becomes more useful than interval running as the competition season approaches, particularly where the 800m and 1500m events are concerned. Athletes tell me that the quality and distance involved and the longer recovery that is allowed equate more closely to the sensation they feel in races.

Fartlek (a Swedish word meaning 'speed play')
This is a natural form of training performed best in woods or parks and similar areas that provide undulating surfaces. The athlete runs fast and slow stretches during the session according to the way he feels and the conditions he encounters. There are no set distances to be run, the pace can vary from sprinting to striding at race pace and there are no set recovery times between the fast surges. He speeds up his running when he feels ready to go again. As with other forms of anaerobic training, *fartlek* must be progressive and as the runner gets fitter so he should increase the number and severity of the fast stretches and reduce the amount of time spent jogging.

TACTICS
With intelligent regular and progressive training the runner will achieve a high level of physical fitness, but if he is to make the most of this fitness he must learn to run cleverly. Some runners seem to possess tactical awareness right from their youngest days, others learn through experience and still others, despite regular lessons, never seem to learn.

In a race where several competitors are evenly matched and are all capable of winning, the eventual winner turns out to be the one who has exploited his physical potential most intelligently.

Each athlete should know his own strengths and weaknesses and run the race according to his strengths. If he also knows the weak and strong points of his opponents then he is in an even better position to prepare some sort of pre-race plan. Factors he should consider about his opponents and himself are:

1 Who is best equipped to handle a fast pace right from the start?
2 Who is likely to try to break away by including fast surges?
3 Who likes to lead but is easily discouraged once he loses the lead?
4 Who doesn't like to lead and will always try to come through from behind?
5 Who is most dangerous in a short fast finish?
6 Who does not possess the sprinting speed to risk a short fierce finish and will attempt a long but not so fast finish?
7 Who is uncomfortable with someone at his shoulders or 'snapping' at his heels?
8 Who is likely to relish physical contact during the race?

An athlete cannot control the way others are going to run but he can be the master of his own fate by making the most of his own strong points. So if he does not possess a fast finish he must attempt either to break away from the field or to make the

Fig 2 (*Overleaf*) One mile: (right to left) Thomas Wessinghage (FRG), Steve Ovett (GB), Philip Deleze (Switzerland) and John Walker (NZ). Ovett and Walker are former Olympic champions and have held various world records at middle distance
Fig 3 Steve Cram (GB)
Fig 4 Women's 800m: Jarmila Kratochvilova (Cze), world champion at 400m and 800m

Fig 2

1

2

3

7

8

9

13

14

15

4

5

6

10

11

12

16

17

18

Fig 3

1

2

3

7

8

9

13

14

15

4

5

6

10

11

12

16

17

18

Fig 4

1

2

3

7

8

9

13

14

15

4

5

6

10

11

12

16

17

18

pace so fast that he runs the finish out of the so-called 'sprinters'.

If an athlete decides to lead he must either set a fast steady pace or also attempt to break away from the field by injecting a series of fast bursts. These bursts should be either fast enough or long enough to make his opponents think twice about staying with him and are most dangerous when they are unexpected. The runner who opts to go for a fast steady pace right from the gun must appreciate that it is quite likely that some runners will hang on like grim death and it may be only in the very closing stages that he is left out in front on his own. Examples would be: the 800m front runner may not get rid of his opponents until the last 150m; and the 10,000m runner may not find himself clear until the last 2000m. The runner who has set a fast pace from the start must not be discouraged if he still has opponents with him in the closing stages of the race but must remember that he is entering the hardest part of the race and ensure that he is not the one to relax the pace.

However, the runner who does possess a fast finish must stay in contact with the leaders so he must ensure that the endurance part of his training will condition him to maintain a very fast overall pace if necessary.

There is no value in a 1500m runner being capable of a 48-second 400m if he is 20m or 30m adrift when the bell rings. This type of runner must analyse himself well enough to know whether he is in fact suited to a short fast finish or is most dangerous in a longer less fast run-in to the tape. If a race is very fast the runner cannot expect to hold a very fast sprint for long, but on the other hand if the race is slow then he must be prepared for a long finish.

If an athlete decides to leave his finishing burst until very late then this burst must be fierce enough not to allow his rivals time to strike back. The athlete who decides upon a longer finish must not let up once he has started his burst. Quite often we see an athlete who has set out on a long finish open up a gap, then relax and be caught up by an opponent who has been gradually closing the gap. The leader then attempts to speed up again only to find that he has lost his running rhythm and is unable to accelerate again. The runner who sets off on a long finish must try to hold

good form and not waste energy by over-straining. In a short fast finish there is no need to worry about conserving energy – it is the fierceness of the burst that counts.

Positioning during a race is vital and a runner should try to take up a position where he can respond quickly to any break by a leader, match any challenges coming up from behind or make a burst himself. The sequence of Steve Ovett (Fig 2) shows him in this ideal position. He is running slightly outside of the leader and just far enough away to allow himself a free run when he decides to make a burst. If he had positioned right behind the leader he would have run the risk of one of the runners behind him boxing him in just as he was about to begin his surge. Thomas Wessing-hage who is running next to the curb inside Ovett will not be able to extricate himself quickly when Ovett makes his burst. In frames 8 to 13 John Walker looks as though he is about to cramp Ovett's position, but he senses this and in 14–18 starts to move away in order to retain his commanding position. This ability to sense danger and immediately react to it is vital to an athlete and, as the race reaches its climax, he must particularly protect his right flank and ensure that he can manoeuvre freely.

It is inevitable that an athlete will find himself boxed-in on the odd occasion and when this happens he should take prompt and decisive action to 'break out' and take up a more favourable position. It is dangerous to sit tight and hope that an opening will occur. Quite often a runner talks about being unlucky enough to have been boxed-in when he in fact allowed the situation to develop through his own lack of action – we often make our own bad luck!

Obviously by running a little wide it means that a runner covers extra distance, but quite often this is worthwhile in order to retain freedom of movement. In the 800m a favourite striking point is the beginning of the final straight and the leader must take care that he doesn't swing out too wide as he comes off the bend, thus giving his rivals a chance of slipping through on the inside. He should make sure that the gap on his inside is too narrow for an athlete to slip through, but at the same time he should be prepared to force any runner coming up from behind on the right to run wide.

3 LONG DISTANCE
Fred Wilt

USA
(Acknowledgements to the Athletics Congress of the USA)

About 20 years ago I made a pilgrimage to deepest USA to meet the great coach and writer on athletics – Fred Wilt. My respect for the man was great when I went there but it multiplied even more when the 140 lb (65 kg) ex-runner took me out hammer-throwing and proceeded to throw the hammer himself as though he had been born to it!

His house is filled with every possible book on track and field, and he must have read every one of them, for he can talk on any event with great authority.

Fred Wilt is a retired former FBI agent who coaches women's track and field and cross-country at Purdue University. He was editor of *Track Technique* magazine from 1960 to 1980, and is the author, co-author and/or editor of twenty books on track and field athletics. During his competitive years he was a member of two United States Olympic teams, won two NCAA and nine national AAU championships, once held the world record for two miles indoors, and received the James E Sullivan annual award as the USA's most outstanding amateur athlete.

Long Distance

INTRODUCTION

It is now generally known that there is no universally applicable 'perfect' method of training. The same may be said of running form of individual athletes. World records have been established by athletes using a wide variety of workout routines. Great athletes are apparently great for reasons other than, but in addition to, their specific training. Successful racing involves not only good training and natural ability, but also – and perhaps more importantly – mental factors such as determination, tenacity, courage, dedication and perseverance. Training makes good performances possible, but these mental factors must be added to natural ability to transform proper training into the reality of successful athletic performances. In the case of both Alberto Cova and Robert de Castella we have examples of world-class athletes who have followed different paths in both training and running to arrive at the oasis of racing success.

ALBERTO COVA (Fig 1)

This photo-sequence was taken during the 1983 European Cup 10,000m, in which Cova finished second with a time of 28:01.13. He was the 10,000m winner at the 1983 World Championships in Helsinki, Finland, in 28:01.04 and 1984 Olympic champion in 27:47.54.

Alberto Cova was born 1 December 1958 in Inverigo, near Como, Italy. He is 1.78m (5ft 10ins) tall, and races at 58 kg (128lb). He is married to the former Anna Molteni, is a member of the Pro-Patri Pierrel Club of Milan, Italy, is coached by Giorgio Rondelli and employed in advertising.

Regarded generally as one of Italy's most popular athletes, Cova's bests are: 800m (1:53.2 in 1978); 1500m (3:42.2 in 1981); 3000m (7:51.0 in 1980); 3000m steeplechase (8:37.2 in 1980); 5000m (13:13.71 in 1982); 10,000m (27:37.06 in 1983); and half-Marathon (1:02:16).

A runner's forward lean is proportional to acceleration (rate of change of velocity). If acceleration is great, the forward lean is pronounced. If there is no acceleration, the forward lean is either slight or non-existent. An athlete's true forward lean is most easily observed when the knees are closest together. In frames 2, 9, and 17 Cova's body appears to be erect, thus indicating he is not accelerating, and is running at a steady speed.

The 'supporting' phase of a runner's stride begins when the foot forward of the body makes ground-contact (with knee slightly bent) about 15–30 cm in front of a point directly below the body's centre of gravity, and concludes when the athlete's centre of gravity passes in front of this foot while on the ground. Frames 8 and 9 show Cova's left foot in the supporting phase of the running stride, while frames 16 and 17 show his right foot during this phase.

The 'driving' phase of the running stride begins when the runner's centre of gravity has passed in front of the foot in ground-contact during the supporting phase, and concludes when the toe of this foot breaks ground-contact behind the athlete's body. Frames 2 to 4 and 18 show Cova's left leg in the driving phase, while 10 to 12 show his right leg during this phase.

The 'recovery' phase of the running stride begins when the foot breaks ground-contact behind the athlete and ends when this same foot again contacts the track to start the supporting phase. Frames 1 to 7 show Cova's right leg in the recovery phase, and 5 to 15 show his left leg during this phase.

The manner in which Cova places each foot on the track appears to be completely orthodox. As each foot approaches the ground, it is moving backward. The outer edge of the ball of the foot makes ground-contact first. Immediately thereafter, the foot rolls inward and the heel comes to the ground to bear the full weight of the body. The knee is slightly bent when the foot rests flat on the ground, as may be observed in frames 1 and 2, 8 and 9 and 16 and 17.

As the toe of the foot leaves the ground to terminate the driving phase of the stride, the heel of this foot rises towards the hip. In general, the faster the running speed the higher the heel will rise towards the hip, and vice versa in the case of slower running speeds. This kick-up behind is highest for any running speed when the knees are closest together. The height to which Cova's heel rises in the recovery phase of his stride, as seen in frames 2 and 3, 8 to 10 and 16 to 18, does not seem excessive and is apparently in keeping with the approximately 67 sec per 400m speed at which he is running in this photo-sequence.

Cova's upper arms correctly move generally forwards and backwards, while the lower arms move slightly around his lower trunk in front. The angle of his arms at the elbows continually alters, and correctly does not remain fixed. The angle of the elbows is greatest when the knees are closest together, as seen in frames 2, 9, and 17 and 18. This angle decreases as the arm continues backwards. The angle at the elbow is least when the hand reaches its highest point in front of the body, although this is not immediately obvious at slower running speeds as seen in 4 and 13.

Alberto Cova's Training
Early-winter training is continuous running on surfaces away from the track, including hills. Except for Sundays, he trains twice daily. Here is a typical week of daily running volume during this period:

Sunday and *Monday* – 25 km at 3:45–4:00 per km
Tuesday and *Friday* – 20 km at 3:45–4:00 per km
Wednesday – 16km at 3:45–4:00 per km
Thursday – 30km at 3:45–4:00 per km
Saturday – 8km at 3:20 per km, followed by 4 km at 3:10 per km

Training during winter competition includes the following types of workouts which are included in the total volume of 170–180 km running per week:

a) 16–20 km continuous running at 3:20–3:30 per km over hilly terrain.
b) 15–20 × 300m in 48–50 sec, with 100m recovery jogging 30–40 sec after each.
c) 15–20 × 400m in 64–66 sec, with 200m recovery jogging in 50 sec after each.
d) 10 × 1200m in 3:30–3:35, with 400m recovery jogging in 90 sec after each.

Typical training prior to major competition during summer takes the following form:

Monday – 20–30 km continuously at 3:10 per km
Tuesday, *Thursday*, *Friday* and *Sunday* – 20–30 km continuously at 4:00 per km
Wednesday – 25 × 400m in 62–64 sec, with 200m recovery jogging in 50 sec after each
Saturday – 5 × 2000m in 5:30, with 800m recovery jogging in 3:15 after each
Alternate Tuesday workout – 4 × 500m in 61–62 sec. 5 × 300m in 45 sec. 10 × 200m in 28 sec. Jog 100m recovery after each
Alternate Thursday workout – 6 × 1000m in 2:35, with 1000m jogging in 4–5 minutes after each
Alternate Sunday workout – morning: 8 km continuously at 3:15 per km. Afternoon: 12 × 300m in 44–46 sec, with 100m recovery jogging in 30sec after each.

References

Bock, Eberhard, 'Alberto Cova (Italien) Neue Taktik nach Wm-erfolg' in *Der Leichtathlet*, No. 45, November 10, 1983.
Bicourt, John, 'Interview with Alberto Cova' in *Athletics Weekly*, Vol. 37, No. 8.

ROBERT DE CASTELLA (Fig 2)
This sequence of Robert de Castella was taken during the 1983 AAA 10,000m championships, in which he finished fourth with a time of 28:27.65. He was the winner of the 1983 World Championships Marathon in Helsinki, Finland, in 2:10:03, after recording successive intermediate 10 km times of 31:22; 1:01:56; 1:33:10; and 2:03:28.

Francois Robert de Castella is of French-Swiss ancestry and was born on 27 February 1957 in

Fig 1 (*Overleaf*) 10km: Alberto Cova (It), world champion 1983

Fig 1

1

2

3

7

8

9

13

14

15

4

5

6

10

11

12

16

17

18

Melbourne, Australia, the eldest of seven children. He is a graduate of Xavier College and Swinburne College in Melbourne. He is 1.80m (5ft 10ins) tall, weighs 65 kg (143lbs) and has a maximum oxygen uptake of 85 ml per kg of bodyweight per minute. De Castella is employed as a biophysicist in the Sportsmedicine Department of the Australian Institute of Sports and is married to former Australian cross-country champion Gayelene Clews.

Regarded as one of the world's premier Marathon runners, de Castella's best marks are: 400m (57.0 in 1980); 800m (1:57 in 1975); 1500m (3:49 in 1981); 3000m (8:04.6 in 1979); 5000m (13:34.28 in 1981); 10,000m (28:12.2); 15km (road) (42:47 in 1983); half-Marathon (1:01:18 in 1982); and Marathon (2:08:18 in 1981).

In this photo-sequence de Castella is running at an average speed of a fraction of a second slower than 68 sec for each 400m of the race. When his knees are closest together, as seen in frame 7, there seems to be a very slight forward lean, indicating he may possibly be accelerating. However, in 15 de Castella's body is nearly erect, indicating he is running at a constant speed.

The supporting phase of the stride is seen in the left foot in frames 6 and 7, and in the right foot in 14 and 15. The driving phase of de Castella's stride in seen in the left leg in 8 to 10, and the right leg in 16 to 18. The recovery phase is seen in the right leg in 3 to 13, and in the left leg in 11 to 18. Both of de Castella's feet are off the ground approximately 50 per cent of the time as seen in frames 3 to 5 and 11 to 13. Each foot is in ground-contact about 25 per cent of the time, as seen in 6 to 10 and 14 to 18 (although these percentages may not be immediately apparent from this sequence). While it is true that each athlete's form in running correctly differs somewhat, it is obvious that de Castella's form is orthodox and correct (for him) in every respect.

Robert de Castella's Training

Typical workouts at age 15 to 17 years:

Sunday - 20-23 km (12-14 miles) continuous cross-country run in the Ferny Creek area of the Dandenong mountains, outside Melbourne

Monday - 10 km (6¼ miles) relaxed continuous cross-country run

Tuesday - 5 km (3 miles) continuously over a course consisting of 6-8 hills, each covering a distance of 180m, followed by 250m of recovery running after each series of hills

Wednesday - 16 km (10 miles) relaxed continuous running

Thursday - 11 km (7 miles) continuous relaxed run, or 6-8 × 200m very fast on the track, each followed by 200m of recovery jogging

Friday - rest

Saturday - race each week, except January and February during very hot summer weather

De Castella's total average weekly mileage during this period was approximately 60-80 km (40-50 miles).

Typical training since 1979:

Sunday - morning: 29-34 km (17-22 miles) continuous run in 2:15-2:20. Afternoon: 8 km (5 miles) easy continuous run.

Monday through *Friday* at 8.00am to 9.00am - 8-10km (5-6 miles) at a reasonably rapid continuous pace, but never at a 'long slow distance' speed

Monday afternoon - 17km (10 miles) continuous relaxed run

Tuesday afternoon - 20km (12 miles) continuous run, including 5km (3 miles) of hilly terrain. Alternate Tuesday workout: 12 laps on a 400m track, running strongly for 100m on each straight and running 100m more slowly and relaxed on the curve after each fast surge on the straight

Wednesday afternoon - 25-30km (15-18 miles) continuous relaxed run in 1:55-2:00 hours

Thursday afternoon - Track session. 5km (3 miles) warmup, followed by 8 × 400m in 63sec each, with 200m of recovery jogging after each, or 8 × 200m at near full speed, with 200m recovery jogging after each

Friday afternoon - 16km (10 miles) continuous relaxed run

Saturday - race or sustained long run of 32km (20 miles) or longer. Average weekly mileage: 185km (110 miles).

'Deek', as he is known to close associates, does no weight training. He and his only coach, Pat Clohessy, scorn the use of 'long slow distance' distance running. They emphasize that all de Castella's continuous runs are performed at a reasonably speedy but not exhausting effort. He does very little stretching as a part of his training routine. His workouts are basically the same throughout the year, in as much as Coach Clohessy does not believe in traditional 'peaking' for a particular race. The intervals he runs on the track are never longer than 400m and never more than eight in number. His 'relaxed' running in terms of speed is 6: 15 to 6: 20 per mile.

One variation in de Castella's workouts comes approximately five weeks before a Marathon when he runs 30 miles continuously in about 3: 20: 00. Much of his training today takes place in the Stromlo Forest, near Canberra.

References

Temple, Cliff, 'King of the Marathon' in *Athletics Weekly*, Vol. 37, No. 18.

Wischnia, Bob, 'Robert de Castella' in *Runner's World*, Vol. 19, No. 4, April 1984.

Personal correspondence with Pat Clohessy, Xavier College, Kew, Victoria, Australia.

COVA VERSUS DE CASTELLA

Some interesting comparisons and observations can be made in the running techniques and training of Alberto Cova (AC) and Robert de Castella (RdC).

RdC is 2cm (¾in.) taller and 7kg (15lb) heavier than AC. This presents a basis for differences in form between these two superior athletes. In terms of the ratio between body surface as compared to body mass for the purpose of eliminating body heat, AC obviously has an advantage.

In successful racing at either middle distance (800m-10km) or long distance (10km-42,195m), efficiency of movement is a factor in avoiding unnecessary fatigue. On the basis of their competitive results, the running form of AC and RC is undoubtedly efficient in relation to the differing physical characteristics of each. For example, it appears that RdC's arms move farther across (in front of) his body than those of AC. This is not an error on the part of either athlete, since runners quite naturally and automatically develop their most efficient form when running distances longer than sprints.

It is well known that the faster the running speed, the longer the stride, the higher the heel rises towards the hip behind the body at the conclusion of the driving phase of each stride, and the higher the knee rises in front of the body during the recovery phase. No meaningful comparison may be made in these aspects of running form by examining the sequence photos of AC and RdC. These aspects of running form may be demon-strated clearly by comparing photo-sequences of the same athlete at different running speeds, which is not possible here. Because every athlete differs at least slightly from another in terms of height, weight, muscle origin and insertion, exact location of centre of gravity, and in numerous other ways, it is obvious that no two athletes should ever display identical running form, even though they all obey the same basic mechanical laws in their movement.

One cannot deny that basic differences do exist between the form of Marathon runners and middle distance specialists. This difference, apart from individual differences in basic running form, results from the variation in speed of movement. For example, if AC were photographed while running at a slower Marathon pace, his kick-up behind of the rear foot, knee-lift in front by the forward leg and stride length would all be somewhat less pronounced than what we see in the photos, and the same would be true in the case of RdC. Slightly different form is used by any athlete when running speed is altered.

An examination of their best marks over distances of 800m through to 10,000m reveals AC is considerably faster at these middle-distance events. AC is not known to have attempted the full Marathon, but his time of 1: 02: 16 for the half-Marathon causes one to suspect that excellence over the full distance is not beyond his capabilities. This, however, is only speculation, since one's maximum oxygen uptake and mental desire may be crucial in negotiating the full Marathon at speeds faster than 2: 09: 00. On the other hand, RdC has an oxygen uptake among the highest ever recorded. It is unfortunate that AC's VO_2 maximum is unavailable for comparison. One may speculate that on the basis of their known racing results, it appears more feasible for AC to race successfully at the full 42,195m distance than for RdC to produce significantly faster results over the middle distances than he has recorded so far.

Theoretically, a 2: 15: 00 Marathon requires a total of 763 litres of oxygen. The Marathon runner acquires 745 litres (97.5 per cent) via oxygen uptake during the race and 18 litres (2.5 per cent) anaerobically via oxygen debt.[1] This suggests that the Marathon runner should train mostly by long

Fig 2 (*Overleaf*) Robert de Castella (Australia), 1983 world champion in the Marathon

Fig 2

1

2

3

7

8

9

13

14

15

4

5

6

10

11

12

16

17

18

runs. An examination of the above workouts reveals Coach Pat Clohessy has wisely guided RdC towards a theoretically correct ratio of continuous fast runs and shorter faster anaerobic training. Clohessy's avoidance of peaking before competition appears to have a logical basis. RdC appears to gradually prepare himself throughout the training year for the stress of Marathon racing, rather than relying on any belated special training efforts just prior to racing.

A 29:00–10,000m theoretically requires 178 litres of oxygen. Ninety per cent or 160 litres, are acquired via oxygen uptake, while the remaining 10 per cent (18 litres) are acquired anaerobically via the oxygen debt mechanism[1,2]. This also suggests that much of the training of the 10km specialist should be of a continuous fast nature, although more of the fast-paced track training is necessary than in the case of training for the Marathon. Coach Giorgio Rondelli has apparently taken this into account, judging by the above description of AC's workouts. It is interesting to note, however, that AC's training is apparently more varied in terms of speed and distances than that of RdC.

In terms of the total volume of running done weekly by these two champions, it appears AC runs about 30km per week less than RdC. This seems logical considering the widely different distances over which they specialize.

References
1 Nett, Toni, *Der Lauf*, Bartels and Wernitz, Berlin, 1960.
2 Robinson, Sid, 'Physiological Considerations of Pace in Running Middle-Distance Races' in *International Track and Field Digest*.

4 RELAYS
Tadeusz Cuch and Jim Alford

Tadeusz Cuch

Poland
(Acknowledgements to Polski Zwiazek Lekkiej Atletyki)
Translation by Janusz Skrybant

Tadeusz Cuch was a world class sprinter and relay runner not so very long ago. He ran a 10.3 100m and 20.8 200m and in 1971, on the second leg of the 4 × 100m relay, he helped Poland to a 39.2sec clocking. Now working for the famous Legia Club in Warsaw, he is Poland's national coach for sprints and relay.

I was privileged to meet Tadeusz at an England versus Poland match in Birmingham, where he told me how he had developed his own version of the 'rolling' start with the emphasis on a drive from the front foot. Tadeusz was a regular second-leg runner in the Polish relay team and this particular start is notoriously difficult in the outer lanes because the incoming runner is obscured by the other teams. Tadeusz found that a relatively passive pull through of the rear foot from the standing-start position allowed him more time to judge the approach of his incoming team member.

Tadeusz Cuch now coaches the likes of Marian Woronin, a sub 10sec 100m runner, and maintains the Polish tradition – of the best-trained 4 × 100m relay team in the world!

4x100m Relay

INTRODUCTION

The 4 × 100m relay is undoubtedly not only one of the most beautiful but also one of the most difficult events of the athletics spectrum. The relay is most often used as the highlight of major games beginning with the Olympics in Stockholm in 1912 when the relay was first run. It is an event all on its own. It is a competition between squads which are chosen for their mental and physical qualities, and victory will be achieved by the squad which has developed the most efficient techniques in starting, running with a baton and passing of the baton. The demands of relay running often enable runners to find hidden reserves enabling them to excel. This can often be verified by a theoretically weaker squad winning against much stronger opposition.

THE RULES IN BRIEF

The 4 × 100m relay is characterized by sequential running with and passing of a baton by the respective members of the squad in the fastest possible time. The baton is in general 28–30cm long, weighs no less than 50g and has a circumference of 12–13cm. The relay is run in lanes which have specific zones or relay boxes marked within which the baton must be passed (Fig 1). The relay box is 20m in length and is marked by lines preferably coloured yellow, across the lane. The line designating the relay box itself is included in the overall length of the relay box.

Takeover zones 2, 3 and 4 have an additional line, the IAAF recommended colour of which is green, marked 10m back from the beginning of the takeover zone. This is called an acceleration zone and the receivers are allowed to start their run from any spot up to the 10m line. Check marks may be made on the track within the competitor's lane but objects must not be used for this, either on the track or alongside it. The meeting organizers may supply special material for this purpose.

The runner must hold the baton at all times during his run and if the baton is dropped the runner who dropped it must be the one who picks it up. If a changeover is deemed faulty then the deciding factor is the position of the baton itself in relation to the box and not the position of the runner or any part of his body which may be in the relay box or outside it at the time that the baton is passed. Having passed the baton the runner should stay in his own lane until all the other runners have finished their part of the race. In the event of a relay runner consciously impeding a member of another team by encroaching into the respective lane then the encroaching team may be liable to disqualification. Any form of physical aid, either by pushing or any other means, is not allowed and if it transpires that physical aid has been given then that will lead to disqualification of the offending team.

TECHNIQUE OF BATON CHANGING

The first runner, starting from a crouch start, holds the baton in his right hand and keeps to the inside of his lane until the end of his respective relay box. The baton is passed over into the left hand of the second runner who then runs along the outside part of his lane.

The baton is passed over into the right hand of

Fig 1 (*Opposite*) Track markings

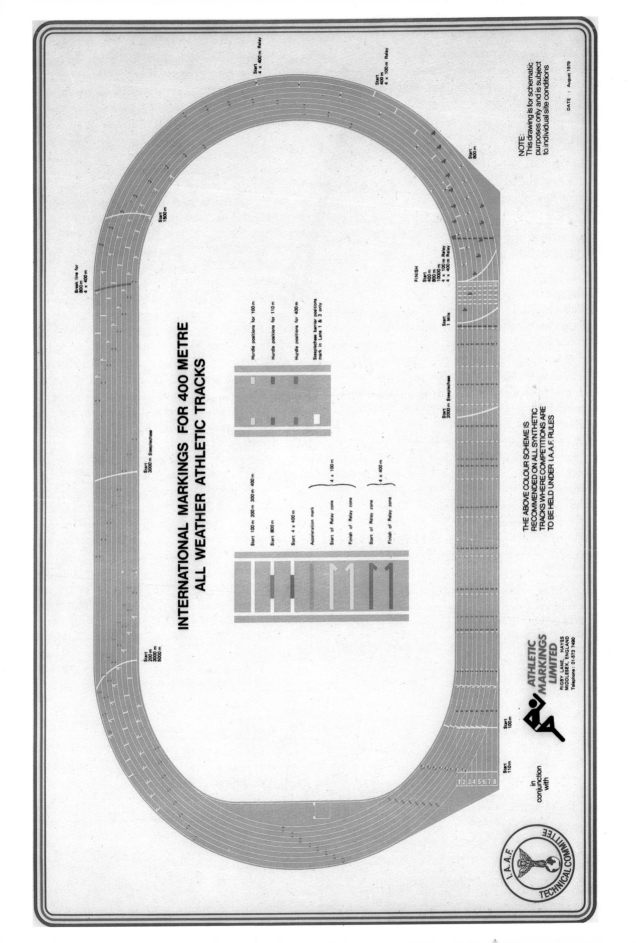

INTERNATIONAL MARKINGS FOR 400 METRE
ALL WEATHER ATHLETIC TRACKS

Start
4 x 400 m Relay

Start
4 x 100 m Relay

Start
400 m

Start
800 m

Break line for
800 m
4 x 400 m

Start
1500 m

Start
3000 m Steeplechase

Start
200 m
3000 m
5000 m

Start
100 m

Start
110 m

Hurdle positions for 100 m

Hurdle positions for 110 m

Hurdle positions for 400 m

Steeplechase barrier positions
mark in Lane 1 & 3 only

Start 100 m 200 m 300 m 400 m

Start 800 m

Start 4 x 400 m

Acceleration mark

Start of Relay zone

Finish of Relay zone

4 x 100 m

Start of Relay zone

Finish of Relay zone

4 x 400 m

FINISH
Start
400 m
800 m
1000 m
4 x 100 m Relay
4 x 400 m Relay

Start
1 Mile

Start
2000 m Steeplechase

1 2 3 4 5 6 7 8

THE ABOVE COLOUR SCHEME IS
RECOMMENDED ON ALL SYNTHETIC
TRACKS WHERE COMPETITIONS ARE
TO BE HELD UNDER I.A.A.F. RULES

NOTE:
This drawing is for schematic
purposes only and is subject
to individual site conditions

DATE : August 1979

in
conjunction
with

*ATHLETIC
MARKINGS
LIMITED*

RIGBY LANE, HAYES
MIDDLESEX, ENGLAND
Telephone : 01-573 7490

I.A.A.F.
TECHNICAL COMMITTEE

the third runner whose running line through the box must give the incoming runner space to pass the baton. On receiving the baton he keeps to the inside part of the lane.

The last relay runner starts in exactly the same position as the second relay runner and he will receive the baton into his left hand and will run along the right side of the lane, ie the outside part.

It is obvious that the efficiency of relay running is dependent upon two factors:

a) the speed at which the runners can cover their respective distances.
b) the technique and speed of passing the actual baton.

The speed at which the distances can be covered by the runners is dictated by certain pre-disposing factors and is related to the individual ability of each respective runner, which is in itself a separate subject. It is wise to point out, however, that the baton itself should not interfere with the freedom of movement of the upper limbs during the race itself. If one observes a novice runner running a relay then some limitation in the movement of the limb holding the baton can be seen and in this case it should be pointed out to the athlete and he should be advised to hold the baton in a more relaxed manner and to try and run imagining that the baton is not there.

Among the relay squads that are most successful in the major games, ie Olympic, European Championships, there can be seen two methods of baton passing:

a) Upsweep method: USSR, German Democratic Republic, France.
b) Downsweep method: USA, Jamaica, Poland.

From the above it can be seen that each respective team has its own technique and style of baton passing. However, recently it is becoming obvious that more and more countries are changing over to the downsweep method of baton passing and examples of these are Hungary and Italy.

The Upsweep Method (Fig 2)

In the upsweep method the changeover takes place between a distance of 120cm to 2m. The passing of the baton occurs in an upward movement by a straight arm. At the same time the baton is received by an arm which is pointing backward and locked at the elbow*. The outgoing runner upon hearing the agreed signal from the incoming runner quickly extends his arm backwards locking it at the elbow, the thumb and fingers are separated and pointing downwards forming an obtuse angle. The fingers are brought together and stiffened slightly. Up to the time that he receives the baton the outgoing runner tries to keep his arm as still as possible. Into this outstretched arm the incoming runner quickly moves his straight arm upwards and in such a way that the outgoing runner can grasp the baton as near to the incoming runner's palm as is possible.

In this way the baton is passed by the right hand to the left and from then on by the left to the right. Too small a surface area between the thumb and index finger creates great difficulties in accurate baton passing. There is another fault in this technique insomuch that in the event of the baton-passing not being very precise then the baton appears 'lost' too far into the palm and this leads to a tendency for the runner to move the baton forwards with the fingers or by hitting the hips with the bottom of the baton and this is a very risky procedure and can result in the baton being dropped.

Fig 2 The upsweep method. Note that the handhold is lower at each changeover

*In the 'classic' upsweep the elbow is at approximately 90 degrees – F.D.

Fig 3 The downsweep method. Note that the handhold remains the same at each changeover

The Downsweep Method (Fig 3)

The downsweep method of baton passing in the 4×100m relay is used with success by several national teams. As in the upsweep method the baton is passed from the right hand to the left and then the left hand passing it to the right. In the downsweep method the baton-change takes place over a distance of 2–3m and this is dependent upon the physical attributes of the respective members of the relay squad. The outgoing runner when hearing the signal from the incoming runner moves the appropriate arm backwards in a positive and slightly angled manner to a level not higher than the shoulder line. The upper arm is straight at the elbow, the back of the hand is facing downwards. The thumb and index fingers are widely spaced forming an obtuse angle. The remaining fingers are separated and slightly flexed. The baton is received into such a palm from the incoming runner with an outstretched arm. In the final phase of the changeover the elbow joint locks quickly and the baton is passed in a downsweep action. At the moment that the baton is passed the free end of the baton is pointing slightly upwards and is placed as quickly as possible into the palm of the outgoing runner.

For the best end result in both techniques, the changeover should occur when both runners are travelling at maximum speed and the actual changeover should be as quick as possible. The majority of experts consider that the speediest changeover occurs when the baton is actually changed over at a distance between 2m and 4m from the end of the relay box. This can be verified by experimental methods during training specifically aimed at efficiency of baton-changing. In the downsweep method an important role is played by the palmar surface area of the outgoing runner insomuch that the changeover between the incoming and the outgoing runner can be finalized over a slightly increased distance*. Analysis of changeover with this method also indicates that the incoming runner often tends to delay actual handing over of the baton and he should aim to pass the baton as quickly as is possible.

TECHNIQUE OF THE OUTGOING
RUNNER AND HIS START

During the course of a 4×100m relay various styles can be seen employed by outgoing runners. There are two basic styles: (a) crouch start (b) upright start.

The Crouch Start (Figs 4 and 5)

The athlete assumes a similar position to that as if he were starting from starting blocks. When the command 'on your marks' is given the head is turned to the side or backwards to observe the incoming runner. When the incoming runner is nearing the check marks the outgoing runner gets set (ie assumes that position), supporting himself on one of his arms whilst the other arm is extended backwards. The head is turned sideways. When the incoming runner reaches the check mark the outgoing runner starts to run out of this position with maximum speed. One of the faults of this method is that the outgoing runner starting in this way can, by excessive movement of the shoulders, unintentionally upset not only the rhythm of his own running but also that of the athletes in the adjacent lane. Another fault of this method is that the outgoing runner starting in this way narrows his field of vision in relation to the check mark.

* The increased distance is due to the extended arm of the receiver in the downsweep versus the lower (sometimes bent) arm in the upsweep. – F.D.

Fig 4 (*Opp. above*) Crouch start, head pointing
sideways
Fig 5 (*Opp. below*) Crouch start, head pointing
backwards
Fig 6 (*Above*) The upright start

The Upright Start (Fig 6)
The technique of the upright start is generally easier to teach and master. In general the outgoing
runner assumes a position to the right of the lane,
the right foot (leading leg) is placed along the outside of the lane and pointing in the direction of
movement. At the same time the left leg (trailing
leg) is positioned 20–30cm behind the leading leg
and the foot is pointing inwards. The upper limbs
are outstretched and are placed slightly below the
shoulder line. The head is turned to the rear.

As soon as the incoming runner reaches the
check mark the legs bend at the knees, the runner
leans forward and transfers the bodyweight to the
left leg. The leading leg initiates the movement and
at the same time the head turns and points in the
direction of movement together with the arm
action which is similar to that of a straight sprint.

The movement can also be initiated by the rear
(left) leg. The arms are raised and point forward

and back, the head is turned backwards looking
for the incoming runner and at the moment that
the incoming runner reaches the check mark the
left leg initiates the movement having transferred
the bodyweight. Until contact is made by the left
foot the trunk is turned sideways and the arms are
still raised and pointing forward and back. As
soon as contact is made by the left foot the head
is turned to the front and the arms are brought
vigorously into action. In such a way the outgoing
runner can observe the incoming runner for a
much longer period.

CHOOSING ATHLETES FOR THE
RESPECTIVE LEGS OF THE 4 × 100M
RELAY
An important factor relating to the choice of athlete for the 4 × 100m relay is the actual distance of
the relay leg which the runner has to cover. In
general the runners chosen for the 4 × 100m relay
are the best runners that are available over the
100m and 200m flat sprint. But certain basic fac-

Fig 7 (*Overleaf*) 4 × 100m relay: Mike McFarlane to
Jim Evans (GB) on first changeover

65

Fig 7

1

2

5

6

9

10

13

14

3

4

7

8

11

12

15

16

Fig 7

17

18

19

20

21

22

23

24

tors determine the choice of a runner for a particular leg. One of these factors is the particular athlete's speed in relation to his relay leg. Together with this basic ability to run the fastest leg possible it has to be noted that the relay legs themselves are of varying distances and also some are on the straight and some are on the bend. It is therefore essential that the runners must be chosen to complement not only themselves but the distances over which they must run and also the nature of the relay lane in relation to whether it is straight or on the bend.

The runner on the first leg, which is round the first bend, has to run a distance of approximately 106–108m. So the lead-off runner must possess excellent starting and good bend-running technique.

The runner on the second (straight) relay leg has to cover a distance of approximately 126–128m. This is one of the longest relay legs and the athlete chosen must have the ability to maintain maximum speed over a much longer distance than 100m. The best choice of athlete for this relay leg is usually one who is excellent at running 200m and he would obviously therefore possess the stamina to maintain his speed over the longer distance.

Similar characteristics should also be possessed by the runner running the third leg and also he should have a very good bend-running technique.

The last runner in the relay has to run an approximate distance of 120m and he should possess very good qualities of mental resilience and competitive spirit in order to be able to fight until the very last moment to the tape. This runner is usually chosen from one of the best runners that is available over the flat 100m.

It can be seen, therefore, that it is essential to choose the most suitable runners for the various relay legs, taking into account not only physical factors but also the mental attitudes of the athletes to the race itself and to the respective relay leg.

McFARLANE TO EVANS (Fig 7)
The photo-sequence shows the first changeover during a 4 × 100m relay when the baton is passed using the upsweep method.

The incoming runner is holding the baton in his right hand and he is running in the inside part of the lane. The right arm of the incoming runner is straight and is ready to pass the baton (frames 1, 2 and 3).

The outgoing runner is running in the outside part of the lane and, at the moment that he hears the signal from his partner, he quickly extends his left arm backwards locking it at the elbow (frames 4 to 12). The palm of the outgoing runner is pointing backwards with an obtuse angle being formed by the thumb which is separated from the fingers which are joined.

Into this 'prepared palm' the incoming runner now tries to pass the baton as quickly as possible, from below upwards so that it sits between the thumb and joined fingers (frames 14 to 19).

The incoming runner tries to pass the baton in such a way that the outgoing runner can grasp it as near to the incoming runner's hand as is possible (frames 18 and 19). Having received the baton the outgoing runner continues his run passing the baton into the next runner's left hand.

KONDRATYEVA TO VINOGRADOVA (Fig 8)
The photo-sequence of the Russian women's 4 × 100m relay squad shows an exceptionally bad changeover. From frame 2 one has to surmise whether or not the athlete running with the baton in her right hand has given the predetermined shouted signal to enable the outgoing athlete to move her left hand backwards to receive the baton.

The actual movement of the left hand backwards by the outgoing runner is shown in frames 3 to 7 and the actual passing of the baton is shown in 8 to 14. The actual changeover occurs over too short a distance (0.5m) and this leads to an inaccurate and slow changeover of the baton.

There are two main reasons for poor changeovers: either a delayed start by the outgoing runner, or one which is far too early by the outgoing runner. The latter will result in the outgoing runner having to slow down so that the baton can be successfully changed over within the relay box. In the case of a delayed start by the outgoing runner the incoming runner should give the predetermined signal for the outgoing runner to reach back for the baton earlier than planned and this will have the effect of compensating, to some extent, for the delayed start and preventing the two runners coming into such close proximity as to impede each other. The runner passing the baton must also remember that the changeover must not take place until she is inside the takeover zone.

Fig 8 (*Overleaf*) Women's 4 × 100m relay: European Cup 1983. USSR team's first changeover, L Kondratyeva to Y Vinogradova

Fig 8

1

2

5

6

9

10

13

14

4 RELAYS
Tadeusz Cuch and Jim Alford

Jim Alford

Wales
(Acknowledgements to the British Amateur Athletic Board and the International
Amateur Athletic Federation)

Jim Alford has been actively engaged in top-class athletics, first as an athlete, then as a coach, journalist, author, lecturer and administrator, for the past 50 years. He set up a unique record in Welsh athletics by winning national titles at all distances from the 440yds to the three miles on the track and the nine miles on the country. In 1937 he captured the World Student Games 800m and 1500m titles and in 1938 at the British Empire Games in Sydney, Australia, he won the mile in a record time of 4min 11.5sec. He represented Great Britain at both half- and one-mile events but his international career was cut short by his RAF war service.

He was AAA national coach for Wales and the West from 1948 to 1961 and was the author of the original AAA instructional books on *Sprinting and Relay Racing* and *Middle Distance Running and Steeplechase*. In the early 1960s he served as Chief National Coach for the then Federation of Rhodesia and Nyasaland (now Zambia, Zimbabwe and Malawi) and later became Senior Lecturer in Physical Education at Shoreditch College of Education.

He is now a consultant for the International Amateur Athletic Federation with the position of Coordinator of the Development Programme, in which capacity he has travelled worldwide, lecturing on athletics coaching and administration.

4 x 400m Relay

In the 4 × 100m relay three superb changeovers can transform a merely good team into a world-beating one. The non-visual exchange used in that event, however, requires supremely accurate timing and perfect technical execution by each runner: teams need a really long period of practice and competition to reach the necessary consistency.

Sheer running ability obviously counts for a good deal more in the 4 × 400m relay. Races are not won because of a perfect changeover technique – but a poor technique can lose precious metres and a really bad changeover can lead to a dropped baton or disqualification.

In the shorter relay the emphasis, during the baton exchanges, is on maintaining or even increasing the speed of the baton. However, in the longer relay a visual exchange is used and the emphasis is now on a safe smooth changeover at a tactically favourable position in the box. The onus for a successful change is much more on the receiver; it is his responsibility to judge the speed and the condition of the incoming runner, which will vary according to the sort of race he has had to run.

The first leg of the 4 × 400m relay is run in lanes and so is the first bend of the second leg; only after crossing the line marking the exit from the first bend are runners free to move to the inside of the track. The first changeover, therefore, is the easier one, since it takes place with each team remaining within its allotted lane. For the last two exchanges, however, the receiver is allowed 'to move to an inner position on the track, provided this can be done without fouling'. The receiver, therefore, must use good judgment to take up a position which offers good visibility and a clear run to his team-mate, whose own judgment may well be impaired by fatigue and the stress of his final effort.

BELOVA TO KORBAN (Fig 9)

There are several variations of the visual changeover. In frames 1 to 16 Lyudmila Belova and Jelena Korban make effective use of the method employed by the USSR women's team in their match against Great Britain and Northern Ireland in 1983. In this method (frames 1 to 10) the baton is carried in the right hand throughout the race. The receiver having taken the baton in her left hand (frames 4 to 10) immediately transfers it to her right hand (frames 11 to 16). In this way there is the least possible disturbance to the outgoing runner's balance and rhythm and there is no risk of a forgetful and confusing switching of the baton from one hand to another at the last moment, as a tired runner is finishing her leg of the race. The one disadvantage of this method is that most athletes find it more natural to receive the baton in their right hands, but there are several compensatory advantages:

1 Most runners find it easier to carry the baton in the right hand.
2 Turning the head and shoulders to the left should permit a good view of the curve of the track and facilitate the approach to the bend.
3 Provided the receiver has moved to the inside of the track, the left (receiving) arm is shielded from collisions with other runners.

Fig 9 (*Overleaf*) Women's 4 × 400m relay: L Belova to J Korban (USSR) in GB v USSR match 1983. USSR won in 3:32.84

Fig 9

4 There is less risk of the receiver being distracted by the movements of other runners.
5 The method facilitates a good reach back of the receiver's hand (frames 5 to 8).

The downward pass into an upturned palm provides very good 'free distance' between the two runners during the exchange, but the method used by the USSR women (unlike the method used in the non-visual change) in which the receiver's head and shoulders are turned so far to the left and the hand is turned counterclockwise, makes it very difficult for the receiver to catch a glimpse of the track ahead of her and to accelerate away along a straight path. The tendency is to move away too slowly and lose baton speed unnecessarily. Frames 15 and 16 show that the apparent free distance evident in 8 is deceptive; in fact, Belova almost overruns Korban. This method is effective enough

Fig 10 West Germany (A team) v Great Britain (B): the Germans use an upsweep pass. The outgoing British runner has misjudged her start

in the sort of situation illustrated, where the USSR team is well clear of the opposition, but it could lead to difficulties in other circumstances entailing many more teams and closer competition.

WEST GERMANY (Fig 10)
Another variation of the visual pass is shown by the West German pair (A team) in Fig 10. This method, basically the same as the upward non-visual pass, has much to commend it especially if the pass is made from the right to the left hand. It obviates the exaggerated turning of head and shoulders shown by Jelena Korban in frames 4 to 8 of Fig 9, and it makes it possible to watch the incoming runner just by a turn of the head and to use peripheral vision to check that the way ahead is clear, so that the receiver can make a fast smooth getaway. Note the slight bend in the receiver's elbow. This, together with the good separation of the thumb from the fingers, makes it possible to offer the hand as a steady clear target for the baton.

Normally the changeover will be an early one, ie it will be completed no later than the mid-line of the 20m zone. The receiver must allow for a possibly fairly abrupt slowing-up by the incoming runner; he should wait until his team-mate is almost upon him, adjust his speed to that of the incoming runner as he reaches back for the baton and really accelerate only when the baton is safely in his hand. A good deal of practice should be carried out with the incoming runner varying his approach speed and with several other pairs of athletes simulating competitive situations. In this way a safe dependable and quite fast changeover can be developed.

Note: Care should be exercised when taking split times for the 4×400m relay. The time should be taken from the moment the outgoing runner reaches the mid-line of the changeover zone to the moment he again reaches it at the end of his leg. The baton exchange should be ignored.

TACTICS

Tactics for the first three runners are straightforward – each runner can do no better than to run his best-possible race in the best-possible time, so that the last runner is placed in the most advantageous position. The last runner still cannot afford to slow the pace or he may allow runners behind him the chance to catch up, but a runner with good tactical sense can pace himself well so that he uses other runners to pull him along and judges his final effort perfectly for the best-possible finishing position. The first three runners should aim for their best-possible time; the last runner aims to win.

ORDER OF RUNNING

The factors affecting the order of running are as follows:

1 The runner on the first leg needs to be capable of finishing within striking distance of the leaders, so that the second runner does not have to waste a lot of effort fighting his way around many other competitors.
2 The runner on the final leg must be an excellent competitor, one who has good tactical ability and pace judgment and who is a good 'fighter'.
3 If the team is one of rather uneven ability, it will generally pay to put the second-best runner on the first leg, the slowest on the second leg, the next slowest on the third leg and the fastest on the last leg.
4 If the team is fairly well balanced, an ascending order of running is effective, ie start with the slowest and finish with the fastest runner.

5 HURDLES
Alexander Ewen

Scotland
(Acknowledgements to the British Amateur Athletic Board)

Sandy Ewen is a British Senior Coach and a Churchill Fellow. In 1973 he studied the art and science of hurdling in Italy, Germany and Poland. He has discussed technique and training with most of the world's best hurdlers and hurdling coaches and he has lectured at IAAF courses, including one in China whose athletic talent is about to enthrall enthusiasts throughout the world.

A mathematics teacher at Marr College in Troon, Sandy has coached international athletes such as Ricky Taylor, Moira Niccol, Liz Sutherland and Norman Gregor.

Hurdles

In 1975, in his book *Hurdling for Women*, the eminent Soviet hurdles coach Boris Shchennikov wrote:

> No other form of female athletics concentrates in itself such an organic inter-relationship of speed, strength, flexibility, precision, high coordination and rhythm as does hurdling. Perhaps it is this peculiarity which demands of women specializing in hurdling high strength of will, versatility and high technical preparation.

When these words were written, they referred to the women's 100m and 200m hurdles events, but they might also have been directed at the women's 400m hurdles as well as the men's 110m and 400m hurdles.

Unlike the field events in which the athlete has only to perform his technique once per round with time between rounds to try to make any adjustments that may be required, the hurdler has to repeat this technique ten times – though not necessarily the same way each time – during his race in a set of circumstances which can change as the race progresses. Consequently, any time-loss in barrier clearance due to inefficiencies of technique may be multiplied by as much as ten if repeated.

How do the circumstances change during the race? These can be grouped under two headings: internal and external.

By 'internal' I mean the changes related to the athlete's own physical qualities - speed, coordination, rhythm and endurance. As the sprint hurdles race develops (this is especially true in the 100m hurdles event and coming more and more into the 110m hurdles) the barriers appear to be getting closer and closer and the athlete finds herself 'crowding' them. Adjustments have, therefore, to be made to adapt to this sensation. In the 400m event the fatigue question is much more obvious and most athletes make the necessary adjustments by 'changing down', sometimes more than once, during the second part of the race.

'Externally', the competition environment can be changed by the presence and actions of opponents (hitting their own hurdles and perhaps other peoples as well – as happened to Thomas Munkelt (GDR) in the 1983 World Championship final), the weather (especially wind conditions) or simply the lane draw. Depending on the individual athlete, any or all of these may affect performance negatively or, sometimes, positively.

In hurdling the main problem is the need to compromise the normal sprinting action in terms of stride length and flight path of the centre of gravity due to the presence, spacing and height of the ten barriers.

The spacing and height of the barriers are laid down by the rules of the event and are the same for everyone in the particular race irrespective of that athlete's height or, perhaps, more specifically, leg length. In the 100m hurdles Kerstin Knabe (GDR) at 1.80m has a different set of problems to face than her compatriot Annelie Ehrhardt who was only 1.66m tall, though they both ran similar times. In the same way in the women's 400m hurdles Chantal Rega (France) brings more basic speed to the event than does Ingrida Barkane

Fig 1 (*Overleaf*) In the women's 100m hurdles the barriers are much lower than in the men's 110m, thus clearance technique is less exaggerated. No. 1 Lucyna Langer/Kalek (Pol) was 1982 European champion. No. 5 is Z Bielczyk (Pol) and No. 2 is Shirley Strong (GB), the British record holder

Fig 1

3

4

7

8

11

12

15

16

(USSR); she is also 20 cm shorter and has a totally different set of problems to solve.

This need for compromise obviously varies from athlete to athlete and from event to event, but the technical requirements are based on certain principles:

(a) the centre of gravity should be raised as little as possible
(b) as little time as possible should be spent in the air
(c) the athlete should land in a position for the continuation of fast running.

To achieve these three objectives certain points of technique should be borne in mind as we begin to look at the sequences.

1 In the 'high' (110m) hurdles the athlete has to lift his hips over the barrier without raising his centre of gravity too much. In the 100m hurdles and in the longer races less lift is required unless the athlete is extremely small (Fig 1).
2 The lead leg, bent at the knee, must be picked up faster than in the normal sprinting action.
3 The same lead leg should not be allowed to deviate from its normal (sprinting) plane of action – although in the 1983 World Championships it was noticeable that both the winner, Greg Foster (USA), 1.90m tall, and runner-up, Arto Bryggare (Finland), 1.93m, have developed lead-leg movements in which the leg is taken out of alignment (to the inside and outside respectively) in the attack on the hurdle.
4 The driving/take-off leg should be recovered no higher than is needed to clear the barrier. Indeed, in the case of many taller 100m hurdlers a technique seems to be developing where the trail knee is allowed to 'drop' after the hurdle in the latter stages of the race in order to counteract the 'crowding' problem; though the technique may also be the result of a coordination endurance problem.
5 The heel of the trail leg should, as far as possible, maintain its normal plane of action while the knee is taken out to the side before being brought back to a high bent position in the direction of the run.
6 No rotations should result from faulty limb movements which take the trunk out of alignment. The arms often reflect such movements and so can be a useful guide to the coach.

7 The arms can be used in this way to absorb the rotations set up by the leg movements, but they can also be used to lead the legs. The very fast bent arm action of someone like Kerstin Knabe (GDR) makes the legs respond with three snappy strides between barriers.

110M HURDLES – RENALDO NEHEMIAH (USA) (Fig 2)

This sequence shows Renaldo Nehemiah clearing hurdle 9 during the race at London's Crystal Palace stadium in 1981 when he set the UK All-comer's Record of 13.17 sec.

In frames 1 and 2 we see Nehemiah completing the last stride before take-off. This stride must be shorter than the one before and Nehemiah achieves this by placing the take-off foot on the track faster than in the previous strides.

Frames 2 to 8 show the attack at the hurdle. In this phase the lead leg holds the key as it moves very quickly from behind the body towards the hurdle, knee first and fully bent to diminish its moment of inertia. If it is done correctly when the thigh has reached its highest point the foot will still be behind its knee. If it has straightened out more than that there will be a transfer of momentum effect as in high jumping and the centre of gravity will rise more than is needed with resultant time-loss.

This lead-leg movement is often made with the toes pulled back, but in Renaldo Nehemiah's case (frames 5 to 8) the toes are extended.

Throughout this sequence the arms have been balancing the leg movements. Very reminiscent of Rod Milburn, the left arm starts bent at the elbow (frames 3 to 5) only to straighten as the right leg does likewise (6 to 8). In many cases the arm on the same side as the lead leg would have been taken farther back, but again Nehemiah displays the pattern of movements of his famous predecessor.

Frames 9 to 12/13 show Nehemiah crossing the hurdle. As soon as his heel crosses the rail it is quickly lowered to the track. This movement is assisted by the forward movement of the arm on the same side. At the same time the trail (take-off) leg is taken to the side in a circular motion with the knee only going high enough to clear the rail (frames 10 and 11). This movement is balanced and aided by the backward sweep of the bent lead arm.

Having maintained his body angle almost constant from frame 5 to 18, Nehemiah now raises his body upwards to produce the action–reaction effect of helping his lead leg's return to the track (frame 13). He lands well up on his toes in a very balanced position with his weight above the point of contact so that there is no braking effect and hence he is in an ideal position to continue running – a position aided by his well-controlled arms which are already very bent in preparation for their short-range work to balance the short-range leg work within the 9.14m space.

Just before the race featured, I had the good fortune to spend nearly a week with Renaldo Nehemiah at the home of his coach Wilbur Ross. I asked Nehemiah to describe what he looks for in a good race:

> The beginning is the slowest part of my race because I am not into the pattern. The first thing I try to do is to really get that out-of-control sensation – when I am really running on my toes with so much momentum and speed that I have to keep running. I must feel a little bit awkward. If I am very comfortable I am probably sitting back flat-footed, riding the hurdle more, spending more time in the air. When I am running fast my legs are up in the air the whole time.

To help him develop this 'out-of-control' feeling, coach Ross had Nehemiah running over hurdles *downhill* on a tarmac road. Initially, runs were done over correctly spaced hurdles 1 to 3 and 8 to 10. This progressed to runs over hurdles 1 to 5 and 8 to 10, and finally all ten hurdles. It is difficult to believe but Renaldo Nehemiah was able to keep running (as if he were running 3s between hurdles) and make the correct take-off point for hurdle 8 despite the space between 3 and 8, and later 5 and 8. 'I just kept my knees up and hit the hurdles (ie got to them correctly – SE). I never had any problems.'

This experience taught Nehemiah to cope with any balance problem which might arise in a race. He knew he had run faster than he would ever need to in a race!

One final thought in connection with the different running stride/rhythm between flat sprints and sprint hurdles, coach Ross says: 'Hurdlers hurdle – sprinters sprint.'

100M HURDLES – MARIA MERCHUK AND VERA KOMISOVA (USSR) (Fig 4)

This sequence shows Maria Merchuk (5) and Vera Komisova (4) clearing hurdles 8 and 9 in the international match GB v USSR at Birmingham's Alexander Stadium on 5 June 1983.

Up to this point Vera Komisova has been just in the lead but from here onwards Maria Merchuk moves to the front and wins in 13.19sec against Vera Komisova's 13.21sec.

We pick up the sequence at the take-off for hurdle 8. Both girls have just completed that all-important shorter final stride and are in the process of driving the thigh at the hurdle with the bent knee in the forefront. Vera Komisova, who seems the slightly more tense, has her legs and arms more coordinated but the more relaxed Maria Merchuk is just ahead. In both cases the thigh is quickly raised to the horizontal when the lower leg begins its swing towards the rail, in Vera Komisova's case with toes well back, while Maria Merchuk has hers well extended.

As the lower leg 'straightens' towards the hurdle, the balancing opposite arm moves out in a parallel direction, going from bent to reasonably straight, as in frame 4 in which both heels have reached the rail. The feet are quickly lowered to the ground with the assistance of the opposite (lead) arm, especially in the case of Maria Merchuk who lowers her arm (frame 7) and quickly brings through the other arm (9 to 12). Vera Komisova sweeps her lead arm back higher (8 to 10) but does get the beneficial push-through of the arm to add to the speed of put-down of the lead leg, which she also seems to attempt to quicken by raising the upper body (frames 12 to 14).

Both athletes land with the heel off the track, though there is the feeling that in Vera Komisova's case a braking effect may have occurred due to the contact point being slightly ahead of the centre of gravity; however, she is working very hard in frames 12 to 14 and is soon fully into her sprinting action.

In frames 11 to 16 one is left wondering about the changing upper-body position of Vera Komisova. As soon as she lands she seems to lean backwards. Is this a belated attempt to speed up the landing of the right foot, an attempt to combat

Fig 2 (*Overleaf*) 110m hurdles: Renaldo Nehemiah (USA) setting the United Kingdom record of 13.17sec in 1981

Fig 2

1

2

5

6

9

10

13

14

3

4

7

8

11

12

15

16

Fig 3

the braking effect of that foot or a postural change to fit her stride more easily into the 8.50m at that part of the race when the hurdles seem even closer? Certainly throughout the race she has shown a characteristic Eastern European tilting of the pelvis, but the signs of tension are in contrast to the freer movements of Maria Merchuk.

In frames 17 to 32 we get a better chance to see the hurdle clearances from a sideways-on position. In 18 to 24 both athletes are using a shortened stride length to combat the 'closeness' of the hurdles and the balancing reduced range of arm movement. Indeed, with many top hurdlers the arms are pumped vigorously through a limited range in the knowledge that this action will reduce the amplitude of the leg movement.

Frames 23 and 24 again show the shortening of the last stride with the faster strike on the ground before the attack on the hurdle. From this angle we can see that in this attack both keep their shoulders square to the front, with Maria Merchuk using more body lean and with strangely extended toes – which do not seem to help in this case as she raps the hurdle.

Again we see the postural changes in Vera Komisova, her more upright attack and seemingly backward lean of the trunk as she leaves the barrier. It might be of interest to add at this point a few of the hurdling routines used by Vera Komisova and her coach – the aforementioned Boris Shchennikov – routines which help to develop the ability to move the limbs correctly in a changing environment:

a) 3–5 hurdles, 3–3.5m apart, running one stride between

b) 4–5 hurdles, 11.5–12m apart, running five strides between

c) 2–3 hurdles, 16m apart, running seven strides between

d) 5–6 hurdles, alternately 11.5m and 8.5m apart, running five and three strides alternately

e) Crouch starts with hurdles 8.4–8.0 m apart

f) 8–10 hurdles at 7, 7.2, 7.8, 8, 8.2, 8.5, 8.5 and 8.5m apart

g) 10 or more hurdles, 8.24m apart

h) 10 hurdles with the first 6 at 8.5m and the last four at 8.25m.

Women hurdlers have to be strong in the legs. Two well-established methods for developing the quality they require are bounding and hurdle-jumping. If we accept the problems caused by the closeness of the hurdles then bounding should be used sparingly since it contributes to a greater stride length. Hurdle-jumping is the key activity, with many of the top 100m hurdlers jumping over 1m hurdles as part of their strength programme.

MEN'S 400M HURDLES - EDWIN MOSES (USA) (Fig 5)

In this sequence we see world champion and record holder Edwin Moses clearing hurdle 9 in one of his many victories at London's Crystal Palace track.

At this point in the race Moses, unlike almost every other 400m hurdler, has dealt with the 'problem part' of his race and we now see him running freely over the last few barriers. Someone once wrote: 'Moses alone in the world possesses the kind of strength and rhythm that is his from the 200m mark to the finish.' At this point in the race he is tired enough, and his stride length has shortened enough, to run all-out and have his steps fit in correctly.

Because of his long legs (94 cm/37 ins), long stride (2.97m/9ft 9ins) and great range of movement, combined with the leg speed and hurdling skill of a 13.5-sec 110m hurdler and the endurance developed by many repetitions over 500, 600, 800 and 1,000m, his 'problems', such as they are, occur in the first part of the race.

Edwin Moses runs 13 strides between barriers throughout the race though it is fairly obvious that he could run 12 for part of the way (as he has in training) before changing down to 13. Ideally, he could run 12 strides to hurdle 3 or 5 so that he

Fig 4 (*Overleaf*) 100m hurdles GB v USSR 1983: 1st Maria Merchuk 13.19 (No. 5), 2nd Vera Komisova 13.21 (No. 4), 3rd Shirley Strong 13.40 (No. 1). Komisova was 1980 Olympic champion

Fig 5 400m hurdles: Ed Moses (USA), 1976 and 1984 Olympic champion, is considered to be one of the greatest athletes of all time. He has run over 100 first-class races without defeat

Fig 6 Women's 400m hurdles: Anna Ambrazene (USSR) running 54.75sec in the 1983 European Cup

Fig 4

1

2

5

6

9

10

13

14

3

4

7

8

11

12

15

16

Fig 4

17

18

21

22

25

26

29

30

19

20

23

24

27

28

31

32

Fig 5

3

4

7

8

11

12

15

16

Fig 5

17

18

21

22

25

26

29

30

19

20

23

24

27

28

31

32

Fig 6

1

2

5

6

9

10

13

14

Fig 6

17

18

19

20

21

22

23

24

is on his normal left leg lead when he comes on to 13 strides.

Early in the race, when he is fresh, Edwin Moses (who overstrides a bit when running on the flat - as if clearing imaginary hurdles) must be careful not to run with his longest stride lest he gets too close to the barrier.

Rather than run 12s (which he hasn't yet done in a race), he has to chop to run 13s, losing momentum and wasting energy. If he stops trying to accelerate after hurdle 1 and is content to restrain himself in the back straight, the second half will become much easier.

As the sequence begins, Moses displays his excellent running form - upright trunk, knee pickup and drive from the other leg with the arms working with the legs (frames 1 to 5). In frames 6 and 7 the take-off leg lands just ahead of the centre of gravity but there is little braking effect as he passes over the point of contact, with a high hurdling-like pick-up of the leading knee (frame 11) and with the compensatory movements of the right arm.

Because of the relative lowness of the hurdle and Moses's height and great leg length, he does not need the exaggerated forward lean of the high hurdler. Instead in frames 11 to 20 we see him lowering his head with the action-reaction effect of raising the lead leg. The leading knee having reached its high point in frames 11 and 12, the heel is driven across the barrier with the corresponding forward-reaching of the right arm.

Having completed its drive, the right leg is folded up and taken to the side, but not in the manner of a high hurdler since the barriers are 15 cm (6 ins) lower. As it comes to the front, the trailing knee is assisted by the pull-back of arm which moves through a greater range to compensate for the additional mass of the leg (frames 22 to 24).

In 23 to 27 we see the trail leg taken far round to the front into the typically Moses stride and run on to the next hurdle.

In these last few frames it is important to notice the very full arm action (so different from that used by tall 100m hurdlers!) which leads the legs into the very full-striding action of this great athlete. If the arm action had been more restricted, the legs would have moved through a similarly reduced amplitude.

WOMEN'S 400M HURDLES (Fig 6)

This sequence shows world record holder Anna Ambrazene (USSR) clearing hurdle 8 in the 1983 Europa Cup Final in London.

Drawn in lane 2, Ambrazene had her main opponent, Ellen Fiedler (GDR) in front of her in lane 4. As usual, Fiedler started out fast - though not quite as fast as she had done in the World Championships final ten days before. This time Ambrazene tried to match Fiedler by running 15s during the first part of the race (instead of her usual 16s) and what happened in the sequence was a result of what had gone before.

In most of her races Ambrazene had problems at hurdle 8 because when she ran 16s to hurdle 7, this was the first hurdle after she had changed down - not in the sophisticated manner of a David Hemery by running wider in the lane or moving the legs faster earlier in the interval between hurdles to facilitate the fitting in of extra strides without having to patter. Indeed, in the race we see here she had run 15s to hurdle 5, 16s to hurdle 7 and we find her changing down once again to 17s as she approaches hurdle 8. Just before the sequence starts she has taken some four or five short 'pattery' strides as she tries to find her take-off point.

Frames 1 to 3 show the last of her short strides, because of which her body is leaning back, her shoulders are up and apprehension is shown in her face. Once she gets her foot on the ground the pattern of movement begins to follow the sequence that has been drilled. In frames 5 and 6 the leading knee comes up with the balancing movement of the left arm. No great forward lean is required in 400m hurdles unless the athlete is very short, so in frames 6 to 9 we see a lowering of her head followed by a slight lowering of the upper body as a whole. Frames 6, 7 and 8 also show one of the characteristics of Ambrazene's technique, namely turning out her right lower leg as she raises it at the hurdle. This she does at other parts of the race but it is never accentuated as much as it is here, with her problem eighth hurdle, which in this particular race may be worse than usual due to the new stride pattern and the position of the hurdle very near the end of the bend, with only a few more strides before the straight begins. Frame 8 shows quite good 400m hurdling technique, although there is a feeling that she lacks range of movement as she drives out across the barrier.

In frames 9 to 12 the trail (left) knee may appear very low, but as in all hurdling the knee only needs to clear the rail, it doesn't need to be horizontal. In the same frames the left arm is perhaps rather high and certainly in frames 13 to 18 the left arm can be seen swinging back with a very straight elbow. A better hurdler would have had the elbow bent and would have taken it back in a lower position to balance the pull-through of the trailing thigh. This sweepback of the left arm may have developed as a result of the pattering just before take-off and the resulting jump at the barrier with the outward-swinging lower lead leg, which however is grounded quickly if with a slight braking effect. This effect is quickly overcome and in frames 21 to 24 we can see her getting back into her sprinting as she tries to pull back at Fiedler – which she had done on their last two encounters, but not this time!

It is unfortunate that Fiedler does not actually feature in the sequence because we would have had an excellent contrast between the superior hurdling of Fiedler and the superior fitness of Ambrazene. To emphasize this I give some statistics at the end of the section to show that over 400m their personal bests are similar but Fiedler had the sprint hurdling experience whereas Ambrazene had shown more endurance in her 800m runs and in the way she finished her 400m hurdle races.

Even after some four years at the highest level, the 400m hurdles for women is still in its infancy and the record will come down a long way yet. What is needed is someone with the leg speed of a sprint hurdler, as shown in many races by Fiedler, who is prepared to do the longer training runs (like Hemery, Akii Bua, Moses, etc) and then to put the two together in terms of stride pattern. The 400m hurdler must work very hard to find the correct stride pattern for him/her for the peak performance aimed at for the particular season, and then work equally hard to consolidate it. You cannot, as someone did in the men's 400m hurdles World Championship final in Helsinki in 1983, try a new stride pattern in the competitive situation!

Anna Ambrazene (1.73m, 61 kg, born 14/5/1955)

	400m	800m	400 mH
1973	58.9	2:28.0	
1974	57.6	2:11.0	
1975	56.9	2:09.1	
1976	57.2	2:08.7	
1977	56.2	2:08.1	59.4
1978	55.8	2:06.0	57.09
1979	53.4	2:02.4	56.2
1980	52.1	2:00.2	55.81
1981			55.51
1982			55.09
1983			54.02

Ellen Fiedler (1.74m, 66 kg, born 10/11/1958)

	100 mH	400m	400 mH
1975	13.4		
1976	13.8		
1977	–		
1978	14.17		58.12
1979			–
1980		52.74	54.56
1981		52.17	54.79
1982		53.09	54.96
1983		52.13	54.20

AMBRAZENE — FIEDLER

World Championships Final (Helsinki 10/8/1983)

24 (Lane 3)	23 (Lane 1)	
R 6.7	R 6.3	Ambrazene pattered at 8, also 9 and 10. Fiedler started too fast resulting in greater fatigue later forcing her to change down to 16s earlier and then to 17s. Winner Fesenko (lane 5) (54.14) and Ambrazene ran past her in the closing stages. (Fesenko used 17s all the way.)
L 10.9	R 10.3	
R 15.3	R 14.5	
L 19.6 (16s)	R 18.7 (15s)	
R 24.0	R 23.1	
L 28.6	R 27.7	
R 33.3	R 32.6	
R 38.1	L 37.6 (16s)	
R 43.0 (17s)	R 42.8 (17s)	
R 48.1	R 48.0	
54.15	21 54.55	
20 (2nd)	(3rd)	

Europa Cup Final (London 20/8/1983)

24 (Lane 2)	23 (Lane 4)	
R –	R 6.4	Ambrazene had to work harder to get in her 15s, 'jumped' hurdles 4 and 5, pattered at hurdles 6, 7 and 8 (some 4–5 short steps). Fiedler was more controlled than she had been in the World final.
R – (15s)	R 10.6	
R 15.6	R 14.9 (15s)	
R 19.9	R 19.3	
R 24.4 (16s)	R 23.7	
L 28.8	R –	
R 33.7	R 32.9	
*R 38.7 (17s)	R 37.7 (16s)	
R 43.9	L 42.8	
R 48.7	R 48.0	
54.74	20 54.20	
(2nd)	(1st)	

* Shown in the sequence

6 STEEPLECHASE
Dr Klement Kerssenbrock and Jan Jurečka

Dr Klement Kerssenbrock

Czechoslovakia
(Acknowledgements to Ceskoslovenský Atletický Svaz)

Dr Klement Kerssenbrock was a senior lecturer in physical education at Prague University and master of physical education at a grammar school. A former pole vaulter, he was coach of the Czechoslovakian women's team at the Olympic Games in 1948, and the national coach of the Yugoslavian team. A leading expert in the application of biomechanics to track and field techniques, Klement is one of the pioneers of the rotational shot. He is the author of about 15 texts and numerous magazine articles on track and field and he is adviser to an international film production team making track and field instructional films.

Jan Jurečka

Czechoslovakia

Jan Jurečka is a teacher at the School of Physical Education for track and field coaches, having been a technical adviser at the Board of Youth and Sports in Algiers. He is head coach of track and cross-country for Czechoslovakian international distance runners. He has written basic coaching texts on running.

Steeplechase

The steeplechase is one of the most attractive events for spectators and one of the hardest for athletes.

The runner has to master 35 hurdles in a race, seven of these are combined with a water jump. A steeplechaser's average speed is of about 6-6.2m/s, which means that the athlete must be a world-class runner at 1500 to 10,000m distances. Training is very intensive and includes work for endurance development and exercises for technical improvement. Clearing the water jump is a difficult affair and as the distance between the hurdles is 78m, the athlete is unable to choose a regular stride pattern. It is self-evident that he must be capable of taking off with either leg.

We are going to illustrate the steeplechase technique by means of photo-sequence analysis of some runners.

WATER JUMP (Fig 1)

In frame 1 Bronislaw Malinowski (Poland) approaches the obstacle and prepares for the take-off. He estimates the distance, his arms prepare a swing action and his take-off heel contacts the ground. The distance of the foot plant from the barrier equals nearly the length of his body. In frame 2 a slight kneebend absorbs the shock of landing and pre-tenses the leg muscles. The take-off is effected by means of an energetic natural armswing and a flexed lead-leg action (frame 3).

During the flight the runner relaxes and watches the landing point on the barrier (frame 4). He places the foot of the lead leg on the hurdle with a 'squeezing' movement. By leaning forward, he gains an advantageous take-off angle for clearing the water (frame 5). He tries to pass over the hurdle rail with the hips as low as possible. The drive off the rail is directed out (not up), as in frame 6.

In frame 7 both arms and the leading leg assist the take-off. The athlete should not lift the arms during the flight, as a hard landing results.

During the flight over the water (frames 8-11) the runner has a moment of relaxation, he tries to keep his balance for landing, watches the other competitors to prevent a collision and looks for an advantageous landing spot. He keeps his arms close to the body and, as he lands, he swings the back leg forward to make the first stride. The first steps are short with an energetic armswing.

Frames 12-16. The forward lean of the trunk helps him to get quickly into full-speed running. Technical performance tends to worsen as fatigue increases throughout the race.

STEEPLECHASE HURDLE - FLIGHT CLEARANCE (Fig 2)

Bronislaw Malinowski approaches the obstacle with good acceleration: by examining the photo-sequences we can see the amount of effort he puts into his driving leg, his leading leg and the armswing. His speed on the flat must be supported by a technical performance similar to a 400m hurdler, as we can observe in his hurdle clearance.

He crosses a little too high, but his performance is otherwise excellent: his body leans forward, his arms are moved with a natural action and his supporting leg is flexed at the correct angle. He clears the obstacle high for safety reasons, but in doing so he lands too short after the obstacle and the heavy landing makes it difficult for him to continue into a normal running stride, his first strides being made with great effort.

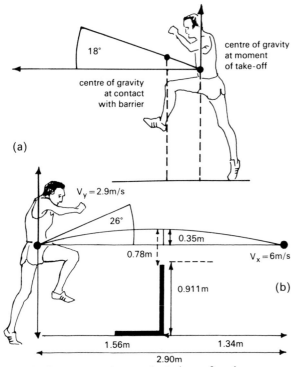

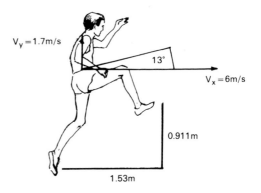

Fig 4a Some approximate calculations of angles, velocities and distances in Reitz's clearance

(a)

(b)

Fig 2a Some approximate calculations of angles, distances and velocities in Malinowski's clearances. (a) water jump (b) hurdle

WATER JUMP (Fig 3)

In this photo-sequence No. 18 is Colin Reitz (GB), No. 6 is Paul Davies-Hale (GB) and No. 15 is Philip Llewellyn (GB).

In frames 1–3 the runners approach the last water jump. We can see evidence of the increasing fatigue in the weaker extension of the drive leg and in the reduced lead-leg action. The trunks and the heads lean slightly forward, the arms are moved in a low position. Their facial expressions show great pain.

Colin Reitz in the leading position tries hard to get to the hurdle rail first so as to make the best of tactical and psychological advantages. But he doesn't achieve a favourable position for clearing the water (frames 5–11). The supporting foot is placed a little way ahead of the centre of gravity. The take-off is assisted by the bent lead leg moving strongly forward and by a swing of both arms.

Looking at the background in frame 4, it would seem that Colin has lengthened the last step before the take-off to the hurdle. Nevertheless his take-off (frame 8) is too far from the obstacle (about 1.82m). In doing so he must stretch his lead leg to

reach the barrier (frame 10) and, as he places his whole foot on the upper part of the hurdle rail his take-off is directed upwards too much (frames 11–18). This results in too short a drive out from the rail and Colin comes down in deep water (frames 20–28).

In frame 29 he wastes much energy in dragging himself out of the water and picking up speed, so by frame 32 he has been caught up by Paul Davies-Hale who has better estimated his last strides. Paul's take-off spot has been some 1.70m from the hurdle so that he gets a satisfactory clearance. His foot will land right on the edge of the water and he can continue straight into a normal running action to challenge Colin Reitz.

STEEPLECHASE HURDLE – FLIGHT CLEARANCE (Fig 4)

In frame 1 Colin Reitz approaches the hurdle with a good running action, the forward lean of the trunk is increasing, the arms are moved with a right angle at the elbows and the fingers are relaxed. The supporting foot is placed almost under the centre of gravity (frame 5). The drive from the back leg is assisted by the bent lead knee moving forward and by a swing of both arms (frames 9 and 10). For safety reasons he clears the obstacle high.

Fig 1 (*Overleaf*) Bronislaw Malinowski (Pol), 1980 Olympic champion – water jump
Fig 2 Bronislaw Malinowski – hurdle
Fig 3 Colin Reitz (GB), No. 18, was 3rd in the 1983 world championships. No. 6 is Paul Davies-Hale (GB) and No. 15 is Philip Llewellyn (GB)
Fig 4 Steeplechase hurdle: Colin Reitz (GB)

Fig 1

Fig 2

Fig 3

3

4

7

8

11

12

15

16

Fig 3

17

18

21

22

25

26

29

30

19

20

23

24

27

28

31

32

Fig 4

4

5

6

10

11

12

16

17

18

Fig 5 Clearance by stepping on the barrier

STEEPLECHASE HURDLE – CLEARANCE BY STEPPING ON THE BARRIER (Fig 5)

The hurdles can be cleared either by flight action as in 400m hurdles or by placing the lead foot on them. The latter method is useful when the athletes are bunched and crossing the barrier together or when the athlete is fatigued and can no longer safely negotiate the hurdle with a flight clearance.

Therefore he takes off a little closer to the hurdle (about 1.40m). His take-off is assisted by a very bent lead leg and by a strong arm action. The runner crosses the barrier as low as possible. He tries hard to drive off the rail outwards (not upwards), so he does not push against the obstacle but slides down in front of it, landing about 1.20m from the hurdle. Kinetic energy aids him to come down into a normal running action and allows him to accelerate.

In clearing the water jump we must note the different hurdle clearance of Amos Biwott (Olympic winner 1968). He pushed off the barrier with the right leg and he came down on the edge of the water with the same leg. His first running step was on the left leg.

CONCLUSION (by Jan Jurečka)

1 The best steeplechasers run the distance at an average speed of 6.0–6.2 m/s.
2 A dynamic evolution of the event is due partly because of increasing speed in running, partly through mastery of technique and the use of good race tactics.
3 A tall athlete with long limbs and less weight is better suited for the race. But more important for his efficient development are his qualities of willpower and high aerobic and anaerobic capacity.
4 The training of a 3000m steeplechaser is similar to that of 1500–5000m runners – in other words a runner has to develop special running abilities and in addition to improve by technical exercises over the obstacles (practice at clearing the hurdles and water jumps). He must also acquire the feeling of competitive pace and its alteration during the training.
5 For an efficient training system we must try to develop not only the physical and technical qualities of an athlete but also his mental qualities.
6 Training should include:
 a) general endurance;
 b) speed endurance;
 c) special pace;
 d) racing pace and maximum speed; and
 e) take-off power of legs and a strong trunk.
There are many methods for strengthening steeplechase runners but the best one remains cross-country. It develops the aerobic capacity of the runner and it ought to represent 80 per cent of the steeplechaser's total running.
7 Some remarks on training for clearing the hurdles:
 – practise clearing without touching and also with pushing off the barrier;
– learn to take off for the hurdle with either leg;
 – try to perfect technique so that the skill does not break down under the stress of great fatigue.

7 HIGH JUMP

Berny Wagner

USA
(Acknowledgements to the Athletics Congress of the USA)

Carl B 'Berny' Wagner, National Coach/Co-ordinator of the Athletics Congress of the USA, was born in 1924 in Fresno, California, and is married, with three grown children. Educated at California Institute of Technology and Stanford University in engineering and education, he received Bachelor's and Master's degrees in education from Stanford.

Berny taught and coached athletics for thirteen years in four high schools, three years in junior college and ten and a half years at Oregon State University as Professor of Physical Education and Head Athletics Coach. He then spent three years planning and directing national sports programmes in Saudi Arabia and served three years as Executive Director of the Track and Field Association of the USA. He assumed the newly created position of National Coach/Co-ordinator with TAC in 1981 to co-ordinate and implement the US national governing body's supervision of national athletics teams, staff selection, development and elite athlete programmes and Olympics preparation activities.

While at Oregon State Berny Wagner developed ten open national and national collegiate champions including four in the high jump. He coached Dick Fosbury from 1965 to 1969 and developed six other jumpers who cleared 2.14m to 2.29m.

High Jump
(Fosbury Technique)

The Fosbury Flop or back-layout style of high jumping was evolved by Dick Fosbury in the mid-1960s while he was a secondary school and university student in the state of Oregon, USA. While he jumped well with the style from 1966 onward, his win in the 1968 Olympic Games with a record height (2.24m) brought his style to the attention of the world. Now jumpers using variations of his technique dominate the high jump event in all parts of the world where rubber or synthetic foam landing surfaces are available.

GLOSSARY OF TERMS

BLOCKING (ARM ACTION): stopping arm and hand movement suddenly.

FRONTAL AXIS: the axis through the body's centre of gravity extending laterally through the left and right hips.

GROUND: the run-up and take-off surface, whatever its composition might be.

INSIDE (ARM/LEG/FOOT): the part of the body nearest to the centre of the circle being run during the curve phase of the approach run. The part of the body farthest from the crossbar at the moment of plant.

LONGITUDINAL AXIS: the axis through the body's centre of gravity extending from the feet to the head.

OUTSIDE (ARM/LEG/FOOT): the part of the body farthest from the centre of the circle being run during the curve phase of the approach run. The part of the body nearest to the crossbar at the moment of plant.

PLANT: the sudden vigorous placing of the heel spikes into the take-off surface at the end of the curved run.

SETTLE: the action of lowering the hips by bending the knees and keeping the upper body upright during the final steps of the approach run.

TAKE-OFF (FOOT/LEG): the foot/leg which last leaves the ground on take-off.

References to Photo-sequences

Fig 1 (F-1) refers to the first frame of the Fosbury sequence. Dick Fosbury (USA) was the 1968 Men's Olympic Champion and record holder. He is shown here jumping 2.22m at the 1968 Olympic Games.

Fig 2 (M-3) refers to the third frame of the Meyfarth sequence. Ulrike Meyfarth (FRG) was the 1972 and 1984 Women's Olympic Champion and record holder. She is shown here jumping 1.94m in 1981.

Fig 3 (T-10) refers to the tenth frame of the Tranhardt sequence. Carlo Tranhardt (FRG) was the

1984 highest-ranked jumper in Europe with a best of 2.36m. He is shown here jumping 2.31m in 1980.

Fig 4 (W-2) refers to the second frame of the Wszola sequence. Jacek Wszola (Poland) was the 1976 Men's Olympic Champion and record holder, breaking Fosbury's mark. He is shown here jumping 2.21m in 1982.

GENERAL

The Fosbury Flop style of high jumping, which most successful jumpers use, involves a J-shaped approach run, the first half or more of which is straight and the last few steps of which describe the arc of a circle, followed by a vigorous heel-toe plant of the foot farthest away from the crossbar. The plant is followed by a vigorous jump off the take-off (plant) foot with a gradual turning of the body around its longitudinal axis toward the take-off foot so that the jumper's back is toward the crossbar as he lays out over it. As the bar is crossed the hips are dropped and the lower legs thrust upward while the jumper descends to impact the landing surface on the upper back and shoulders.

One of the distinct advantages of this technique is that the rotation around the frontal axis of the body, which rotates the athlete over the crossbar, comes from checking linear motion (stopping one end of the body with the foot plant, while the other end, the head, continues to move toward the bar) rather than by eccentric thrust (jumping off-centre toward the bar). The total force of the jump can be directed up through the body's centre of gravity rather than partially toward the bar as must be done in other styles to produce the rotation. This, plus the fact that the crossbar can be crossed with the jumper's centre of gravity at or even below the bar's height, leads to the conclusion that this is the most efficient technique for high jumping yet used.

Another definite advantage of the Flop is that it is a simpler technique to master than are other high-jumping styles. The human being is bilaterally symmetrical, and since all the actions of the Flop in the air are bilaterally identical they are easier to master than the asymmetrical actions of other techniques.

THE RUN

The purpose of the run is to generate horizontal velocity which the athlete can convert into vertical velocity. Another purpose is to put the athlete in a position at the beginning of the take-off so that upward force may be exerted through the body's centre of gravity until the moment when contact is lost with the ground. To achieve these purposes the athlete must execute the run so that the take-off point is arrived at with the athlete moving at the fastest speed which can be converted into upward movement. The athlete's strength and skill will govern how much speed can be used. Also, the body must be in a position which will allow the upward thrust to be directed through the body's centre of gravity and at the same time initiate rotation around the frontal axis so that the jumper rotates over the bar.

Attempts have been made to use straight, semi-circular and parabolic curved runs, but the most success has been achieved using the J-shaped run devised by Fosbury himself. It allows the jumper to achieve more speed with a more consistent stride pattern through its straight part than is possible with completely curved runs. The curve at the end of the run puts the jumper in the needed position at the beginning of the take-off so that more thrust is used for achieving upward velocity than in other techniques.

Since the jumper must arrive consistently at the same predetermined take-off point, the starting point of the run must be determined exactly and the same starting action should be used for each run, whether it be from a stationary start or from several walk-in steps to the start of the run. While it is important that the stride pattern is the same throughout each run, most problems occur from varying the length of the first stride.

Fosbury used an eight-step approach, starting at a point which was 5.95m to the left of the left standard and 12.95m perpendicularly out on the run-up area. This measurement is given as an example only, since each athlete's stride length, speed and strength will determine the starting point.

A run of from eight to ten steps has proved very successful for most jumpers. Athletes who are inherently faster can use shorter runs and generate the speed needed but taller or slower athletes may need longer runs.

The run can be considered in two parts: the straight speed-gathering phase and the curved positioning phase of the last three to five steps.

Straight Phase

The straight phase should be started with exactly the same action on each run and should consist of rapidly accelerating, rhythmical, bounding strides using high knee action with as much relaxation as possible during acceleration. The same speed should be generated at all bar heights, and the same stride pattern should be used so that the jumper will be consistent at arriving at the take-off point. The direction of the straight phase of five to seven steps should be perpendicular to the crossbar or toward the back corner of the landing surface. Both techniques have been used with success. In either case a target marker should be placed at the edge of the run-up surface in a line extended from the crossbar. The athlete should look at the target marker during the straight phase of the run.

Curve Phase

The straight part of the run must be blended smoothly into the curved last three to five steps. The jumper must not step sideways to the inside or outside of the curve but must run a path which, on a smaller scale, resembles the curve of a track as it leaves the straight. Some jumpers prefer to begin the curve with the outside foot and others with the inside. Fewer steps on the curve should result in a tighter turn with more lean toward the inside of the curve resulting in the jumper having a longer period of time to rock up from heel plant to take-off from the toes to the take-off foot, since the centre of gravity has a longer distance to travel to arrive at a position directly over the point of take-off from the toes. This is advantageous for the athlete who uses a more extended (and slower) lead leg action.

During the curve phase the outside arm should move across the body somewhat on its forward swing as in any curve sprinting (F-2, 3; M-5 to 8; T-2, 3; W-5 to 7). The curve must be continued right into the plant for take-off (F-4) since to 'straighten out' the last stride and to lose the lean away from the bar negates one of the advantages of the Flop over other techniques. As the curve is entered the eyes should leave the target mark and gradually be raised to the bar, or above it (F-1 to 4; M-3 to 13; W-1 to 19).

In running the curve the entire body should lean to the inside of the arc; lean from the ankles, not the waist. The body should not have any lateral bends in it from the top of the head to the ankle supporting it while the curve is being run (F-3, 4; T-2, 3; W-6 to 12).

The jumper 'settles' on the last two strides by lowering the hips and landing on the heels (F-1; M-9 and 12; T-6, 7; W-9 to 14). Also, the last two strides must be quickened as much as possible. These actions will result in two strides run with bent knees in the support phase, low knees in the flight phase and two steps which have a heel-toe or flat-footed action (W-3 to 13). During this action the hips must be kept under or ahead of the shoulders so that there is no forward lean with the upper body (F-1, 2; M-11 to 17; T-3 to 8; W-8 to 16). There must be no loss of speed; on the contrary there should be an increase in speed if possible. Only the speed at which the athlete is travelling on the last step of the run has any effect on the jump. The take-off heel should touch the ground on the plant very quickly after the last touch of the outside foot.

The jumper should push vigorously with the outside foot with strong ankle extension in a forward direction into the plant (T-8; W-15 to 18). The centre of gravity must not be raised and then lowered during this last stride but should travel directly forward, or forward and slightly upward (F-1 to 4; T-8 to 10; W-12 to 17). During this final stride the body must continue to remain leaning into the centre of the arc from the ankles and may be inclined slightly backward (F-3; M-14 to 17; T-9 to 11; W-13 to 20). A slight backward lean gives the less-quick athlete more time to bring the free leg through on take-off (W-16 to 20).

During the last two strides the jumper's arms must be put into position for a single-arm or double-arm take-off action. If a single-arm action is used, the arms continue the natural running action through the plant (F-1 to 4). If a double-arm take-off action is used, one of two methods to position the arms has been found most effective. In one variation the jumper keeps the outside arm forward during the penultimate stride while the inside arm moves naturally forward so that both arms are forward as the outside foot contacts the ground. During the last stride both arms are pulled back and then swung forward and up on take-off (M-9 to 19; T-6 to 12; W-8 to 19). In the second variation, natural running action is maintained until the outside foot touches the ground the last time. In the last stride the inside arm moves back naturally but the outside arm is not moved forward. From this position with both arms back they are swung forward and upward on take-off. Care must be taken not to slow down during the variation from normal sprinter's arm action to the double-arm action positioning.*

The run so far has brought the jumper to a take-off point 90 to 120cm perpendicularly out onto the take-off surface from the nearer standard (F-4; M-18, she is not near the standard. Note where she clears in M-29 to 32; W-19). The reason for taking off in front of the standard rather than nearer the centre of the crossbar is that this take-off point will allow the jumper to clear the crossbar at its lowest point near the centre, since forward momentum created by the run will carry the jumper along the bar. This take-off point also decreases fear in the jumper of missing the landing surface and allows concentration on correct technique. The distance from the crossbar to the take-off point is determined by the speed and strength of the jumper, and will vary with these factors and the angle of the jumper's curve with respect to the crossbar at the moment of plant.

The speed or direction of the run should not be changed as the height of the bar is raised.

THE PLANT
The take-off foot must be planted† vigorously heel first‡ as the first aspect of the take-off (F-3; M-15, 16; W-16, 17). As has been described, the last stride of the run must be initiated by a vigorous push-off from the outside foot. The plant of the inside heel follows. The inside (take-off) leg is almost completely extended, the knee is not locked, however, with the foot well in advance of the knee (F-3; M-16; T-10; W-17). The plant is made directly in line with the circular arc which has been run, with the toe pointing slightly toward the bar in the direction of the arc (F-4). The angle should be approximately 15 degrees from parallel to the crossbar.

The plant is a vigorous, sudden stopping of the lower end of the jumper's body. It is important to

*There is also another variation of: third-last stride, arms forward, second-last stride, arms back, take-off stride, arms forward - F.D.

†The action is a dynamic striking action. Actually there are two main Flop take-off techniques (Tancie), with a third which is a compromise between the two. The author is describing one of the techniques - F.D.

‡Some jumpers take off from a ball-of-foot plant, eg Dwight Stones in film of 1976 Olympics - H.P.

note that the upper part of the jumper's body will continue forward as a result of the run, and toward the bar as a result of the inertia generated by running a curve. The athlete must not step inside or outside of the arc being run. The plant foot should not be parallel to the crossbar due to the danger of injury to the foot and the common result of a clearance with one hip lower than the other when this type of plant is used. Planting with the toe pointed away from the crossbar results in the two problems just mentioned, plus it tends to cause the athlete to lean back into the bar and not direct all the jumping force upward through the centre of gravity.

The knee of the take-off leg will flex as the heel is planted, although the jumper should resist this motion (F-4; M-17 to 19; T-11, 12; W-18, 19).

THE TAKE-OFF
As the jumper's weight is transferred from the plant heel to the plant toe a number of things happen. The knee and the ankle of the take-off leg are extended strongly (F-5, 6; M-20 to 22; T-13, 14; W-21 to 23). During the approximately 0.12 seconds necessary to rock up from the heel to the toe, the jumper's body will change position from leaning inward to being straight up and over the toes of the take-off foot (F-5, 6; M-19, 20; T-13, 14; W-21 to 24). This is caused by the fact that the vigorous plant has checked linear motion at the lower end of the jumper's body. As forward velocity is converted into upward velocity by the vigorous extension of the take-off leg at the knee and ankle joints, the force is directed up through the body's centre of gravity. Had the jumper been upright instead of leaning into the circle at the moment of heel plant, the body would have been leaning toward the crossbar by the time the upward thrust was generated and not nearly as much energy would have been expended in gaining vertical height, since the thrust would not have been directed through the body's centre of gravity.

If a correct body position has been reached at the moment that the plant is made, no effort to jump toward the crossbar is necessary. All effort should be made to jump straight up. The body's inertia, which causes the head and shoulders to move toward the crossbar when the foot plants, creates the necessary velocity for the jumper to travel toward the bar and to rotate over it.

It is most important to keep from bending for-

Fig 1 Dick Fosbury, originator of the 'Fosbury flop' technique, is shown here winning the 1968 Olympics high jump (*Photo-sequence by Toni Nett*)

ward or sideward at the waist during any part of the take-off action. The hips must be kept under the shoulders (F-6; M-20; T-14; W-22 to 24).

The outside leg, which on the last stride vigorously thrust the jumper forward in a horizontal direction into the plant, now becomes the free leg. In Fosbury's original technique it is brought through as quickly as possible with a low knee action and accompanying dorsi-flexion of the ankle (F-3 to 5; M-16 to 19; T-11 to 14). After the heel of the take-off foot has been planted, the knee is driven upward rapidly and strongly to a position at which the top of the thigh is parallel to the ground (F-5 to 8; M-19 to 23; T-11 to 14). The free foot should be kept in a dorsi-flexed position and back under the knee. Its movement out in front of and to the side of the body should be

resisted, although most jumpers cannot completely resist this movement (F-5 to 8; M-20 to 24; T-13 to 16).

A variation of the above technique of free leg action is the use of a semi-bent (W-21 to 25) or straight free leg. This results in a slower rock-up action from the heel plant to the take-off from the toes, therefore decreasing the vertical velocity which can be generated from a quick 'explosion' of the take-off leg. There is an advantage, however, in that more force is exerted against the ground, because of the slower, long swinging lead leg, and therefore an increase in upward thrust because of the action. As in the straddle technique the advantage/disadvantage of the bent-leg quick-rock-up versus the straight-leg slow-rock-up is a trade-off.*

To use the straighter lead-leg technique effectively, the backward lean on the last stride of the run must be accentuated as must the lean away

* This is related to the type of plant used – F.D.

120

from the crossbar, to allow for the slower rock-up (W-16 to 20). These positions are necessary so that the jumper's body does not reach the vertical position in which the upward thrust can be directed through its centre of gravity before the rock-up is completed. If the body passes the vertical and begins to lean toward the crossbar before take-off from the toes, the force will not be directed through the centre of gravity and less upward velocity will be generated.

It is not necessary to drive the knee across the body to initiate rotation around the longitudinal axis. The turn is initiated as the jumper 'wills' it*. During the brief moment that the toes of the take-off foot are in contact with the ground, the athlete brings into play the muscles which rotate the take-off leg inward. Since the foot is anchored by the spikes to the ground, the body rotates toward the leg rather than the leg rotating inwardly

* There must be a biomechanical reason for this, nevertheless - H.P.

toward the body. It is sometimes mistakenly thought that because the outside arm comes across the body in curve sprint action and the outside (free leg) knee swings across on take-off that one or both of these actions are necessary to take-off to achieve the rotation around the longitudinal axis of the body to turn the back to the crossbar.

Four arm actions have been used with success, each having some advantages and disadvantages. The technique which will cause the fewest problems is a single-arm action in which running arm action is used all the way through the take-off. The inside arm is swung forward and up in a normal running action as the free knee is punched

Fig 2 (*Overleaf*) Ulricke Meyfarth (FRG), 1972 and 1984 Olympic champion, who has been responsible for helping to push up the world record
Fig 3 Carlo Tranhardt (FRG), leading European high jumper in 1984
Fig 4 Jacek Wszola (Pol), 1976 Olympic champion, here jumping 2.21m

Fig 2

1

5

9

13

2

6

10

14

3

4

7

8

11

12

15

16

Fig 2

17

18

21

22

25

26

29

30

19

20

23

24

27

28

31

32

Fig 3

Fig 4

1

2

3

7

8

9

13

14

15

4

5

6

10

11

12

16

17

18

19

20

21

25

26

27

31

32

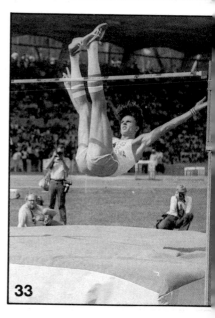

33

22

23

24

28

29

30

34

35

36

upward, is stopped (blocked) when the hand is at about eye level and then is dropped to the side as layout occurs (F-5 to 9). This is the simplest, and possibly least effective in helping produce upward thrust, of the arm actions used.

The second single-arm technique departs from the first in that the arm continues straight up in a reaching motion rather than being stopped. This raises the centre of gravity slightly to the advantage of the jumper if it is done before take-off is completed. There is no problem if the upper arm is positioned adjacent to the ear of the jumper and kept there until clearance is achieved. If the arm is allowed to reach out over the crossbar, however, the jumper has a tendency to lean or dive into the bar, losing some upward velocity.

During single-arm action the jumper must concentrate on not dropping the outside (nearest the crossbar) shoulder (F-5).

The double-arm techniques parallel those of the single-arm style in that: (1) The arms are raised vigorously until the hands are at forehead level, blocked suddenly and then dropped to the sides (M-20 to 27; T-13 to 16, both variations in which one arm is then raised before being dropped). The double block, if done before the take-off toe leaves the ground, will assist in generating upward thrust, (2) Both arms are raised over the head, reaching up on take-off (W-22). This action will raise the jumper's centre of gravity more than a reach with just one arm and will mean that in order to clear a given bar height the jumper does not need to generate quite as much upward velocity.

THE RISE

As the toe of the take-off foot leaves the ground, the parabolic curve which the jumper's centre of gravity will follow and the jumper's rotation around his longitudinal and frontal axes are fixed. If the jumper's strength, speed and take-off position are good, the body will be launched into a nearly vertical path with relatively slow turns around the longitudinal and frontal axes (F-6 to 9; M-20 to 23; T-13 to 18; W-22 to 24). The turn around the longitudinal axis should be gradual enough so that the back is not to the crossbar and the hips not parallel to it until the jumper is well off the ground (F-8 to 10; M-19 to 26; T-14 to 18; W-24 to 28).

The free knee is not straightened in the bent-leg quick-rock-up technique. As the body begins to

lay back due to rotation around the frontal axis, the rest of the body 'catches up' to the bent leg, and the take-off leg is bent to match it (F-7 to 11; M-21 to 26; T-13 to 19). (See W-25 to 28 for the straighter leg action.)

Head position can be completely neutral (W-26) with the neck a straight extension of the spine, or the chin can be positioned near the clavicle nearest the centre of the bar (F-11; M-24). The latter position allows the jumper to see the crossbar out of the corner of the eye, a confidence-builder some jumpers need. There seems to be no disadvantage to looking at the crossbar in this manner so long as the chin is kept down near the clavicular area.

No effort to arch the back should be made at this point. As the body rotates backward the hips should be thrust forward and the buttocks tightened (F-8 to 11; M-24).

THE CLEARANCE

Fosbury and the majority of successful male jumpers have used a passive clearance of the bar with the hips thrust forward causing only a moderate back arch (F-12 to 14). The layout position should be such that the jumper's frontal axis is parallel to the crossbar. If either hip is lower than the other, adjustments should be made in the take-off action to increase or decrease rotation around the athlete's longitudinal axis.

A number of successful female jumpers and some male champions have used a marked back arch (M-25 to 28; T-19; W-27, 28). Women seem to have more flexibility in the back than men, on the average, and can use this to their advantage in this jumping technique. If the arch is begun before the take-off foot leaves the ground, however, it is not possible to generate the maximum upward velocity. The jumper can slow down rotation around the longitudinal axis by spreading the knees while in the layout position. This is sometimes necessary in order to keep the hips parallel to the crossbar while the body is crossing the bar (F-11 to 13; M-26 to 28; T-18 to 20; W-29).

During the layout, if a passive clearance is used the jumper's head should be kept in the same attitude that it was during the rise to the bar, either a straight extension of the spine or with the chin on the clavicle and the eyes continuing to look at the crossbar (F-12 to 14). If a more pronounced back arch is used, the head is usually thrown back (M-25 to 28; W-28).

The arms should be at the jumper's sides or extended beyond the head during clearance, depending upon arm action at take-off. The hands and arms should not be appreciably higher (eg a greater vertical distance from the ground) than the jumper's body during the layout (F-12 to 14; M-27 to 29; W-27 to 29).

While the path of the jumper's centre of gravity cannot be changed after the last contact with the ground, the paths of parts of the body can be changed. Some very successful jumpers take advantage of this fact by executing a 'flip-flop' over the bar. As the head crosses the crossbar, it is immediately thrown back and down and the hips are lifted. The legs stop rising momentarily and an extreme arched or 'draped over the bar' position is achieved. Rotation and motion over the bar toward the landing surface continue and as the hips cross the bar they are dropped vigorously causing the legs and feet to rise making it possible for them to clear the bar.

Precise timing and quickness are necessary and the action must become one of reflex, since there isn't time to think it through during a jump.

In a clearance using this action it is possible for all parts of the body to go over the crossbar without dislodging it, even though the body's centre of gravity passes through or actually under the bar. The action is explained by Newton's Third Law of Motion regarding freely suspended objects in which for every action there is an equal and opposite reaction. In this case when the head and legs are lowered the hips can be raised. When the hips are lowered the legs can be raised. This action also markedly slows down the body's rotation toward the landing surface, thereby precluding a head-first landing.

In each of the clearance techniques described above, the hips must be dropped quickly as soon as they cross the bar so that the thighs and particularly the lower legs can be raised, again according to Newtons Third Law of Motion (F-15, 16; M-29 to 31; W-31). The action must be initiated as the hips are still over the bar to compensate for human reaction time and will actually start them down a fraction of a second later at which time they will be across the critical point.

THE LANDING
The dropping of the hips and bending at the waist to do so raises the legs and markedly slows further backward rotation through the frontal axis. The effect on the upper body is to raise it with respect to the body's other parts (F-16 to 18; M-31, 32; T-22; W-32 to 34). Regardless of which clearance form is used, the head is now inclined forward with the chin on the front of the neck, and the arms are thrown out laterally and sometimes up (F-16, 17; M-30 to 32; T-22, 23; W-32 to 35). Landing will occur on the upper part of the back and the shoulders (T-24; W-36).

The landing from this style of jumping with an adequate landing surface of rubber or synthetic foam is not dangerous. Vaulters descend safely onto their shoulders and back from much greater heights than do high jumpers. The Committee on the Medical Aspects of Sports of the American Medical Association made a thorough investigation of the Fosbury Flop. The Committee's conclusion was that: '... When performance is according to recommended coaching techniques, the Fosbury method of high jumping does not bear greater risks than other methods of high jumping, pole vaulting, or gymnastics ...'

8 POLE VAULT

Maurice Houvion

France
(Acknowledgements to the Fédération Française d'Athlétisme.)

Maurice Houvion was France's top pole vaulter in the early- and mid-1960s and he was national record holder at 4.87m just as the world's pole vaulters converted from the rigid pole to the fibre-glass pole. The books on technique had to be rewritten since the flexible pole with all its problems and challenges required new thinking. No one can doubt that the pole vault is the most technical and exciting of events.

Maurice was in the forefront of these developments and from his own vaulting to his coaching, innovating and writing he has made France one of the world's leading pole-vaulting nations. His athletes, some of whom are mentioned in this chapter, have included many world record holders.

Maurice, as well as being a master of vaulting technique, also combines those valuable abilities of being able to motivate athletes and instill a sense of good sportsmanship in those he coaches.

Pole Vault

GENERAL

The development of pole vaulting is dependent on equipment and facilities (hall, jumping pits, poles, etc), on extending and devising specialized training techniques and also on logistical support to allow the growth and blooming of latent talent. This is why it is not universally practised: it has always been the privilege of technologically developed nations (USA, USSR, France). But many athletics clubs even in these so-called rich countries have difficulties: a 'poor' club cannot afford to train pole vaulters. However, despite these restrictions, the number of 5.70m vaulters is growing rapidly (17 in 1984), whereas in 1979 Houvion and Abada led the world ratings with 5.65m and the world record itself, held by the American Roberts, stood at 5.70m.

What has caused this growth? Motivation in this sport is one source of progress and the increase in competition is pushing the world record inexorably upwards towards the 6m mark, which is foreseeable in the not-too-distant future. Psychological training by coaches is much emphasized in order to create, maintain and develop the necessary motivation. Technique has not evolved much, but there is a slightly wider range in the movements resulting in better execution of the vault.

ACHIEVING THE GREATEST LEVERAGE

The Approach Run

The aim is to develop the highest speed for the plant that permits perfect control (Fig 1). It is essential that the vaulter is able to plant the pole accurately and make an efficient take-off. This is why it is noticeable that most vaulters are relaxed but alert, distribute their efforts carefully and take care over their running action.

At no time must the desire for speed destroy the correct running action or prevent relaxation. This is why all vaulters place such a high value on perfecting their run-up in their training programme.

The Plant

The pole must be placed in such a way that the

Distribution of Effort in the Approach Run

	LENGTH: between 14 and 20 strides DISTRIBUTION: progressive acceleration	
Preparation either – by walking – by a little hop or step – by jogging	Get up speed by increasing length of stride and quickening of rhythm. Vaulters are careful about their running action. This part of the run is important as ultimate efficiency very often depends on it	Strive for alertness by relaxing and increasing the stride rhythm. In this vaulters should show much determination
Variable	8–14 strides	4–8 strides

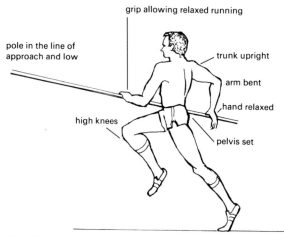

Fig 1 Try to 'run tall'

energy developed in the run-up and at take-off is put into the bending of the pole.

Vaulters have two complementary aims then: to make the pole bend and to give it the speed to straighten up again. They resolve these problems by keeping the pole in line with the approach run (an early plant is necessary), by adopting a wide grip (60cm to 100cm plus) and by opening the ground/pole angle to a maximum at the moment

Fig 2 (a) The static take-off point (b) The dynamic take-off point

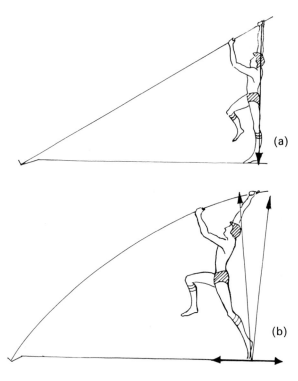

(a)

(b)

of take-off. The energy developed in the run-up is transferred and put into the flexion of the pole by means of the take-off sequence: foot, pelvis, shoulders, hand-grip.

The position of the take-off point in relation to the upper hand hold used is one element that can determine the success or otherwise of the vault. Checking the point of take-off after each vault shows the importance attached to it by the vaulter. It is useful to add two definitions of the take-off point to the vaulter's vocabulary:

a) The static take-off point (Fig 2a). The vaulter places his pole in the box without bending it, increases the ground/pole angle to the maximum and then marks the take-off point in a vertical line with his upper hand.

b) The dynamic take-off point (Fig 2b). This is the true point of take-off which according to vaulters can be situated further from the box or closer in relation to the static point (this gives full meaning to the expression 'to be underneath').

What criterion should one choose to assess the efficiency of the take-off? The static point, the dynamic point, or the visual impression of the vault? To decide this, we must realise that this efficiency is influenced by a number of related details:

In Relation to Mechanics

The Soviet coaches Maljutin and Manzwetow have calculated the loss of speed brought about by a take-off point that is 'underneath':

80cm = 3.50m per second and a pole plant time of 0.14 to 0.16sec

30cm = 1.40m per second and a pole plant time of 0.12 to 0.14sec

The loss of speed is less if the dynamic take-off point is close to the static take-off point. On the other hand, a point close to the box decreases the horizontal movement of the upper hand grip (by 20 to 24 per cent), as well as the distance that the pole/vaulter combination must cover to reach the bar.

In Relation to the Dominant Physical Qualities of the Vaulter

SPEED – SPRING Vaulters having these qualities normally take off at distance (ie farther from the box) eg Abada and Vigneron with a handhold of

4.80–5m have a take-off point at about 4.20m from the box. Slusarski's in Moscow was 4.10. Take-off at distance allows the vaulter to direct his take-off upwards and forwards without feeling resistance to the penetration of the pole. The vault is thus faster; the vaulter appears to soar.

POWER – STRENGTH   This ability allows the vaulter to 'force' the penetration while maintaining a good control of the take-off sequence and by keeping a rational direction in take-off while being 'underneath'. We are talking of a power vault as executed by the Finn Kalliomaki, and to a lesser degree by the Pole Buciarski.

Between these extremes there is room for all

degrees of strength. It is, however, noticeable that it is more and more common for the best vaulters to take off at distance, the result of research and the development of speed-spring techniques.

In Relation to the Mental Character of the Vaulter

Mental attitude directed towards *attack–audacity–determination* directly influences technical attitude, particularly in the link between run-up–plant–take-off. Without it the vaulter is unable to accelerate his run-up, to move forwards on take-off.

In Relation to All-Important Technical Elements

SPEED OF APPROACH RUN   This factor determines the amount of energy developed. Jean-Claude Perrin, in his conclusions drawn from the study of

Fig 3 Action of the lower arm. (a) Kozakiewicz (b) Volkov (c) Vigneron

(a)   (b)   (c)

mechanics, reveals the necessity for a compromise between the maximal run-up speed and the ability to control take-off.

To do this, the vaulter must have very early on the perception of gradual, calm acceleration. Accuracy of run-up allows him to find the ideal take-off point without having to adjust by lengthening or shortening the last strides. This kind of adjustment always causes faults in the final approach, such as lowering of the centre of gravity, straightening-up of the body and loss of balance.

PLANT TECHNIQUE There is a very close interdependence of the movements of the top part of the body and those of the lower. This means that activating the plant too late brings about an automatic lengthening of the last stride, hence a take-off point 'underneath' and a 'freeze'. Good coordination between arms and legs is the aim.

TAKE-OFF LEG CYCLE Between the time when it leaves the ground at the time of his penultimate stride and the time it regains it for the last time, the take-off leg reaches the greatest segmental speed. The vaulter seeks an action that is dynamic, driving, clawing, in order to keep down the loss of speed brought about by a 'freeze', as well as maximum distance. The pressure exerted on the ground is felt in the toes of the take-off foot.

ACTION OF THE FREE LEG An energetic movement of the knee of the free leg forwards and upwards aids the efficiency of take-off, and improves pelvic position.

However, vaulters frequently pay little attention to this point in their attempt to find extra length and extension that will help the hang position eg Kozakiewicz and Houvion.

ACTION OF THE ARMS Force exerted on the pole by the lower arm varies from one jump to another according to possible modifications of the handhold, of take-off point (ie at distance or not), of speed of approach, of stiffness of pole and of mental and technical attitude. (See Fig 3.)

An experienced vaulter will possibly not be aware, in a good vault, of exerting any force on the pole. If the arm extension, the force exerted on the pole and the take-off are well coordinated

the vaulter will not feel that he is exerting force with the lower arm.

To conclude, I think that the attitude of the body at the moment of take-off is a more important criterion of quality than the point of take-off. In the final phase the vaulter's shoulders must be in line with the pit. When running, they are above the foot plant position and so bring about a movement forwards and upwards which will maintain his angular speed and make the pole bend.

If arm extension, force exerted on pole and take-off are well coordinated, the vaulter has the impression of leaving the ground without 'shock'.

Hang/penetration is the result of the run-up-plant-take-off sequence. The further the take-off point is away from the box the greater it will be, and its speed is conditioned by the run-up speed and also by the stretching of the muscular chain in the front part of the torso. Usually this 'whiplash' is accompanied by a recoil of the shoulders, by gripping the pole or by pushing with the lower arm. The result of this action allows a) acceleration of the hang, b) greater flexion of the pole, c) keeping the centre of gravity behind the pole and d) more effective use of the pole.

HOW TO USE THE POLE TO MAXIMUM EFFECT

Good use of the pole is possible only when it has sufficient straightening speed. This being said, the rockback aims at placing the body in a position that will favour recovery of the energy stored in the pole, so that it will be catapulted to the greatest possible height. The hang phase introduces a rotation around the axis of the shoulders to bring the back parallel to the ground and then face on to the bar (vaulters describe this as 'staying on the back'). The legs go through a phase of quite pronounced flexion of the knees towards the hands. The last part of the rockback is an extension of the legs and hips in time with the extension time of the pole. The body is practically vertical. Notice that at no time is the head extended to aid rockback.

The vaulter being catapulted upwards means that the pull-up begins automatically and the turn occurs simultaneously with the pull-up, bringing the front of the body to the bar in an attitude which favours the movement through the air. A last push by the upper arm completes the lift of the body. Clearing the bar is the obvious conclusion to the catapult. The vaulter should be on his stomach, chest hollowed, head down, elbows drawn backwards and upwards. Efficient clearance depends on effectiveness of those factors leading to the pole being raised to the vertical and the influence of the bar on the vaulter. The latter can cause him to make errors in his position in relation to the pole leading to premature clearance (ie unsuccessful). This is why a good vaulter tries to vault according to the pole he uses and not according to the height to be cleared.

FACTORS AFFECTING PERFORMANCE IN POLE VAULTING

The following is a useful reminder of the factors necessary to produce maximum impetus upwards.

VERY WIDE ANGLE   The ground/pole angle should be the greatest possible at take-off.

POWER AT TAKE-OFF   The take-off not only contributes to the development of the necessary energy but also gives the pole the speed to reach the vertical.

OBJECTIVE JUDGMENT   The pole must bend, but don't choose just any pole – the choice must be one which will allow most energy to be stored without breaking, ie the stiffest possible for the athlete.

SPEED OF RUN-UP   The speed and weight of the vaulter are the essential factors in this energy storage in the pole bend. However, for better catapulting, the speed factor is particularly important.

RELAXATION AND ALERTNESS IN EFFORT   The linking of run-up-plant-take-off is the key technical phase. It must be carried out with accuracy at high speed.

COURAGE AND DETERMINATION   Psychologically, mental attitude has a direct influence on the technical attitude of the vaulter.

PECTORAL GIRDLE POWER, COORDINATION AND BALANCE   After take-off, the vaulter becomes a gymnast who works on the pole as on a piece of apparatus, in order to create a good relationship. He tries to turn over to put himself in the best

position for catapulting. Waiting for pole-time*, he finishes his upward movement by a pull-up and a turnover in order to cross the bar in the most effective position.

PHYSICAL HEALTH (TOUGHNESS) AND MORAL HEALTH (MOTIVATION, WILL TO SUCCEED)   The range of qualities needed for a good level of performance at this event is very wide. Improvement is thus possible thanks to many elements which can be realised if the vaulter works hard and consistently.

MAIN AREAS IN THE TRAINING OF A POLE VAULTER

When to Start

Considering the size of the task, it is best to start athletic training relatively young (at 12 to 14 years) to ensure a gradual development of all the factors affecting performance.

The selection of possible talent must include an evaluation of the physical potential of the future vaulter. He must be strong and supple so that he can work consistently. Selection must not merely take into account present physical reality but must consider probable subsequent development. It must also take psychological factors into account: it is useless to try and make a pole vault champion out of a youngster who would not have the strength of character and the mental resistance which are essential if he is to succeed.

Basic Training

There is an age to train the body, the character and the mind; it does not just suddenly happen on reaching adulthood. As a precaution, the muscles supporting the spinal column (dorsal and lumbar) must be developed, as must the abdominal muscles, and the shoulder joints must be strengthened. No serious progress can be made without good control of running and speed. Learning running techniques is fundamental to basic training. In pole vaulting motor skills in various combinations are called for. So multidiscipline training is needed at a young age (7 to 11 years), using progressively varied and precise movements taken from athletics gymnastics and apparatus work.

*This phrase 'pole-time' is the literal translation from French and will be very clear to expert pole vaulters. It refers to the natural frequency of the pole/athlete system which determines if, and when, the pole will straighten - H.P.

When athletic training begins the aims must be to learn the form of the movement, to develop willpower and to respect the rules, other competitors and the officials.

General Physical Condition

Health is probably the most precious possession of the top-class athlete. Maintaining and/or developing it are a constant worry throughout his career. Periodic medical examinations are necessary, and since in order that it can be assimilated, each area of training must be followed by a recovery period, the athlete should not hesitate to use methods such as massage and hydrotherapy.

Steps should be taken to avoid, as far as possible, accidents which might hinder continuous training. Strengthening the antagonistic muscles (hip extensors), the abdominals, dorsals and lumbars, the feet and the shoulders, already an important part of basic training, must carry on throughout his career. Training capacity improves with time if it is based on continuous and varied sporting activity.

Perfecting Technique

SAFETY Improvement in technique and training of the pole vaulter are determined by the amount of consistent effort he puts in. This effort is dependent on his character and the *equipment* he uses.

The landing area must provide every guarantee of safety and inspire sufficient confidence in the vaulter that he can attempt all exercises without fear.

Growth of physical potential and technique depends necessarily on changes of pole. The vaulter must have a range of poles at his disposal which will allow him to deal with the demands of training and improvement.

BALANCE A balance must be maintained between technique and physical potential. Indeed, certain technical movements can only be made if the vaulter has the physical ability to carry them out. This

potential must be determined by a series of tests as must its use in the vault so that its position in the training scheme can be worked out.

The physical qualities essential in the ideal vaulter, as we have seen, are strength and speed.

PROGRESS All problems cannot be resolved at once. There must be a gradual progression throughout the athlete's career as well as during the annual training programme.

This progression is from the most simple to the most difficult and from the principal to the secondary.

The speed of progression depends on individual capabilities, influenced by age, physical and mental characteristics, accumulated physical skills, amount of training, and the assimilation potential of the athlete. The main stages in the progression are shown below.

The 'seeds of dedication' are sown when specialization begins, taking into account elements already mentioned concerning equipment, safety and basic training.

TEACHING CONSIDERATIONS

a) Measure out degrees of difficulty according to limits of the athlete so as not to ask more of him than he can give.
b) Be patient – everything cannot be done at once.
c) Quality – demand work of quality by applying the following principles:
   – do technical training when the vaulter is at his freshest
   – allow complete recovery time between each vault
   – a vault which involves overcoming fear uses up more energy
   – a period of concentration before a vault when the vaulter pictures mentally the execution increases efficiency of technical training
   – question the athlete on his perceptions and feelings.
d) Vary training. The vaulter must be able to

	TECHNICAL	PHYSICAL
Initiation	Doing a long jump with pole in the sandpit. This short first stage perfectly reveals latent skill	Multidisciplinary training. Control of stride in running. Strengthening of abdominals, and spine-supporting muscles

	TECHNICAL	PHYSICAL
Beginning of Specialization	Search for *accuracy* and *amplitude* a) Move from long jump to high jump b) Master the run-up-plant-plant-take-off sequence so as to increase handhold height safely. Begin all sessions with a range of plant and take-off exercises. Make use of the suppleness of the pole c) Standardize the start of the approach run d) Establish a good relationship with the pole in the overall vault	Multidisciplinary training – high jump – hurdles – sprint – javelin – aerobics etc Continue preventative strengthening of muscles
Specialization	a) Work on approach run to increase maximal controlled speed without overtension b) Improve rhythmic structure of vault for the best development of pole bend c) Use of progressively stiffer poles	Continue multidisciplinary training – long jump – hurdles – sprint Improve strength and speed. Gymnastics
Perfecting Technique	Increase level of technique by using potential of strength and speed to its best advantage. Develop experience in major competitions	Bring together specific speed and absolute speed. Develop specific physical potential

adapt to all circumstances that can affect the execution of a vault. This faculty is developed by varying the conditions: length of approach run; stiffness of pole; and place of training.

e) Develop an individual style. If basic principles of biomechanics are to be respected, it is better to develop the style of the vaulter himself, rather than to copy that of the champion of the moment.

When the objective is understood, the vaulter develops a personal style of vaulting. The trainer only needs to intervene to put him back 'on the rails' if he strays.

f) Repetition. This is an essential element in training-consolidation and automatization. Here, too, the coach must be aware of the limits and avoid fatiguing the vaulter, whose system would then revolt against any new exercise: group the repeated exercises in series, and separate the series by rest periods. In this way, the reinforcement process begun in the repeated exercises will carry on in the rest period. This is known as the maturation phase.

g) Motivation. Competitive pole vaulting is a combat sport demanding great mental commitment. The psychological influence of the trainer is important. He must create the competitive spirit through dynamic lively group activity, evaluation of the vaulter and competition. It is always possible to find positive points even in a bad vault. The athlete must be treated firmly so that he will become equally hard on himself.

Preparation for competition goes beyond the training ground. Effective logistical support is needed in the areas of equipment, medicine, social and publicity.

TWO TYPICAL TRAINING SESSIONS

1 Methods
(a) Average and varied approach runs (4 + 12 or 4 + 10 or 4 + 8 strides).
(b) Range of adapted poles.
(c) Adapted handholds with perhaps slight progression.

Composition
(i) Warm up with technical exercises related to run-up, plant and take-off outside the pit, then in the pit followed by loosening-up.
20 to 25 vaults:

(ii) Aiming at unhurried acceleration over the main part of the run-up then forward posture at take-off. Raise the handhold gradually. Apply more and more pressure on take-off before carrying out dynamic tuck extension.

(iii) Reduce the run-up by two to four strides in order to *attack* better.

(iv) Raise the handhold and change pole by use of springboards ranging in height from 5 to 10 to 15cm.

2 Methods
a) Competition run-up (possibly − 2).
b) Range of poles.
c) Seeking highest handhold.

Same composition as in previous session but do fewer vaults, 10 to 15, making them higher.

Try to find the rhythm for run-up/vault. Move progressively, in preparation for competitions, from technique to efficiency. Vaults with bar. Note the percentage of success.

Rockback - Extension. If the run-up–plant–take-off sequence is correct, the rockback is relatively easy. Rotation occurs around an axis situated at shoulder level. During rockback, particularly at the beginning, the vaulter tries to keep this axis far behind the pole by pushing with the lower arm. This action not only keeps the vaulter's centre of gravity behind the pole, but allows him more easily to find the pole-time which provides all its harmony and effectiveness in the suspension phase.

Rockback Extension Exercises
1 (Fig 4) Starting from plant-take-off exercise number 4, put the end of the pole 50cm to 100cm away from the base of a wall or a tree. After take-off, balance two feet against the wall at shoulder level, with the body perpendicular to the pole. Hold this position so as to control the balance of the pole/vaulter combination, and to be able to correct, if necessary, the position, particularly at arm level (lower arm stretched) of the shoulders (behind the pole) and of the pelvis (at pole level).
2 (Fig 5) Same start as the previous exercise but facing a soft landing area so as to continue the swingback and the rotation until the vaulter is parallel to the pole when he lands on his back.
3 (Fig 6) In order to give more height to this

movement, start from a raised point (the higher it is, the higher will be the movement and the more useful). The pole is planted in a sandpit. After take-off swing back the take-off leg and push with the lower arm so as to make the pole bend.
3b Same exercise but end the rockback by a dynamic extension of the legs and hips lengthened by a pull-up and a turnover.

PLANT–TAKE-OFF

It is possible to pole vault without worrying too much about take-off, but it is not the best way.

The pole vaulter, after all, is a jumper. If he doesn't cultivate the form and intensity of his take-off, he will never be able to use the large poles, without which great height cannot be achieved. Take-off is like that of a long jumper. To be complete, ie to allow complete freedom for the foot, the take-off point must be at a distance from the box and the hand, approximately in line with the upper hand.

This is why in take-off exercises the vaulter will be asked to exaggerate this aspect by taking off before the pole is planted.

The 'clawing' action of the take-off leg and foot is coordinated with the widest possible ground/pole angle by means of placing the pole in a throwing position above the head, with the upper arm and the lower arm and a rigid torso to ensure transmission.

Plant - Take-off Exercises
1 (Fig 7) Hold the pole at the end, arm above head, feel the leg rise at same time as arm: (a) when walking (b) running on the spot and (c) jogging.
2 (Fig 8) When jogging with the pole held normally to the side, throw the top end upwards and forwards using the upper arm to make it go through the vertical. Catch it at the other end and repeat.
3 (Fig 9) Pole vertical. Standing upright, stretch up to grip the pole then add 5cm. Walking with the pole to the side, plant the pole to bring it to the vertical position then walk by on the right-hand side for righthanded/sided vaulters, and on the lefthand side for lefthanded vaulters. This vertical position of the pole is achieved by a

Figs 4–6 (*Opposite*) Rockback and extension exercises

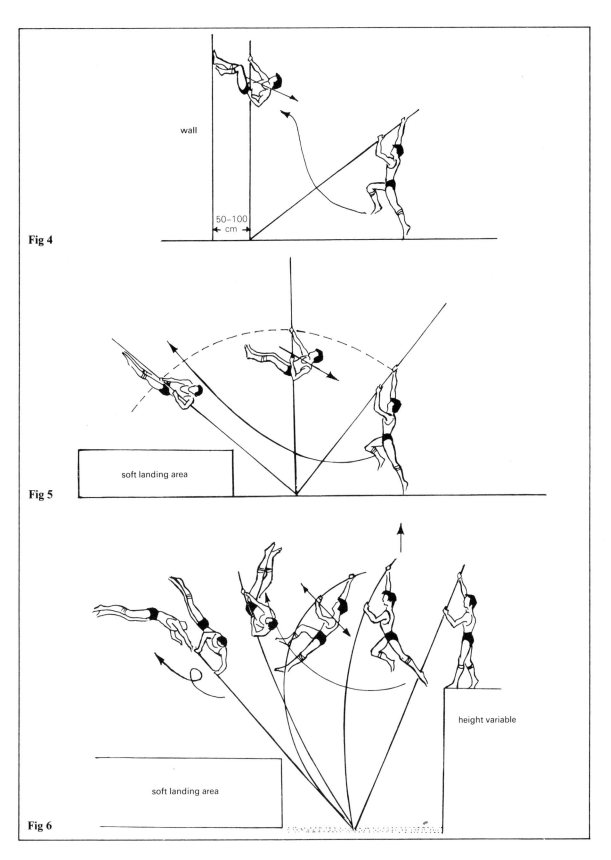

Fig 4

wall

50–100
cm

Fig 5

soft landing area

Fig 6

soft landing area

height variable

143

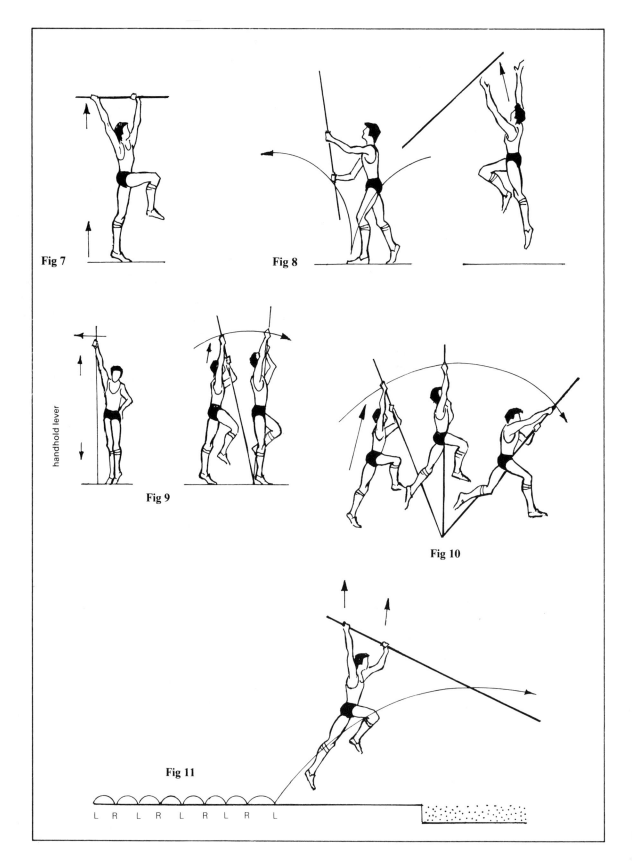

Fig 7

Fig 8

handhold lever

Fig 9

Fig 10

Fig 11

L R L R L R L R L

144

complete and intense extension of the whole body.

4 (Fig 10) Same exercise as above but with 30cm higher handhold. Plant at a jog. Vertical position of the pole is achieved by driving up on the take-off foot. Do not hang on to the pole but rather stretch to the maximum to bring the pole to the vertical, and ground it.

5 Same exercise again but try to jump further. If during these exercises the lower end of the pole slips on the ground, this is because the vaulter is not stretching enough or because he has grasped too high.

6 (Fig 11) After a four-, six- or eight-stride run-up, do a long jump with the pole in the long-jump pit. These vaults allow the vaulter to concentrate on take-off which takes place before the pole is planted in the sand, avoiding the problems posed by accuracy of take-off point. Maximum possible angle at take-off should be stressed.

SUPPLEMENTARY TECHNIQUE EXERCISES

Exercise 1
OBJECTIVE   To devise a run-up in which, by means of vaulting exercises, the accuracy and rhythm will be improved.

EQUIPMENT   6 to 14 check marks.

EXECUTION   Choose an interval adapted to the aim in view and to the length of stride of the vaulter. From take-off point count three intervals then put down the first marker, then an even number of markers. After a preparation phase place the take-off foot before the first marker.

Exercise 2
OBJECTIVE   Improve forward thrust at take-off. Dynamic building-up of the hip extensors.

EQUIPMENT   One or more 4m elastic straps held at one end by an assistant and fastened at the other to an ankle strap on the vaulter.

EXECUTION   Fix the lower end of the pole in the box: a helper will hold the elastic straps creating

degrees of resistance. The pole is held by the vaulter in the take-off position. Claw with the take-off leg while raising the pole with both arms.

Exercise 3
OBJECTIVE   Improving plant without vaulting.

EQUIPMENT   One box and one relatively soft pole.

EXECUTION   With the pole in the box use maximum handhold height, locate the take-off point slightly below the line of the back hand, then step backwards three steps so as to have the foot of the free leg in front.

Do three small dynamic strides while planting the pole in the box. Insist upon: early launch (from the beginning); rhythm and determination; placing the pole above the head; shoulder line perpendicular to the pole; a firm pelvic girdle and clawing of the take-off foot.

Exercise 4
OBJECTIVE   To consolidate good movement during the run-up–plant–take-off sequence.

EQUIPMENT   One mobile box, ie an inner tube filled with 10kg of sand or a wooden box.

EXECUTION   After a run-up of 3, 6, 8 or 10 strides with or without check marks, link into the run-up–plant–take-off sequence paying attention to firmness and attack. This will make the mobile box slide.

Exercise 5
OBJECTIVE   To improve transference of the energy developed at take-off into the pole.

EQUIPMENT   Vaulting pit, adapted pole.

EXECUTION   On a short- or medium-length run-up, take a higher and higher handhold. The plant is powerful, directed upwards and coordinated with a powerful thrust of the take-off leg. Make the pole bend without straining it, concentrating on lifting and take-off. Do not attempt to turn over.

Exercise 6
OBJECTIVE   To give more and more height to the vault by taking high handholds, by taking off at

a distance and by making the pole bend by thrusting with the lower arm during the swing phase.

EQUIPMENT   Three springboards 5, 10 or 15cm high.

EXECUTION   Using a longish run-up perform the run-up–plant–take-off sequence, taking off from the springboard to do a complete vault. When using springboards, avoid exercises without them in the same session.

Exercise 7
OBJECTIVE   To improve take-off. To improve balance in the rockback.

EQUIPMENT   Jumping pit, rigid pole.

EXECUTION   After a 6- to 8-stride run-up, perform run-up–plant–take-off sequence, making sure that the take-off is at a distance, and then that the rockback is carried out about the shoulders, which should remain behind the pole. Finish parallel to the pole. Perhaps do a complete vault.

Exercise 8
OBJECTIVE   To coordinate in the hang phase the hang–tuck position and the pushing of the shoulders away from the pole by lower-arm thrust.

EQUIPMENT   Beginner's pole Lerc unbreakable (80 × 4.20m). Sandpit.

EXECUTION   After a short 6- to 8-stride run-up, pole held at the end (4.20m handhold), vault, then during the hang phase push down into the pole, so as to be able to pass the take-off foot between the arms and end up astride the pole.

DEVELOPING THE STRENGTH OF THE POLE VAULTER*

Main Principles of Strength Work
The pole vaulter is a sprinter–jumper–gymnast,

*** Editor's Note**   Maurice Houvion at this stage wrote a very comprehensive account of a pole vaulter's strength, speed and mobility training requirements. Efficient technique is inextricably bound up with, and dependent upon, these physical attributes as every coach and athlete knows. However, as these aspects go beyond the intended range of this book, which is primarily concerned with technique and its acquisition, only some important principles which relate specifically to pole vaulting are extracted – H.P.

thus strength is a deciding factor in performance. Certain postural and technical abilities can only be realised if the corresponding level of strength is there. Improving necessary strength for comfortable execution of a vault is dependent on the following factors:

PRIORITY TO BE GIVEN TO RELATIVE STRENGTH

$$\text{Relative strength} = \frac{\text{Absolute strength}}{\text{Bodyweight}}$$

If in certain cases there is a link between the development of this strength and the stabilization or even reduction of bodyweight, an increase in muscle bulk should not give rise to alarm unless it is excessive.

RELATIONSHIP BETWEEN STRENGTH AND COORDINATION   Increase in strength is not an end in itself; its aim is to allow comfortable execution of the movement the vaulter wants to make. As well as this, great specific ability/skill must be maintained or developed. For this reason:

a) Choice of strengthening exercises is varied.
b) They are chosen specifically for their usefulness in developing strength for pole vaulting.
c) Their execution is balanced out by suitable compensatory exercises (stretching, relaxing).
d) The balance between agonistic and antagonistic muscles is maintained.
e) Strength training is carried out along with training specific to pole vaulting.

PROGRESSION RESULTING IN EXPLOSIVE STRENGTH (POWER-SPRING)   Spring means the ability of the neuro-muscular system to overcome resistance by the quickest possible contraction. This state can only be attained after general physical conditioning, with pride of place given to support strength (abdominals, dorsals, lumbars, etc) as well as an improvement in endurance strength: eg choice of 8 to 10 exercises covering all the muscle groups, with loads allowing about ten repetitions (60 to 80 per cent of maximum load) and rhythm ensuring good movement technique. If possible the exercises should be in the form of a circuit, repeated two or three times.

The essential prerequisite for attaining maximum speed in the execution of a movement is a

Load as percentage of maximum –	70%	80%	90%	100%	90%	80%	70%
Repetitions –	10	7	3	1	3	7	10

high level of strength (as subsequent base for work).

After the general physical conditioning phase, strength is sought with the aid of the Pyramid method: ie progressive sets with increasing poundage and reducing repetitions.

When preparing for competition the strength potential is optimized by intra- and intermuscular coordination. Intramuscular coordination and speed of contraction are optimized by dynamic effort training. Intermuscular coordination is improved by specific technical training.
– Average loads (70 to 80 per cent) maximum speed of execution.
– Rests (2 to 3 mins) between difficult series or plyometrics.

Some Rules to Remember
1 Any method used in one form only becomes habitual, the athlete gets used to it, and it loses its effectiveness. It is very important to change the form of work from time to time.
2 Strength training which has quick results in terms of growth will bring about a similarly quick decline if exercise is stopped. The reverse is equally true.
3 An intensive short exercise with weights followed by a springing exercise produce in this order more effect on spring than in the reverse order.
4 Ultraviolet rays (sun) have a favourable effect on the effectiveness of training.
5 In the long term adopt the following progression:
  (i) Jumping exercises
  (ii) Building strength in legs using weights
  (iii) Jumping exercises with a weighted jacket
  (iv) Plyometrics
6 Efficiency of method is not the only criterion. Continuity is fundamental to the viability of training. Injury or illness spoils efficiency.

It is sensible to avoid methods or exercises which could cause trauma to those areas of the body already much used in pole vaulting (lumbar regions, joints, tendons).

This is why I only recommend plyometrics in prescribed doses, and for the heavy muscling in the legs, I prefer **diagonal press extension** to standing upright squats.

DEVELOPING THE SPEED OF THE POLE VAULTER

TECHNICAL REMINDER The pole vaulter aims to get to the box in the quickest possible time while being in a suitable position (control of speed) to effect the run-up–plant–take-off sequence in an accurate and efficient way. Controlled maximal speed of the vaulter depends on his absolute speed, his ability to adapt to running while carrying a pole and careful distribution of efforts in the run-up.

Factors Determining Speed
1 Speed of reaction: reaction time which is vital in a timed sprint has much less importance in the vaulter's run-up.
2 Acceleration ability: here, too, there is no direct relation between this ability and the search for controlled maximal speed in the run-up. However, it must be noted that maximal running speed is obtained usually after 4 to 6 seconds of effort which for a sprinter represents about 30 to 50 metres of the race. There is a very close relationship between acceleration ability and strength of leg.
3 Action speed: this is by far the most important factor for the vaulter seeking controlled maximal speed. Best results come from a good coordination between length and frequency of strides.

When the drive is greatest, the length of the stride increases and the ground contact time decreases which brings about an increase in frequency. Quality of action speed, then, is greatly influenced by the drive, as long as it works with the other essential features.

Methodology
LENGTH OF RUN-UP The optimum distance depends on the aim of the training. If its purpose is to improve acceleration ability, distances corresponding to the level of the sprinter in this area must be chosen (25 to 35m). If its purpose is to

147

improve the maximal speed, distances (20 to 45m) must be run when this speed has been achieved (full-speed runs) eg 25 to 35m acceleration plus 20 to 45m full-speed sprint.

INTENSITY OF EXECUTION Speed work operates at a very high level. However, at the beginning and end of a session effort can be less than maximum so that a good running action can be sought, as well as good coordination and relaxation.

RECOVERY TIME Leave the maximum amount of time before beginning the next run: every 20 to 30m needs about 3min; if the run is longer then rest time can extend to 6 to 8min. Whilst making sure that recovery is complete, the rest time must not be too long lest the excitability of the central nervous system is affected. The best thing is to use active rest periods (walking, relaxation exercises).

NUMBER OF TIMES EXERCISES SHOULD BE REPEATED The principle is straightforward: no speed training when the athlete is tired. Usually 5 to 10 repeats in one training unit are enough. As soon as rhythm drops, speed training must stop.

PREPARATION All speed training must be carried out when the athlete is completely warmed-up. Raising body temperature can increase contraction speed by 20 per cent. Warming up can be done using slow running exercises, technical exercises, relaxation and suppleness exercises, short jumps and bursts of acceleration.

PROGRAMMING Speed training is necessary throughout the year though in different proportions ie keeping athlete ticking over in general conditioning period and developing this area in pre-competition period. In a micro-cycle it is best to train for speed in the first or second day after rest.

THE SPEED BARRIER AND CONSOLIDATION OF THE RUNNING ACTION The method used for developing speed contradicts the fact that the more a movement is repeated the more 'barriers' are set up. In fact it is known that many repeats form a stereotype which results in a 'grooving in', or consolidation, of the movement pattern which includes frequency and speed. This disadvantage can be avoided by taking a number of precautions during apprenticeship and training:

(i) Give the beginner a general physical training with the stress on **strength-speed** exercises, and using many different exercises in varied situations.

(ii) For established athletes find ways of carrying out the main movement which will allow them to exceed normal speed and achieve new sensations, eg running downhill, sprinting and vaulting/jumping using a sunken box.

(iii) Decrease the amount of work done on the major movements in favour of work on **speed-strength** and work specific to the event. A pole vaulter can be advised, in the period devoted predominantly to developing physical potential, to use training methods which vary the execution of vaults and help develop adaptability, eg change length of run-up, use poles of varying strengths and use facilitating methods such as planting in the sand, sunken box, raised run-up, springboard, etc.

These methods by bringing new technical elements into play, favour progression when the vaulter seeks height in his vault. The process known as 'extinction' which involves non-practice of the main movement can help the 'barrier' to disappear. It has often been said that a short break of 2 or 3 weeks from technical training 4 to 6 weeks before a major competition has a positive effect on the level reached in the competition.

ADJUSTING TO SPRINTING WITH THE POLE The efficiency of run-up and take-off is the main factor behind the energy produced by the vaulter. Speed at the moment the run-up–plant–take-off sequence takes place must be at its greatest. This is achieved by perfect balance in running. The best thing is to reduce the difference between the absolute speed and the speed while carrying the pole. It is vital to have maximum control of running with the pole – this is achieved by frequent sprint repetitions, by a range of exercises and by increasing acceleration, sprint and run-up with pole.

RUNNING EXERCISES
1 (Fig 12) Standing holding pole near the top and parallel with the ground. Legs straight and together. Move forward alternating feet.
2 (Fig 13) Standing holding pole as above. Hop with dynamic action of the foot. 30m alternating right foot (8) then left (8).

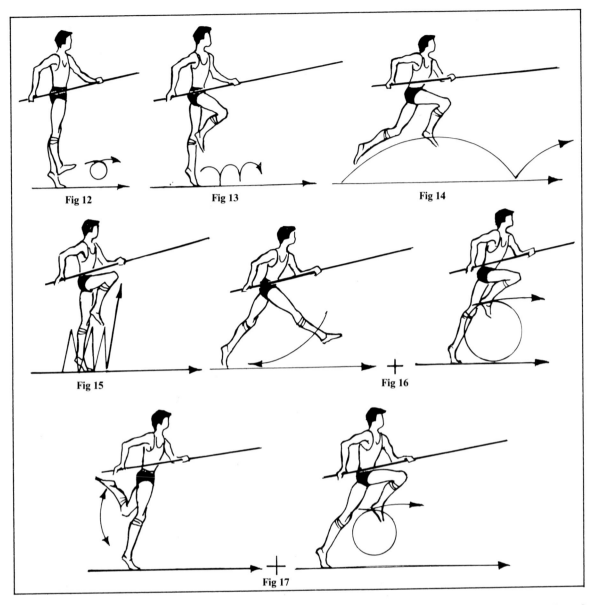

Fig 12

Fig 13

Fig 14

Fig 15

Fig 16

Fig 17

Figs 12–17 Running exercises

3 (Fig 14) Same starting position. Do 30m of multi-jumps. Each jump should be 'lively'. Pay attention to the balance of the vaulter/pole combination and the firmness of foot contact.

4 (Fig 15) Same starting position. Do high-knee-lift running over 30m. Keep pelvis as high as possible (don't sit). This exercise can be fully felt if the heel of the free leg is raised to the top of the take-off leg.

5 (Fig 16) Same starting position. Run, stretching the legs by pulling with the foot. Get maxi-

mum length, then finish the run with a series of quick knee-lifts.

6 (Fig 17) Same starting position. Run slowly for 30m, with the heel of first the right and then the left foot striking the buttocks. Keep a firm forward lean. Between each exercise, run for about 30m with the pole. This run should be easy – relaxed – high. The legs 'cycle' as though the vaulter's feet were on a wheel.

To improve still more balance and awareness, the pole can be carried by starting with it high and progressively lowering it, by lowering and raising the pole several times, aiming at gradual acceleration, etc.

DISTRIBUTION OF EFFORT DURING RUN-UP This varies according to vaulter: some run quickly and powerfully from the start; others increase the rhythm gradually after a relatively slow start; and others aim to reach their highest speed a few strides (3 to 4) from take-off so as to devote the end of the run-up to alertness which will give them the best run-up–plant–take-off sequence.

Whichever way and whatever number of strides necessary to reach controlled maximal speed, the preparation phase should not vary from one run-up to another. This means that the first run-up strides change little and a high balanced posture is established straight away.

Run-up preparation can be as follows:

a) Walk up to the starting mark, then start running.
b) Do a jump with the free leg so that the take-off leg is positioned on the starting mark and then run.
c) Set off with 4 small springy strides before the starting mark.
d) Take a longer distance (9 to 12m) to set off in.

A few trials will show the vaulter which method to choose, the one he feels happy with.

Attaining controlled maximal speed is usually done by having an equal number of strides with check marks on the side of the track corresponding to the take-off foot. The number of strides after preparation is 10–20, and they are gradually and calmly speeded up so that controlled maximal speed is reached before take-off, and so that the vaulter can concentrate on the accuracy of the run-up–plant–take-off sequence.

If relaxation is one essential element in the pole-vault run-up, the other is determination: the vaulter must attack, keep on attacking whilst remaining alert. Posture aids balance and can in an experienced vaulter affect speed. The vaulter leans slightly forward, not too far, he remains erect, runs high, with the knees bringing the thighs to the horizontal position particularly in the last strides. The last stride is slightly shorter with the aim of accelerating the last foot contact.

The choice of run-up length is affected by the vaulter's powers of strength, speed and training as well as the maximal speed at which he can effect an accurate plant and an efficient take-off. Obviously he adjusts the flexibility of the pole he uses to this last element.

CHECK MARKS Most vaulters use a starting mark as well as a check mark which is usually more useful for the observer (trainer/coach) than for the athlete. In France for many years we have used a mark 6 strides from take-off. This helps us to assess the character of the vaulter and the ways we can correct his faults.

EXERCISES HAVING AN INFLUENCE ON FORM, REGULARITY AND RHYTHM OF STRIDE

(i) 400m runs to obtain a regular stride.
(ii) 30 to 50m run with pole.
(iii) free run over 3 or 4 low hurdles to ensure an accurate and rhythmic stride pattern.
(iv) layout markers on the run-up to help stride length, accuracy and rhythm.

COUNTING TECHNIQUES Some coaches, in order to establish a regular rhythm, a regular stride and a stable run-up, recommend counting each time the take-off foot touches the ground. At each foot contact, the speed increases until the penultimate stride. To get used to this method, it should be done every time the vaulter runs.

METHODS OF IMPROVING THE RUN-UP Over the full run-up (between 14 and 20 strides).

Seeking technical control with acceleration of the plant Starting from the principle that sprinting is the result of posture, relaxation, good distribution of efforts and rhythm, concentrate on these elements rather than on speed which can sometimes have a negative effect on these elements.

eg concentration on posture or concentration on relaxation or on rhythm of knee-lift etc } use poles of average stiffness

Seeking terminal rhythm (by accelerating) Mark out the 6 final strides quite short. After powerful acceleration of the stride rhythm in the first part of the course, try and attain high frequency of knee-lift over the final 6 strides. Gradually move back the 6-stride mark so that the new length can generate linear speed.

Seeking controlled maximal speed These exercises are carried out in the pre-competition period.
a) After the run-up stick the pole into a sandpit

(accuracy being not so important, more energy can be put into getting up speed).

b) Run-up ends with pole in a sunken box, a raised take-off zone (5 to 10cm) a lower hand-hold, a soft pole so as to inhibit resistance from the pole lever. Concentrate on the run-up in 'training' competitions where motivation is good. Choose competitions which have good atmospheric conditions, surroundings and opponents.

METHODOLOGY CONCLUSION Intensity – it is best to start a session in a low-key way, choosing a softer pole for the first few vaults and for the end of the session.

Repetition – during vaults off a full run-up calling for great concentration or mastery of nerves is very tiring. They quickly bring about a lowering of speed. Limit of 7 to 12 vaults once or twice a week. Warm-up – same as for a sprint session.

MAINTAINING OR DEVELOPING SUPPLENESS

Suppleness is a characteristic of a functional anatomical group composed of muscles, ligaments and capsules which allows, during physical exercise, good segmental displacement based mainly on muscular elasticity without ruining its strength and power.

But suppleness seems to go beyond these mechanical considerations: the whole bearing can be improved by suppleness. An important factor in progress, it allows better balance for the individual. Eliminating unnecessary contractions will improve the movement in the event and the athlete will feel better. However, athletes often ignore this aspect of training. Since motivation is a problem in this kind of work, the athlete often lacks not only the conviction but the time necessary and the work is essentially individual.

Some factors act positively or negatively on the sensitivity to stretching of muscular fibres. Tiredness raises the threshold of sensitivity, so it is better not to force stretching exercises when this point is reached. In the morning just after getting up the threshold is equally high – compensation is thus necessary in the form of longer and more intense muscle warm-up. On the other hand through pre-competition concentration and after a good warm-up session, the sensitivity threshold is lowered.

Methodology

a) Active stretching exercises with or without time allowed for recoil. This kind of work, although not the most effective, can play an important role in the warm-up for example.

b) Slow and gradual stretching of muscles preceded by a resistance. A helper exerts the force. The athlete exerts first of all moderate resistance to the manipulation, say for about 10 seconds, before giving way to the pressure. The manipulator uses this relaxation time to stretch the muscle a little more.

c) Concentration on the stretched muscles in order to control relaxation.

d) Global relaxation work. This kind of work is done after training when the muscles are warmed up. Breathing plays a leading role, breathing out allowing the muscle to relax. Avoid distress which could bring about reflex contraction.

MENTAL TRAINING

The history of pole vaulting shows that progress often comes as a result of the breakdown of psychological barriers. 2.25m separate the 3.69m world record held by the Frenchman Gonder in 1904 from the 1984 world record held by Sergey

Fig 18 (*Overleaf*) Alexandr Krupski (USSR), European champion 1982, is shown here winning the European Cup in 1983. He appears slightly uncomfortable in his run-up, but has excellent body extension at take-off, even though his take-off point is a little ahead of his upper handhold. The rest is perfection as he clears the bar, set at 5.50m, by about 25cm

Fig 19 Daley Thompson (GB), Olympic decathlon champion, takes off too close to the box which results in his body moving too close to the pole in the hang. His left arm is too passive, although the soft pole bends, and his strength allows him to 'muscle' to the vertical. His high point is reached too early and in spite of raising himself some 30 cm higher than the bar, he narrowly misses it on the way down

Fig 20 Thierry Vigneron of France is Olympic bronze medallist and has set several world records. In this excellent vault the plant is particularly good with a take-off at distance, an active lower arm which continues the pole bend, and a well-timed action to the vertical. Perhaps the only criticism to be made is the over-twisting of the body at clearance which brings the right side of the chest close to the bar

Fig 21 Vladimir Polyakov raised the world record to 5.81m in 1981. His technique here is flawless and his timing exact. Note how he has the confidence to let his head go back in frame 18, but allows himself a quick look at the bar in 19

Fig 18

Fig 18

17

18

21

22

25

26

29

30

19

20

23

24

27

28

31

32

Fig 19

1

2

5

6

13

14

3

4

7

8

11

12

5

16

Fig 19

Fig 20

Fig 21

Bubka. Evolution of equipment and training methods do not entirely explain this considerable gap. Today's barriers - handhold 4.80-5m, performance 5.94m - are also short-lived barriers which will make vaulters smile in the year 2000. Mental training means crossing these barriers, thinking like vaulters of the future. This is a job that concerns the coach, but more than that it concerns autosuggestion, and personal ambition. These reflections (that the Eastern countries in particular have studied) convince us that we must think in the future to progress, and thus complement the physical training by improving the athlete's temperament. The quality of training is directly proportional to the motivation of the vaulter and his capacity for concentration.

TACTICAL PREPARATION

A vaulter must know the length, the number of strides and the distribution of his full run-up of about 20 strides and his reduced/short run-up of 12 to 14 strides. Depending on current form and material conditions (wind, track etc), he must decide upon the pole to use, the height of his grip, the distance from the posts and the first height of the bar and subsequent heights he is going to attempt.

In the competition period he has to work out the nature and intensity of final sessions and decide the amount of rest on the last day or days. A well-trained athlete could usefully do, 24 hours before a minor competition, either a heavy strength training session or a sprint session. He should pay attention to the activities of the last evening or the hours preceding the event and the time and contents of his last meal. It is important to work out the nature and intensity of the warm-up, know how to fill in the last moments before the vault and what to do between vaults. Thus with a particular event in view the coach and athlete must work out in advance the strategy to acclimatization, accommodation, problems posed by food, the time of the event and the variability of the break between vaults. These things are worked out by deduction and trial and error. They depend on the individual. Experience is the only way to find out.

Adapting to Circumstances Peculiar to Some Competitions

The athlete should, when competing, be in conditions that suit him. This is not very often possible so he must know how to adapt to the conditions of each competition, especially when these conditions are unfavourable. A vaulter confronted with problems he is not used to solving will lack competitive drive, he will not wish to vault. It is important then to recreate unfavourable conditions in training, in order to inoculate him against them. These situations are usually the same for all vaulters. Every vaulter is sensitive to something or other. It is the coach's job to discover what and try to find a way of dealing with it.

9 LONG JUMP
Dr Jim Hay

New Zealand and USA
(Acknowledgements to the Athletics Congress of the USA)

Dr James G Hay has the strongest credentials as the author of this chapter, not only because he is a former long jumper and pole vaulter himself, but also because he is one of the world's foremost experts on the biomechanics of sports who has made the science of long jumping one of his specialities.

Coach to the New Zealand athletics team in 1969, Jim was elected president of that country's Coaches' Association in 1970. Now a professor of physical education at the University of Iowa, his research and writings have taken him to the positions of president of the American Society of Biomechanics and president of the prestigious International Society of Biomechanics.

Jim Hay's books *The Biomechanics of Sports Techniques* and *The Anatomical and Mechanical Bases of Human Motion* are known to physical education students throughout the world.

From 1981 to 1984 he was research consultant to the USA Olympic Committee with specific responsibility for the horizontal jumps.

Long Jump

GENERAL

The long jump may be considered to consist of five consecutive phases: the approach; the transition from approach to take-off; the take-off; the flight; and the landing. In the course of performing these five phases, a long jumper's goals are to: (a) develop near-maximum speed in the approach; (b) perform the transition from approach to take-off with little loss in speed and place the take-off foot level with the front edge of the board; (c) drive vigorously forward and upward into the take-off; (d) control during the flight any forward rotation acquired at take-off; (e) extend the feet well forward for touchdown in the sand, and pass forward over the feet without reducing the distance of the jump. A failure to satisfy any one of these goals invariably results in a less-than-optimum performance.

DOMBROWSKI (Fig 1)

Frames 1-13 show the last three strides of the athlete's approach. These three strides are of critical importance in determining the ultimate success of the jump.

Well-trained long jumpers perform many full-effort repetitions of the approach-run in training. The object of such training is to acquire the ability to arrive at the board with as much speed as can be handled effectively during the take-off into the jump itself. In the course of this training an athlete develops what specialists in motor behaviour refer to as a 'motor program' – a structured sequence of movements that can be executed as required. Skilled long jumpers use such a programme in performing the same 14–20 strides that normally precede those last three strides. Then, during the last three strides, they use visual feedback – their visual perception of how far they are away from the board – as a basis for adjusting the length of their strides to ensure that they land appropriately on the board.

It is during these last three strides that the athlete must also make the adjustments necessary to obtain an effective transition from the sprinting action of the approach to the jumping action of the take-off. Many potentially fine jumps are lost because the athlete fails to make these adjustments or because he (or she) makes them only at the expense of a very large loss in horizontal velocity.

Frame 1. The athlete has landed on the outside of the ball of the foot – as is characteristic of good sprinting – and with his centre of gravity (cg) about 25–30cm behind the toe of this foot. This latter figure is a little larger than is usually the case with top sprinters.

Frame 2. The completely extended position of the left leg, the high lift of the right knee and the full-range action of the arms indicate that the athlete has driven off vigorously into his third-last stride – albeit perhaps a little more vertically than desirable. This latter, and the slightly longer-than-usual cg-to-toe distance referred to earlier, are possibly indications that the athlete is making adjustments in his stride lengths as a result of finding himself a little too far from the board with three strides remaining.

Frame 3. With the possible exception of some excess tension in the shoulders and arms, the athlete is maintaining good sprinting form during the flight phase of the stride. He appears to be a little higher in the air than is commonly seen at this stage in the stride cycle – a further indication that the preceding take-off may have been a little more vertical than usual.

Frames 4-6. Another ball-of-the-foot landing followed by a vigorous driving-off into the next stride. The driving leg does not appear to be quite as completely extended, and the recovery leg not lifted quite as high as in the take-off to the preceding stride. (Note: Frames 2 and 6 appear to have been taken at well-nigh identical instants in the stride cycle.)

It is at the instant depicted in frame 6 – the instant of take-off into the second-last stride – that well-trained long jumpers almost invariably attain their maximum horizontal velocity. From this point onward, some of the horizontal velocity previously developed is reluctantly sacrificed in the interests of obtaining the vertical velocity at take-off necessary for a successful jump.

Frames 6-8. The second-last stride of the approach. Although maintaining good sprinting form, the athlete still appears to be struggling a little to reach the board.

Although photo sequences like those included in this book are not ideally suited for obtaining measurements, it is often possible to obtain rough estimates of values of interest. In the present instance, the length of the athlete's second-last stride appears to be in the order of 2.65m – an estimate that tends to support the notion that he is struggling to reach the board.

Frames 9-11. After a landing on the heel or the flat of the foot – somewhere between the instants depicted in frames 8 and 9 – the athlete lowers his cg by flexing the hip, knee and ankle joints of his left leg. He then drives forward and upward into the last stride, but with rather less vigour than in the preceding strides. This relative lack of vigour is reflected in the positions of the limbs in frame 11, a moment before take-off.

Frames 12-13. Although the last stride of the approach often appears to be longer than those that preceded it – because the take-off foot is well forward of the athlete's centre of gravity at touch-down – in reality it is usually considerably shorter. In this instance, the last stride appears to be close to 2m, or about 65cm shorter than the second-last stride.

In the course of a normal running stride, an athlete's cg rises and falls during each flight phase. As it falls, it acquires vertical velocity which is arrested and reversed during the next support

phase. In a long jump take-off, the skilled athlete tries to keep the downward vertical velocity of his cg at the instant he plants his take-off foot to a minimum so that all the vertical forces he exerts at take-off can be used to generate the upward vertical velocity he needs. To this end, he strives to get his take-off foot planted before his cg has begun to descend from the peak of its flight. As a direct consequence he curtails the time that he is in the air and thus shortens the length of his last stride.

Frames 14-18. The take-off. Once the take-off foot has been planted, the athlete seeks to pass forward over it and into the jump itself without flexing excessively at hip, knee and ankle joints.

The athlete's actions immediately following the planting of his take-off foot have two contrary effects. Because his cg is well behind his take-off foot at the instant of touchdown, the forward and upward rotation of his body over his take-off foot tends to raise his cg. However, at the same time this is happening, the hip, knee and ankle joints of his take-off leg are flexing to cushion the shock of the impact with the ground. This flexion tends to lower his cg. Thus, to ensure that the first of these two effects is the dominant one, the athlete should try to keep the flexion of his take-off leg to a minimum.

The force that a muscle can exert is augmented if it is forcefully stretched immediately before it begins to shorten. This augmented response depends, however, on the shortening taking place soon after the preceding stretching of the muscle. The short stretch–shorten cycle associated with a limited range of motion at hip, knee and ankle joints thus makes it more likely that the athlete will have the benefit of an augmented muscular response if he does not flex these joints more than is absolutely necessary.*

Frames 19-25. The athlete uses an orthodox hang technique during the flight phase of the jump. In this technique he extends the knee of his free leg shortly after take-off (frames 19-20) and then sweeps the leg forcefully downward and backward (frames 20-22). This downward and backward motion – clockwise in the sequence –

---

*The flexion is forced so it may be misinterpreted if it is suggested that the action is one of flexion, as this implies a voluntary act when it is in fact involuntary - F.D.

Fig 1 (*Overleaf*) Lutz Dombrowski (GDR) won the 1980 Olympic long jump with 8.54m

Fig 1

produces a counter-clockwise motion of the athlete's upper body, in accord with Newton's law of reaction. With both arms overhead (frames 22–23) and his legs partially extended, the athlete has a relatively large moment of inertia about a transverse axis through his cg. Because the forward angular momentum he acquired at take-off is equal to the product of his moment of inertia and his forward angular velocity, this relatively large moment of inertia ensures that his forward angular velocity is relatively small. In short, because he has kept his body fairly well extended, his forward rotation is kept to a minimum.

As the athlete nears the end of his flight, he flexes his knees and draws his feet up towards his buttocks (frame 23). Then with the mass of his legs close to a transverse axis through the hips and the mass of his arms and trunk as far from the same axis as he can get them – note that the arms are high overhead and the trunk fully extended in frame 23 – he swings the legs forward in preparation for the landing. This counter-clockwise action (as seen in the sequence) produces a contrary reaction in the upper body (frames 22–25). However, because the legs are much closer to the axis than are the trunk and arms, the legs swing through a much greater angle than does the rest of the body.

The method used by Dombrowski to bring his legs forward in preparation for the landing is simple, easy to learn and the one most frequently employed by hang-style jumpers. Another technique sometimes used for the purpose is the one demonstrated by Lorraway (Fig 2). In this technique the legs are kept essentially straight and swung outward, around and forward in a circular, or rather conical, motion. Because the legs are kept close to the transverse axis through the hips in this process – picture a horizontal line through both hip joints and extending outward beyond the limits of the body – the mass of the legs is again kept closer to this axis than is the mass of the rest of the body.

Once the athlete's trunk comes into contact with his thighs (frame 25), and further motion of the two is effectively halted, the arms continue their clockwise motion (frames 25–26). The reaction to this continued motion of the arms is a further lifting of the legs and a concomitant extension of the time that the athlete spends in the air.

Frames 26–27. The landing. Ideally the landing is made with the knees extended, the trunk near-erect and the arms level with, or slightly behind, the hips; and with the athlete retaining just sufficient forward momentum to carry him forward of the first marks he made in the sand. How close the landing in the jump shown here came to this ideal is difficult to judge because the instant at which the athlete first made contact with the sand is not shown and it is difficult to judge how easily he made it forward over his feet. Assuming that frame 26 shows the athlete already beginning to rotate forward over his feet, it appears that his position at landing was quite close to the ideal one described here, except perhaps with respect to the position of his trunk which seems to be somewhat forward of the position described.

Summary. With the exceptions of the apparent overstriding in the third-last and second-last strides and a relatively minor improvement that might be made in the landing position, the hang technique shown here is a model of its kind.

IONESCU (Fig 3)

Frames 1–17 show the last four strides of the approach. In the first three of these the athlete exhibits a curious high-bounding action rarely seen in top-class sprinters and long jumpers. This action is characterized by a near-straight arm action (see especially frames 4–8), an apparently high centre of gravity at the peak of each flight phase and a wide separation of the thighs in mid-flight (frames 3,7 and 11). An examination of videotapes showing Ionescu jumping on other occasions suggests that the characteristics shown in this sequence are regular features of her technique rather than a response to being too far from the board with four strides remaining. (Note: Given a running action of this kind, it would require a considerable familiarity with the athlete's 'normal' technique before one could determine with confidence that she was overstriding in an effort to reach the board.)

The touchdown at the end of the second-last stride (between frames 12 and 13), the last stride (frame 15–17) and the take-off into the jump (frames 18–21) have many of the same characteristics as the corresponding parts of the Dombrowski sequence discussed earlier. The touchdown at the end of the second-last stride is apparently made on the heel or on the flat of the foot; the athlete's cg is lowered much more than in the preceding strides by the flexion of the hip, knee and ankle joints; and the touchdown at the end of the last stride is made with the cg again well behind the take-off foot.

Frames 18–21. The take-off shows a minimal flexion of the take-off leg, followed by a forceful extension and a similarly strong action of the free leg. The arms, however, appear to contribute very little to the lifting action at take-off and seem instead to serve only a balancing function. The body positions shown in frames 21 and 22 suggest that the angle of take-off was a relatively high one.

Frames 22–28. The athlete in this sequence uses a 2½-stride hitchkick technique during the flight phase of the jump. (Note: Although coaches and athletes seem to be in total agreement concerning the manner in which one should count running strides, for some inexplicable reason there is no such agreement concerning how the 'running strides' used in a hitchkick technique should be counted. Some, with evident logic, count the strides in exactly the same way as they would if the athlete was still running on the ground. In this counting system, the technique used by Ionescu is referred to as a 2½-stride hitchkick. Others, with logic not so apparent, use a counting system in which the same technique is referred to as a 1½-stride hitchkick. The first of these two counting systems will be used here.*)

The first part of this in-the-air technique is similar to that in the hang technique. Immediately after take-off the athlete extends the knee of the free leg (frames 22 and 23) and sweeps the leg downward and backward (a clockwise action in frames 23 and 24) to complete the first in-the-air stride. In reaction her trunk moves in a counter-clockwise direction – compare the erect, or slightly forward, position of the trunk in frame 22 with the backwardly inclined position in frame 24.

In concert with these actions of the free leg, the take-off leg is flexed at the knee and swung forward and upward (a counter-clockwise direction in frames 23–25) to complete the second in-the-air stride. At the forward limit of this swing and, in this case, with the thigh well above the horizontal (frame 25), the knee is extended. The other leg is brought forward to complete the final half-stride of the 2½-stride hitchkick action (26–28).

* Dr Hay is quite right in his stride-counting system. Nevertheless the usual (non-logical!) convention somehow ends up with one less stride – H.P.

Contrary to what is sometimes thought, a long jumper's in-the-air actions cannot increase the distance of the jump by propelling the athlete through the air. The flight path followed by the athlete's cg is determined at take-off – ignoring the usually trivial effects of air resistance – and nothing that the athlete can do subsequently can alter that. Instead, the athlete's actions are designed to control the forward rotation, which is almost inevitably imparted to the body at take-off, so an effective landing position can be obtained.

The hitchkick technique shown in the sequence appears to be completed earlier than is desirable. The athlete achieves a truly superb position with her legs horizontal and almost fully extended at the completion of her 2½ strides in the air (frame 28) but this deteriorates considerably during the remainder of the flight. There are at least two things that might be done to remedy such a situation: the range of motion of the first stride in the air might be increased and thus cause that stride to occupy more time; and the clockwise motion of the arms that slows to a halt in frame 27 might be continued until the hands are level with or behind the hips. This latter adjustment would tend to keep the legs up longer.

Frames 29–30. The landing. Although it does not match the promise implied in the position shown in frame 28, the landing is still a good one. The legs are fairly well extended and the trunk is nearly erect. The landing technique used here differs from the traditional technique shown in the Dombrowski sequence. In this case, the athlete has flexed her knees and driven her buttocks down into the hole created by her feet. Although it appears to offer no obvious advantages over the traditional technique and would seem to impose potentially hazardous loads on the athlete's knees (note the position of extreme flexion in frame 30) this technique is now fairly widely used, especially by athletes from Eastern European countries.

Fig 2 (*Overleaf*) Robyn Lorraway (Australia), who was a 1983 world championships finalist, uses a variation of the hang technique in which she brings her legs sideways and forwards for the landing. This leg movement helps prevent undesirable forward rotation

Fig 3 Vali Ionescu (Romania) was number one in the world in 1982 with a world record of 7.20m

Fig 4 Carl Lewis (USA) winning the 1981 World Cup. Lewis was 1984 Olympic champion and 1983 world champion

Fig 2

1

2

3

7

8

9

13

14

15

4

5

6

10

11

12

16

17

18

Fig 3

Fig 4

4

5

6

10

11

12

16

17

18

LEWIS (Fig 4)

Frames 1–2. The last part of the last stride. The athlete's trunk is twisted rather more to his right than would seem to be desirable at this stage. This may be because he has found himself a little too far from the board with one stride to go and has stretched to reach it. If this is the case, the slightly exaggerated actions of his lower body in one direction would logically be matched by a corresponding reaction of his upper body in the opposite direction. It may also be due, at least in part, to the athlete's efforts to shift his cg laterally so it will be in the same vertical plane as his take-off foot. In this way vertical forces exerted by the ground on his foot have no tendency to produce unwanted rotation about his frontal axis – the axis through his cg in the forward–backward direction.

The lateral shift of the cg in preparation for take-off provides a suitable excuse to mention that the side view favoured by most observers – including sequence photographers! – is not the only view from which the long jump can be observed to advantage. The view from directly in front or behind can often reveal important features of an athlete's technique. Some athletes step to the side on their last and/or second-last stride thereby subjecting the joints of their supporting leg to large lateral stresses and possible injury. Some in the same process, or by directing their free limbs (and particularly the free leg) across the body, also initiate undesirable rotations about their longitudinal axes. These and other similar faults in technique are much more likely to be detected from a front or rear view than from a side view.

Frames 3–5. Here the athlete is running powerfully off the board and into the jump itself. The driving actions of the free limbs, culminating in the position shown in frame 5, are superb. So, too, is the forceful extension of the take-off leg. (Note that the knee of the take-off leg has flexed relatively little during the course of the take-off.)

Frames 6–17. The athlete is using a 3½-stride hitchkick technique. The number of running strides that can be usefully taken while the athlete is in the air is a function of his (or her) ability. Athletes who jump less than 7.50m are rarely in the air long enough to complete a 3½-stride hitchkick effectively.

The first in-the-air stride begins as the athlete leaves the board with his trunk inclined forward (frame 6) and ends, after a strong downward-and-backward sweeping action of the free leg, with the trunk inclined slightly backward (frame 9).

The second in-the-air stride (frames 9–13) does not involve the large ranges of motion at the hip and knee joints evident in the first stride and, as a consequence, does not have as pronounced an effect on the inclination of the athlete's trunk. Indeed, if one compares the trunk positions in frames 9 and 13 it is difficult to discern any real change. The limited ranges of motion at hip and knee joints in the second stride might be attributed to several factors. It could be that the athlete's trunk is already in the optimum position for the landing to follow and all that he needs to do is to maintain that position against the contrary tendency of the forward angular momentum he has acquired at take-off. It could be too that even an athlete of Lewis's ability has insufficient time in the air to permit him to execute 3½ full-range strides and he must therefore reduce the range of one of them to complete the task.

Some credence is given this suggestion by how close he comes to landing and still does not have both feet together at the end of the final half-stride (frame 17). (Note: It is not clear from the photosequence whether the athlete gets both feet together while still in the air or lands on one foot and brings the other alongside a moment later.)

The third in-the-air stride (frames 13–15) consists of a swinging forward of the left leg into position for landing. In this process the athlete keeps the mass of his left leg close to the axis about which it is rotating – a transverse axis through the hip joint – and the mass of the rest of his body as far from this same axis as he can. (Note the well-flexed position of the left knee and the well-extended positions of the right arm and leg in frames 12–14.) In this way, the athlete is able to bring his left leg forward without seriously compromising his trunk position. The final half-stride (frames 14–17) is performed with an action akin to the trail leg action used by a hurdler.

Frame 18. The landing. This photo shows the athlete shortly after his heels have cut the sand. Assuming that he was able to avoid falling backward without undue difficulty, the positions shown in frames 17 and 18 suggest that the landing might have been delayed and the distance of the jump improved a little if his arms had continued on their clockwise path until they were in line with (or behind) the trunk.

10 TRIPLE JUMP
Yukito Muraki

Japan
(Acknowledgements to the Nippon Rikujo-Kyogi Remei)

Yukito Muraki represented Japan in the triple jump at the 1968 and 1972 Olympics, during which period he was Asian record holder with a best of 16.63m. He ranked in the world top ten in 1969. Since 1970 he has coached his national team in all jumping events and in the heptathlon. As an associate professor he teaches and researches sport sciences at the University of Tsukuba in Japan.

Yukito's reputation as one of the world's best coaches has involved him as a visiting coach at the 1976 Russian national training camp, as a visiting coach/faculty member for 1982/83 at San Diego State University, USA, and as a present member of the JAAF's National Coach Development Committee.

Triple Jump

MECHANICAL PRINCIPLES OF THE TRIPLE JUMP

The prime driving impetus in the triple jump is generated by the approach run as horizontal velocity. That means the final run-up speed at the moment of take-off is of much greater importance than any phase in the entire course of the approach run. The triple jump might be likened to a pebble skipped across the surface of water. The distance reached by a pebble after three bounces on a pond is determined by its approach velocity, the approach angle into the first touchdown and the shape of the bottom of the pebble – if air

Fig 1 Take-off model of the triple jump (step and jump). The 3 basic elements to generate vertical lift are: a) Hinged body rotatory movement during the first half of the phase b) Explosive leg extension during the second half c) Transference of free body segmental (arms and swing leg) momenta during the second half, while shock absorbing at touchdown. The actual take-off movement starts slightly before the touchdown to ensure an active foot placement

KEY
- - -⊙- - - body's centre of gravity path
V_1 approach velocity
β approach angle
V_2 take-off velocity
α take-off angle

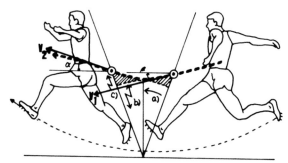

resistance is ignored and if the surface of the water is sufficiently smooth. The pebble bounces on the water, generating vertical velocity from the approach velocity. The shape refers to the posture of the jumper, his movements and alignment of supportive body segments (head, trunk, hips and take-off limb) and effective use of non-supporting leg and arms.

The horizontal velocity during the triple jump, which is a result of the final velocity of the approach run, is constantly decreased during each phase of take-off (hop, step and jump) in order to generate a vertical velocity. Thus, prime importance should be placed on a well-controlled final approach speed into the first take-off, and maintaining as much of this speed as possible especially during the first and second take-offs (hop and step).

On the other hand, as in other jump events, the total vertical momentum of the whole body during each take-off is compounded as follows (Fig 1):

1 During the first half of the take-off phase, angular momentum of the trunk and take-off leg is generated by a hinged movement, or a checking of linear movement at the take-off thus utilizing the horizontal approach velocity as the prime driving factor.
2 Explosive extension of the hip, knee and ankle of the take-off leg occurs immediately after the ballistic, eccentric contraction of the muscles.
3 Momentum from the segmental movement of the lead (swing) leg and the arms is transferred to the whole body.

The last two components are effective during the second half of the take-off period, but they also

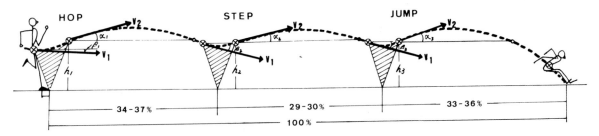

HOP   STEP   JUMP

— 34–37% —   — 29–30% —   — 33–36% —

— 100% —

KEY
--⊗-- body's centre of gravity
h height of cg from the ground
    at each take-off

V_1 approach velocity
β approach angle
V_2 take-off velocity
α take-off angle

Fig 2 Schematic illustration of the running triple jump and jump ratios

have the important role of absorbing shock at the touchdown during the first half of the take-off phase (amortization eccentric phase). However, according to precise and detailed biomechanical analysis, the last component does not play as great a part in the total vertical momentum as do the first two components, though it does play an indirect role in absorbing the shock at the touchdown, as mentioned before, and in preserving the horizontal velocity.

In the past there were many significant misunderstandings that prevented progress of triple-jump performances, eg overstressing the second component of the flexion/extension of the take-off leg, like a piston-type leg action during the take-off. This form is still often observed in unskilled jumpers, especially during the early stages of athletic development and also in athletes doing bounding/hopping exercises. However, after the introduction of the synthetic all-weather surface on the runway in the late 1960s, this old-fashioned so-called 'piston' type of power jump has disappeared in the jumping of top-level athletes. The modern jump technique has been developed to adapt to the elastic surfaces which is more in keeping with the scientific, biomechanical jump mechanism which utilizes more of the horizontal velocity with extended active foot placement at the take-off. This is called the 'rowing-thrust type' of technique and replaces the 'piston type' of leg action.

During the take-off the path of the jumper's centre of gravity is changed by an amount which is the sum of the approach angle and the take-off angle: the approach angle is about 1–2 degrees, 16–18 degrees and 14–17 degrees in the hop, step and jump respectively, while the take-off angle is about 15–18, 15–17 and 18–20 degrees in the hop, step and jump respectively. The resultant sum of

the above two are about 16–20, 31–35 and 32–37 degrees in the hop, step and jump respectively. That means the last two take-off movements (step and jump) especially require vigorous impulses (force × time) through the take-off leg, about double that of the average vertical force in the first take-off (hop). Thus the movement in the first take-off is closer to the take-off in a flat-flight long jump. The other two take-off movements are similar to a depth or drop jump up and forward (Fig 2).

Actual take-off movements appear slightly before the moment of touchdown while still in the air. There is a stretching forward of the take-off leg, a pullback of the swing leg and arms, then a striking or clawing action of the straight take-off leg, and a pulling of the swing leg and arms forward simultaneously. Previously stretched muscles are activated to produce more strength and power and to provide firm supportive body alignment (active foot placement) with the least amount of horizontal speed loss and unpleasant impact at touchdown. This clawing action should be continued throughout the take-off into the air with a powerful drive and lift of the swing leg and arms. During the first half of the take-off phase the clawing take-off leg is forcibly slightly bent by the momentum of the body, even though the athlete should consciously try to keep the take-off knee straight. During this phase the body's rotatory hinged action generates most of the vertical momentum to lift the body's centre of gravity. This take-off leg thrust works to generate ballistic leg extension during the latter half of the take-off phase.

The jumper should develop his technique with various drills and exercises emphasizing the following points:

1 During the final stage of the run-up, maintain the maximum run-up and leg speed as this is the action which drives the jumper into the first take-off and enables him to get a flat and well-controlled jump with good balance and relaxation.

2 Each of the three take-off movements requires 'active foot placement' into the touchdown in order to generate vertical momentum with the least loss of horizontal velocity. Active foot placement means:

  - Preparing to generate sufficient backward angular momentum of the take-off leg at touchdown.

  - Preparing an appropriate backward body-lean with straight body positioning, and not reaching too far forward with the take-off foot.

  - Preparing a powerful swing action of the lead (swing) leg with good timing just prior to the touchdown and the smooth passing through of the arms and the lead leg while rotating the body forward on the take-off foot during the contact period.

  - Executing a shallow and quick eccentric–concentric action of the knee extensors to effect a ballistic leg extension on the ground, while driving the body forward with the movements of the lead leg and the arms.

3 During the take-off the jumper should keep his trunk straight, and above, the take-off foot, not leaning his body axis laterally or sagittally. This makes it possible for a jumper to develop greater effective impulses on the ground with the least off-centre thrust to prevent generating useless rotatory movement.

4 The active foot placement and the straight body positioning make it possible to get a powerful ballistic explosive leg extension during the latter half of the take-off phase. A short take-off time and the least knee-bend with an active foot placement make it possible for the jumper to generate the greater explosive leg power with the least waste of energy.

5 The lead leg and arm actions have a significant indirect role in generating vertical momentum while maintaining horizontal velocity and absorbing the shock at the touchdown. They have less influence on the direct role of generating vertical momentum than the take-off leg, especially in jumps with full run-ups, but function more in a preparatory manner.

IMPORTANCE AND EFFICIENCY OF THE APPROACH RUN

Most experienced jumpers agree that, in a very practical sense, at least 90 per cent of the result of the jump will be determined by the approach running. In other words, mechanically speaking, it is most important for the jumper to move his body through the approach run to enable him to get into the correct position with maximum velocity at take-off. If the approach is correct the jumper is able to get a perfect take-off movement leading to a good performance. The jumping events have common fundamental mechanical characteristics: ie, that the direction of the horizontal momentum must be shifted to upward and forward; and that the jumping (take-off) motion must be a modified extension of the sprinting motion. Every element of each motion should join together in a coordinated organic continuity that is the successful jump.

The athlete's aim in the approach run is to reach the maximum possible horizontal velocity with well-controlled body positioning which leads to an efficient take-off movement at the right spot on the board. The basic requirements to improve the approach run are the same as those required in efficient sprinting during acceleration and coasting. These are as follows:

a) A relaxed high stride frequency related to maximum drive.

b) Appropriate stride-lengthening with least waste of energy or effort: maximum effort does not necessarily lead to the highest speed. On the other hand, less effort may lengthen the stride and lower the frequency resulting in an inefficient build-up.

c) Think 'centre'! Focus attention on the centre of the body. Concentrate the energy in the lower abdomen for perfection of movement, that provides a good relaxation and balance during the movement.

d) Maintain efficient leg movement; fold the recovery leg up, heel to buttock, pick up the knee and contact the ground high on the ball of the foot, especially when running at coasting speed.

The technical aspects of the approach run are as follows (Fig 3):

1 Find the most comfortable combination of stride frequency and length, especially during the first 6–7 steps, to allow maximum controlled

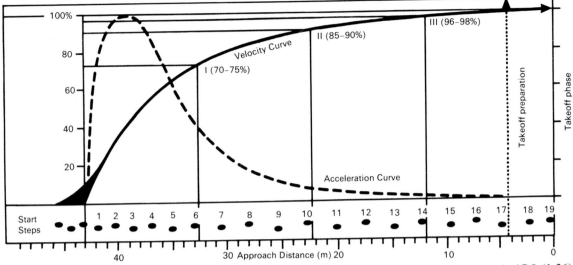

Fig 3 Schematic model of approach running; changes of running velocity; and acceleration (% to max) according to approach distance, and the number of steps. The second mark should be placed at the sixth or seventh step from the start to lead and stabilize a smooth and well-controlled build-up rhythm. Standard distances from the start to the sixth step are approximately 10–11m for men

speed with the least waste of energy. The first 6–7 steps can easily vary due to mental pressure, varying effort, wind, etc and lead to an erratic approach to the take-off. A balanced stride and controlled speed are vital.

2 Once again, over-intensity may not give the best result, neither will too little effort. Find the best suited build-up rhythm in the first 6–7 steps and take good note of it. A suitable distance for the first 6 steps is about 10–11m.

3 Accelerate smoothly up to the two steps before take-off and then just try 'coasting'. The pre-paratory movement into the take-off during the last two strides, with a relatively longer penultimate and shorter last step, should not be overemphasized as in the long jump.

CHARACTERISTICS OF CONTEMPORARY WORLD-CLASS TRIPLE JUMPERS

Research with top-class jumpers provides some valuable information on finding and developing jumping talent. The following are the averages and standard deviations of parameters (bracketed) relating to the development and characteristics of world-class jumpers (n = 25, x = 16.98m, SD = 0.23):

1 Age to start specific training (years): 17.8 (1.36)
2 Age to reach a high performance level (years): 21.8
3 Age to reach a personal life-best performance (years): 25.7 (1.94)
4 Body height (cm): 182.4 (6.62)
5 Bodyweight (kg): 76.9 (6.99)
6 100m sprint personal best (sec): 10.65 (0.18)
7 Long jump personal best (m): 7.78 (0.26)

Table 1 shows various parameters and standards of physical requirement for the development of triple jumpers from the experience of the USSR. Statistics show averages (and standard deviations) of distances and jump ratios in each part of the hop, step and jump of contemporary world-class jumpers as follows (n = 11, x = 17.25m):

	HOP	STEP	JUMP
Distance:	6.28m (0.22) +	5.04m (0.24) +	5.89m (0.26)
Ratio:	36.5% (1.26) +	29.3% (1.35) +	34.3% (0.93)

TECHNIQUE AND STYLE

High-performance jumpers do not always show good technique, but all of them show some unique attributes such as historical background of motor learning processes, the developmental stages, physique, body proportion, physical resources (muscular strength, power, flexibility, etc) and so on. However, at the same time most of the high-performance jumpers do show excellent mastery of technique. In observing their movements we must differentiate the basic correct movement pattern

Table 1. Control Tests for the Triple Jumper

TEST EVENTS		Standard marks							
		12.50	13.50	14.50	15.50	16.00	16.50	17.00	17.50
1) 50m dash (sec)		6.6	6.4	6.2	6.0	5.8	5.7	5.6	5.5
2) Long jump (m)		6.00	6.30	6.80	7.00	7.20	7.50	7.70	8.00
3) 150m dash (sec)		19.0	18.3	17.8	17.0	16.5	16.2	15.9	15.7
4) Long jump from 10-step approach (both feet)	-TOF-	5.40	5.50	6.30	6.50	6.70	7.00	7.15	7.50
	-OPF-	5.10	5.20	5.85	6.20	6.30	6.50	6.65	7.00
5) Triple jump from 10-step approach run (m)		12.50	13.20	14.00	14.80	15.20	15.60	16.20	16.60
6) 5-hopping from 7-step approach (both feet)	-TOF-	18.00	19.00	20.50	22.00	22.50	23.00	24.00	24.50
	-OPF-	17.50	18.00	20.30	21.30	21.80	22.50	23.50	23.50
7) Depth triple jump from 50-90cm high with 2-step app.		9.00	9.50	10.00	10.50	11.00	11.30	11.70	12.00
8) 5-full squatting with 60kg (time = sec)		9.5	8.0	7.0	6.0	5.5	5.0	4.8	4.5
9) Maximum barbell clean (kg)		–	75	86	95	105	117.5	125	130
10) Double-handed shot put with 7.257kg (m)	-Back-	9.50	11.50	13.00	14.50	15.50	16.00	17.00	17.50
	-Forw-	9.00	11.00	12.50	13.50	14.50	15.00	15.50	16.00

Abbreviations: TOF—to jump with a take-off foot; OPF—to jump with the opposite foot; Forw—to throw a shot forward in front of the body; and Back—to throw it backward over the head

from the individual style of jumping and running. Therefore, the technique should obey the bio-mechanical rules or principles characteristic of the triple jump itself, while still taking account of individual differences.

There are at least four different types of combinations of arm actions with the two basic styles of 'double' and 'single (or running)' arm actions in hop–step–jump: double–double–double; single–double–double; single–single–double; and single–single–single.

The first three styles are now most commonly employed. The kinematogram (Fig 4) shows a typical example of the second type (R. Liverse, USA). However, most attention in jumping should be focused on the essential leg actions and body alignments for each of the take-off phases. Arm action is also important, but mostly in terms of indirect roles such as: shock absorbing; preserving

horizontal velocity; keeping balance; and helping to generate vertical momentum, etc.

The photo-sequence of Ken Lorraway, AUS, (Fig 5) shows an example of the double-arm action in jumping. He shows good active foot placement with powerful clawing leg actions during each take-off (frames 3–7, 10–16 and 20–26). However, in this trial he seemed to have inefficient body alignment, especially during the third take-off (22–25). This unbalanced body alignment was probably produced from the beginning of the hop (frame 9; over-tense airborne posture) and then magnified through the step.

The photo-sequence of Willie Banks, USA, (Fig 6) also shows an example of the double-arm action in jumping. His use of full range of motion is excellent. However, his excellence in the jumping action is often disturbed and the efficiency reduced because of his mistiming of the take-off move-

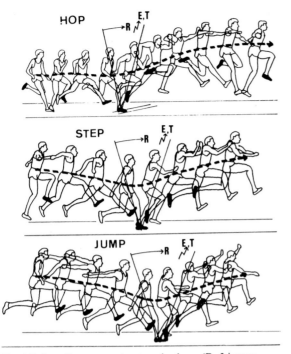

HOP

STEP

JUMP

Fig 4 Take-off movements at each phase (R. Liverse, USA) with a running (single-) arm action in the hop and a double-arm action both in the step and jump, generating the vertical momentum by R: Rotatory, body's hinged movement   E: Explosive leg extension   T: Transference of free body segmental momenta of arms and swing leg

ment, which starts in the air slightly before the touchdown. That may be due to his overstriding approach run (frames 1–3). This overstriding is often shown on his last 3–4 steps into the take-off and reduces his run-up velocity. During the jump his take-off foot is often placed too far forward on the ground from the vertical position of his body's centre of gravity (11–12 and 20–21).

In his other successful jumps, at least those over 17.50m, the inefficient movements have never shown so clearly as seen in this trial. Even if a jumper uses a double-arm action during the first take-off (hop), he should not overemphasize the arm action as this reduces speed and tempo.

The photo-sequence of the world record holder J de Oliveira, Brazil, (Fig 7) also shows a typical example of the second type, single–double–double arm action. His world record jump of 17.89m set in 1975 had a jump ratio of 34.1–30.2–35.7 per cent in hop, step and jump respectively. He also excelled both in sprinting (10.4sec in 100m) and long jumping (8.35m), with a body height of 186cm and weight of 75kg.

His outstanding success in triple jumping re-

sulted from his fluency of movement as well as his ability to preserve horizontal velocity from the first flight to the second (frames 2–11), which allowed him to maximize his jump (12–23). However, it can be said that had he improved the effectiveness of the active foot placement for the second take-off (5–9) he would have improved his total performance. Similar improvement would have resulted from a lengthening of the hop.

It was very unfortunate that he could not maximize his potential because a serious car accident ended his competitive career. He was the most likely person to be first over the 18m barrier.

TRAINING

The higher the level of athletic performance, the more the training should be specific to the task, and the higher the intensity of exercise load required. There is no substitute for actual competitive jumps or jumps with fast run-ups in training for higher technical mastery and specific muscular strengthening for top-level jumpers. In the specific jump exercises employed in practice, such as pop-ups or jumps from short run-ups, there are many differences in timing, speed and coordination among the body segmental movements from the actual competitive jump movements.

As a matter of fact, these jumping exercises generate greater body segmental momenta by the transfer of momentum from the legs and arms to the whole body than would be possible from jumps with full run-ups. Jumping exercises in practice can usually be performed perfectly while maintaining relaxed motions, good body positioning, balance, timing and a full range of movement. We must, therefore, find a way to enable the jumper to execute such effective powerful movements of the lead leg and the arms in actual competitive jumps with a full run-up.

It is desirable that the jumper realises these advantages in the high-speed competitive jumps, even though there is a deep gap between the movement in practice and in the competition. The best methods to close this gap are as follows:

Fig 5 (*Overleaf*) Ken Lorraway (Australia) jumping 17.46m for a new British Allcomers record
Fig 6 Willie Banks (USA) jumping 16.66m in the 1979 World Cup. Banks was 2nd in the 1983 world championships
Fig 7 Joao de Oliveira (Brazil), world record holder in the triple jump

Fig 5

1

2

5

6

9

10

13

14

Fig 5

17

18

21

22

25

26

29

30

19

20

23

24

27

28

31

32

Fig 6

1

2

7

8

9

13

14

15

4

5

6

10

11

12

16

17

18

Fig 6

19

20

21

25

26

27

31

32

33

22

23

24

28

29

30

34

35

36

Fig 7

a) Understanding the characteristics of the specific movement structure and the principles of the technique for selecting the specific training exercises.

b) Executing those exercises with an effective training method, such as an 'analytic/constructing method', and applying high intensive loads varying from 90 degrees to super maximums.

c) Rationalizing the training process throughout a year, including a competition calendar and a long-term training programme for individual athletic development.

The following are examples of basic and specific workouts, methods (–) and some suggestions (=) on training to develop a jumper's specific strength and power and to improve technical mastery of the triple jump.

Bounding
– Successive jumps with alternate legs, on stairs, hills, benches etc.
= Lift the thigh high and rotate the arms. Vary from 10 to 15 jumps consecutively or about 30m on a flat surface.

Hopping
– Same as in the bounding work, but hopping on one leg.
= Continue about 30m on flat, or 10 to 15 times, avoiding a strong braking action with the take-off foot but stretching forward as far as possible.

Clawing Action Drills
– Lift up the thigh and swing the lead leg to kick forward strongly, striking the ground and clawing to drive through the body.
= Key point of the clawing exercise is on the active foot placement and the acceleration at the final stage of the kick. The direction of the kick is not upward but forward.

Development of a Sense of Kicking for the Take-off
– Depth jumping from a box 40–60cm high. Take off with either leg from the box, then take off with the same leg on the ground (step), and take off again with the other leg (jump). Landing in a sandpit.
– Long jumps with the opposite (jump) foot from 6–10 steps run-up into the pit.

= Concentrate mainly on the timing of the take-off to integrate all the body actions: active foot placement, free leg/arms swing, and body alignment, etc. Use 90cm-high box for advanced level.

Development of Jump Power
– Use same exercises of bounding and hopping over 30m within 10 steps.
= Start from 6–7 steps approach runs, repeat and use the imitation clawing action drills in between these exercises.

Combination Exercise for the Triple Jump
– Repeat the combinations such as 'hop + step', 'step + jump' and 'step + hop' from 6–7 and 10–11 steps approach.
= Land in the pit with both feet during the 'step + jump' work. But run through after the last take-off during the other exercises.

Learning Basic Movements of the Triple Jump and Strengthening the Hopping and Stepping Phases
– Three hops (firstly use only with the take-off leg, then use the opposite leg) from 6–7 and 10–11 steps approach run.
– Alternative leg triple bounds from the same number of steps of approach.
= To get a perfect clawing action at the take-off use a springy leg action with active foot placement. Do not hurry the kick.

Learning the Whole Successive Movements of the Triple Jump from the Short- and Medium-length Approach Run
– Triple jump from 6–7 and 10–11 steps approach run. Try to make a flat and long path in the jump.
= Better to do this on grass or a similar soft surface.

Learning the Triple Jump Rhythm
– Triple jump with check marks from 6–7 and 10–11 steps of approach run.
= Place the check marks at the most efficient jump ratios: 36.5% + 29.3% + 34.2%.

Running Hop Work
– Successive take-off drills followed by 2–4 hops, over a distance of 50–100m; in advanced-level jumpers, include the second take-off (step), ie 'running hop-step drill'.
= Try to maintain speed or try to build up the

speed gradually while keeping good balance and full range of motion.

Approach Running
- Practise the first half (at threequarters maximum speed).
- Practise the last five steps into the board (about 11–13m) from an easy and springy extra run-in.
- Jump over 5 medicine balls placed at 140–150cm intervals from a 15–20m approach.
- Build-ups with ascending rhythm and number of steps (20–24).
- Complete approach running.
= Decide the approach distance depending on the stage of development. It should be enough for beginners to take 12–14 steps for the approach, but top-level jumpers should take 19–22 steps.

Completion of the 'Hop' and the Connection with the Approach Run
- Take off with a fast and flat lead-leg action from a 6-1 stride approach. Hop work from 6 steps approach, then extend up to 12–14 steps.
= Attempt to carry out the clawing action of the swing leg with good timing at the initial stage of the hop. Landing into the pit with one leg. Employ the exercise before the last one.

Learning the Triple Jump at High Speed
- Triple jump from 6–8, 10–11 and 14–15 steps approach, then from a full approach distance. The 14–15 steps approach jump fills the gap between the short and long approach jumps.
= Desirable to practise on grass or similar springy surface.

Complete Triple Jump in a Competition
- Make full trials in a competition, trying to make a flat and long path of the jump from fast approach runs.
= Select different types of competitive loads and conditions, and simulate them in jump workouts and minor competitions as specific preparation for the most important competitions.

11 SHOT
Peter Tschiene

Federal Republic of Germany
(Acknowledgements to the Deutscher Leichtathletik Verband)

Peter Tschiene was born in 1935. He studied in the German Democratic Republic and now lectures on the Theory of Training at the University of Darmstadt.

Peter has coached the throwing events for over 15 years and is the Federal coach for hammer in West Germany. He is very much involved in the literature of track and field athletics: he is a member of the instruction and documentation staff of the German Track and Field Association, he is a member of the Centro Studi and Ricerche, FIDAL, and he edits the review *Leistungssport* of Frankfurt. In addition to all that, he has found time to write books on the preparation of young athletes.

Peter is a valuable member of the IAAF Development Programme coaches panel and has lectured at coaching courses in many parts of the world.

Shot

There is no universal technique of shot putting. International practice shows us the different concepts of both the traditional linear putting and the rotational technique. However, the coach and his athlete have to observe certain common factors operating within these concepts.

REFERENCES TO PHOTO-SEQUENCES
Fig 2 (B-3) refers to the third frame of the Beyer sequence.
Fig 3 (S-8) refers to the eighth frame of the Slupianek sequence.
Fig 4 (O-12) refers to the twelfth frame of the Oldfield sequence.

THE MAIN PRINCIPLES OF MOVEMENTS IN SHOT PUTTING AND ITS TECHNICAL VARIANTS

We proceed from the fact that the flight distance of the shot depends on:

a) its height of release (ie the highest contact of the shot with the fingers above the ground).
b) its angle of release (ie the angle between the flight direction of the shot and the ground as it leaves the hand).
c) its release speed into the direction of throw.

The most important of these is the release speed (V_0). A tall body height of an athlete enables a high release point of the shot and consequently a smaller, more favourable angle of release (40 ± 1^0), whereas the release speed of the shot is the result of all the forces the athlete uses to accelerate the shot. The release speed depends upon the impulse ($F \times t$) resulting from the summation of forces from the extension of legs, trunk and arm and

from trunk rotation completed in the shortest time range possible. The impulse applies a certain amount of kinetic energy to the shot for its flight.

But since a long path of acceleration of the shot has great importance, the connection between the neuro-muscular factors (power) and the body physique within the technique is evident.

The athlete's explosive power will be produced and applied to the shot under the limiting conditions of his physical potential and the available space (diameter of the circle 2.135m).

The athlete is subject to the laws of biomechanics. In order to obtain a better understanding of the interpretation of world bests' techniques, shown in this book, we will deal with the main biomechanical principles.

THE PATH OF THE SHOT IN THE ATHLETE'S HAND RESULTING FROM THE STARTING STANCE

It is not possible to move the shot through the optimum angle (ie angle of the final phase) right

Fig 1 The path of the shot. I start of shift or turn II final throwing action (a) Slupianek (b) Beyer (c) Baryshnikov (d) optimum path

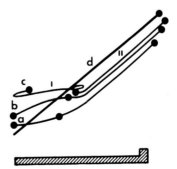

Fig 2 Udo Beyer (GDR) winning the 1976 Olympics shot

from the starting stance. However the athlete has to keep its deviation of direction (ie change of angle) as small as possible.

What are the possibilities for this? (See Fig 1.) In the traditional linear technique of shot putting athletes employ two forms of the start, causing different effects upon the path and the acceleration of the implement.

First Form of Start
Beginning in a slightly bent position with the following angles (righthanders): right knee 100–110°;

200

right hip 85–120° (B-2, 3 and 4), the athlete pushes himself (in a backward facing position) towards the centre of the circle using his right ball-of-foot or heel (B-5).

Thus the path of the shot describes a slight curve. For this reason in the following body shift the shot velocity has a different direction from that in the final throwing position (B-7). The result is a certain loss of shot velocity at the end of the shift. The push by the ball of the foot gives a

Fig 3 (*Overleaf*) Ilona Slupianek (GDR), 1980 Olympic champion
Fig 4 Brian Oldfield (USA) using the rotational shot technique

Fig 3

4

5

6

10

11

12

16

17

18

Fig 4

4

5

6

10

11

12

16

17

18

Fig 4

19

20

21

25

26

27

31

32

33

22

23

24

28

29

30

34

35

36

higher curve and more loss of speed. An advantage of this 'high start' has to be seen in an unforced and easy muscular activity of the right leg at the beginning of the shift and at the beginning of the final position (B-8). E Sarul (Poland), World Champion 1983, uses a similar technique.

Second Form of Start

Beginning in a very low and deeply bent position with the following angles: right knee 75–80°; right hip 80–70° (S-1, 2, 3 and 4), the athlete usually breaks right-foot contact with the ground from the right heel (S-5). At the beginning of the shift the chest almost touches the right thigh (S-1). Finishing the shift, the right foot still lands in the rear half of the circle (S-7 and 8).

This difficult form of start depends on a very powerful right leg, but aims at two essential advantages: the shortening of the shot path in the shift in favour of the extension of the final shot path, and less deviation between shot (velocity) direction in the shift and in the final delivery (by lifting the trunk). (See Fig 3 – Slupianek.)

The choice of the technique especially affects the right-leg work at the beginning of the throwing phase (S-9), and this has important implications for the training of the athlete.

A common factor of all linear start techniques is the work of the left leg and the position of the free (left) arm during the start and shift: the left foot has to be pushed forward - down to the stop-board (B-5, 6, 7 and S-5, 6, 7), the leg muscles remaining tense for the delivery. The action of the left side provides an additional momentum to the system 'athlete and shot', assisting its movement towards the centre of the circle. The thrower keeps his tensed free arm across the chest or parallel to the right lower leg (S-1 to 6), supporting in this manner the right-angled position of the shoulder axis in relation to the direction of throw.

Third Form of Start

This is characteristic of the rotational technique, where we actually can distinguish two variants: with a fairly high trunk position, like Baryshnikov (Fig 1 and Fig 8c); and with a lower trunk position and deeper bend of the knees, like Oldfield (O-1 to 12).

A start with deeply bent knees meets a) the demand of a rotation plane providing an angle near to the optimum in the final throwing phase and b) the demand for a long effective acceleration path

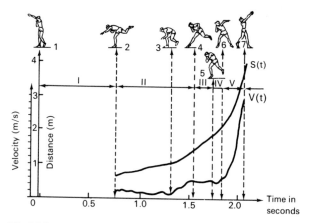

Fig 5 Movement s(t) and velocity v(t) of the shot (Susanka, 1974). I preparation II start III shift IV landing or intermediate phase V final or delivery phase

for the shot. However, there are problems concerning the rotational speed and the leg and trunk extension. They are slow and they cause a loss of velocity after the spin. A start with an upright position causes the well-known differences in the velocity directions of the shot, but facilitates a faster turn right from the start. Oldfield prefers the first variant (O-1 to 12).

Though the speed of the shot in the rotational start is slower than in the linear technique, the swing of the right leg (kicking with the lower leg) provides the rotational momentum of the system, athlete and shot (O-9 to 15).

In any case the nature of the path of the shot in the athlete's hand, ie his technique of shifting and turning, has to be seen in conjunction with his level of explosive leg power and its development and exploitation at the beginning of the final throwing phase.

THE SEPARATE PHASES IN SHOT ACCELERATION AND THEIR RELATION TO LEG ACTION

Initial Acceleration

The start and shift or start and turn form the 'phase of initial acceleration' (ref. to Tutjowič 1969), of the system athlete and shot. The shot speed obtained in this phase is 2.0–2.5m/s; the difficult point in each variant of shot put technique is the transition to the 'phase of final acceleration' (Tutjowič) first of the system, athlete and shot, and then of the implement only at the end. After land-

208

ing with the right foot the main acceleration of the system, athlete and shot, and the change of shot direction (ie increase of angle) begin (see Fig 5). However, in the short time between right and left foot landing (ca. 0.09–0.1sec) at the final throwing position no further acceleration can be gained; the shot maintains a steady velocity (B-7 and 8; S-7 to 9; O-20 to 25). This is a characteristic of top-level throwers; a decrease of shot velocity denotes a poor level of skill.

The phase of initial acceleration develops about 15 per cent, but the phase of final acceleration contributes more than 85 per cent of the release speed (V_0) of the shot (in a similar range for both men and women - ref. to Tutjowič, 1969). So we can state the principle:

The phase of initial acceleration is second in order of importance, although necessary for the increase of acceleration in the final phase.

In the rotational technique the contribution of the initial acceleration (ie turn) is smaller.

The right leg and hip muscles have to be regarded as the engine of acceleration, though they are heavily loaded: after the shift they have to catch up with the system, athlete and shot, during which time they resist vertical forces of 3–4 times bodyweight. But immediately after this they have to accelerate the whole system, athlete and shot, (ie the extension and turn of right leg and hip)

Fig 6 Dynamograms of the vertical (R_y) and horizontal (R_x) forces of the right leg upon the ground during the final acceleration phase (Lanka and Shalmanov, 1982)

KEY
____ advanced putter (19.60m)
- - - - beginner (12.74m)

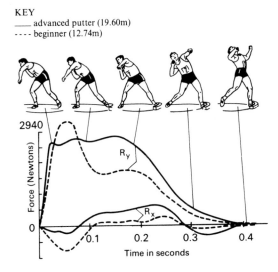

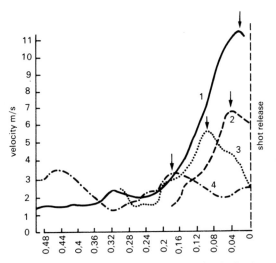

Fig 7 The velocity of the key body parts in the final acceleration phase. 1 right hand 2 right shoulder 3 right hip 4 right knee (arrows mark the maximum in each joint)

into the direction of throw (B-10 to 13; S-10 to 13; O-28 to 30).

The neuromuscular disadvantage of the leg drive is highly overcompensated by a sudden stretching of the already tensed leg and hip extensors (pre-tension). When the left foot touches the ground, a pre-tension of the back muscles takes place too, as the trunk turn is transferred to the chest. Next principle, deriving from the above:

The phase of initial acceleration has to provide the conditions for a sudden stretching (pre-tension) of muscle extensors at the beginning of the final acceleration.

The result will be an enormous increase of the neuromuscular working effect (compare the differences in performance of standing and shifting throws!).

A condition of using the pre-tension effect after the phase of initial acceleration is that the putter must land upon his right ball-of-foot (B-7; S-7; O-22 to 24)! Otherwise a sufficient pre-tensioning of the leg extensors and a quick leg and pelvis turn cannot be obtained.

Fig 6 demonstrates the importance of effective work with the right leg in shot putting.

Final Acceleration

There is a further increase of the vertical force in the phase of final acceleration, about 70 per cent more than the athlete's bodyweight (at the

beginning of knee extension). The horizontal force of the right leg has two peaks too, always coming soon after the vertical peaks and being caused by the right foot and knee turning into the direction of throw, thus affecting the right hip. A large positive horizontal force component is a characteristic of top-level putters.

During the phase of final acceleration the left leg 'blocks' against the kinetic energy of the system, athlete and shot, in order to ensure the lift of the centre of mass and the shot, ie the vertical force component, which is developed in a very short time, is emphasized (B-9 to 11; S-11 to 13; O-26 to 29) as demonstrated by E Sarul. However, some athletes break foot contact by an active push-up (B-13; O-30).

The effect of the right leg in the phase of final acceleration depends on its coordination with the hip, trunk and arm movements, to summate their partial forces, as shown by the velocities of the right hand, shoulder, hip and knee in Fig 7. Principle:

> The work of the right leg pushes the body upwards and turns the right hip forward into the direction of throw, whereas the use of the trunk and of the free arm depends on the individual method of shot putting.

First 'Method'
By accentuating the right-leg extension, the trunk will be actively thrown with its left side into the direction of throw, followed by the shoulder and arm push (B-8 to 11).

If at the beginning of the throwing stance the right hip is 'open', the system, athlete and shot, requires far more horizontal speed, thus causing a late vertical impulse and a shortening of the shot path. The external sign is a left knee bending before blocking for right-arm action (in the past demonstrated by A Feuerbach).

Second 'Method'
This involves accentuating the trunk rotation with the participation of a long free-arm action swinging forward and sideways. This variation of technique is mostly executed with double support of the feet (demonstrated in the past by Randy Matson).

Third 'Method'
Proceeding from a wide span between right and left foot placement (S-10 to 14), the right hip can be accelerated through the optimum angle. However, after having extended the right leg breaks ground contact, which enables the body to move forward over the left leg and provides a long path for shot acceleration (S-14 and 15). But a very high level of explosive muscular ability is necessary. The trunk rotation can be used too. A characteristic of this variant is the left foot support in delivery (S-15).

Fourth 'Method'
Continuing the trunk rotation after the turn and using the free arm as means of movement control, momentum is maintained (O-24 to 29). General principle:

> In each variant of technique the succession of body segment movements have to be observed: from the lower to the upper; ie after having finished its muscular activity the lower limb must be fixed by muscular tension, to permit impulse transfer to the next higher body segment.

The free arm regulates 4 technical elements:

(i) By swinging upward–left–down, a low shot position at the neck is held as long as possible (B-8 to 10; S-9 to 11).
(ii) It controls the pre-tension of the chest muscles (B-10 and 11; S-11 and 12; O-28 and 29).
(iii) It aids the fixing of the left side of the body (B-12 and 13; S-13 and 14; O-30 and 31).
(iv) It helps to time the delayed strike with putting shoulder and arm.

The reverse depends on the explosive left-leg blocking. Breaking foot contact must not be a result of real jumping (B-14 and O-31). A conscious effort to reverse should not be necessary.

Fig 8 gives a final survey of the shot putting variants for instant comparison.

References
1 V. Tutjowič, *Teorija sportivnych metanijach* (*Theory of throws*), F.i.S. Moscow 1969.
2 J.A. Lanka, A. Shalmanov, *Biomechanika tolkanija jadra* (*Biomechanics of shot putting*), Moscow 1982.

12 DISCUS

Dr Gudrun Lenz and Dr Paul Ward

Dr Gudrun Lenz

German Democratic Republic

(Acknowledgements to the Deutscher Verband für Leichtathletik der DDR)

Translation by Jim Alford

Dr Lenz, who was born in 1956 in Chemnitz, was herself an active thrower specialising in the discus. She is now a senior lecturer in charge of the throwing events in the Department of the Science of Track and Field Athletics at the Deutscher Hochschule für Körperkultur (German Democratic Republic Academy of Sport and Physical Education). Her main responsibility is the study of problems of technique and technical development in the throwing events.

Dr Lenz is a member of the Commission for further development of training principles for the throws.

Discus

SUMMARY

From the technical point of view performance in the discus throw is determined by:

a) A long preliminary swing, which produces the first twist between hips, shoulders and throwing arm and creates the conditions for a long path of acceleration.

b) An effective starting position to introduce the turn, which results in the initial acceleration of the thrower and implement system and provides a powerful preparation for the turn phase.

c) A flat turn covering the ground in the shortest possible time, in the course of which a pre-stretched position of the body is established.

d) An effective transition phase with the minimum delay between the landing of the right and left legs.

e) An explosive throwing action, imparting maximum possible velocity to the implement.

CHAIN OF MOVEMENT

(Numbers prefixed 'L' refer to sequence of Armin Lemme, Fig 2.)

Starting Position

The thrower stands upright, or with the knees slightly bent, at the back of the circle with his back towards the direction of throw, and with his feet slightly more than shoulder-width apart.

The implement is held so that the last joints of the fingers of the throwing hand grip the under surface of the rim. It must facilitate a good transfer of momentum to the implement. The thumb is spread apart a little and lies along the upper sur-

Fig 1 Holding the discus

face of the discus in order to stabilise it. (See Fig 1.)

The upper edge of the discus lies lightly against the lower arm, so that the back of the hand faces outward. Thus the wrist should not be too bent. The handhold should be a relaxed one, it should create no overtension of the hand and arm muscles and must facilitate a free arm swing with a wide range of movement.

Preliminary Swing

The preliminary swing brings the implement into a starting position which facilitates a long path of acceleration. The preliminary movements should be simple and purposeful. After a relaxed swing to and fro of the throwing arm on the right side of the body or one or two swings to the left, the throwing arm is swept well back at shoulder height. This is accompanied by a shift of the body-weight onto the slightly bent right leg, the head and the right hip meanwhile being turned only

Fig 2 (*Overleaf*) Armin Lemme (GDR) shown from side and rear views. He has a best throw of 68.50m

Fig 2

slightly to the right. A powerful stiffening of the right hip ensures a strong twist between the axes of shoulder and hips. Meanwhile, to maintain continuity in the preliminary movement the left heel is raised and the foot turned in the direction of the movement (L-1).

The Turn

The turn begins with the 'two-legged' phase in which the dynamic work of both legs starts the preliminary acceleration of the system, thrower and implement. With a quota of about 35 per cent, of the total time of the throwing movement, this phase should be the longest one in time. The turn begins with a lowering of the centre of gravity by bending both legs. With this there is also a turning of the feet to the left. Of special importance for this is the active turning of the left foot (on the ball of the foot) with a definite loading of the bodyweight on the bent left leg. Meanwhile the implement is held well back and should deviate only very slightly from the horizontal.

A delayed action of the trunk and a great deal of twist results when, at the end of the two-legged starting phase, the left shoulder is positioned behind the left knee (L-14). A slightly delayed lifting of the right foot which leads into the beginning of the 'one-legged' phase, and to the 'bandy-legged' position, facilitates the creation of stretch in the leg muscles and provides the conditions for the following powerful swing of the right leg.*

As the right leg leaves the ground the one-legged phase begins. It assists the extensive acceleration of the total system and also prepares for the following jump-turn. Consequently this phase, taking up about 30 per cent of the total time of the throwing action, is similarly a relatively long one.

In order to maintain a good amount of torsion the discus should still be visible behind the thrower's body when viewed from the side. The upper body meanwhile remains upright or inclined slightly forward. The bodyweight in this phase rests squarely on the well-bent (100–110°) left leg which, while avoiding any substantial opening of the angle at the knee, is turned further in the direction of the throw (L-3).

In order to create a large angular momentum – as a forerunner to the great acceleration of the lower body and with it the further build-up of

* The timing of the footwork is described in Paul Ward's section, p. 221.

torsion – the right leg is swung on a wide but flat arc around the left leg. Then the right knee leads the movement, until the left leg has been overtaken. Next the lower leg is brought forwards and downwards in an active 'grasping' movement, so that the foot is turned inwards towards the direction of the throw (L-4).

When the turn on the left foot has reached the point when the thrower's face is turned fully in the throwing direction the jump-turn phase is begun with a low drive from the left leg (not a complete leg extension). This movement phase provides a **build-up of torsion** between lower body, trunk and throwing arm as a basis for an explosive throwing action. Provision for this is provided by the lower body moving well ahead of the implement. The throwing arm should, therefore, during the turn, be held well back while the right leg, in conjunction with a turn-in of the foot, is brought dynamically **forward** to the ground.

The support and non-acceleration phase should be completed as quickly as possible (one should strive for a proportion of the total throwing action of not more than 10 per cent, ie under 0.15sec) by working for a high angular velocity. This is facilitated by bringing the left leg and the free arm quickly close in to the body, with a consequent decrease of the moment of inertia and increase of angular velocity (L-4 and 5).

The Transition Phase

The transition phase (L-5) begins with the plant of the strongly bent (about 100°) right leg. In this phase after the absorption of the negative acceleration force, a second positive acceleration force follows. For this purpose the right leg after the plant on the ball of the foot (foot pointing back about 110–120°), in immediately and actively turned further in the throwing direction. The throwing arm is consciously held back, so that the strong torsion between the lower body, as it 'hurries' ahead, and the trunk and throwing arm is maintained.

The prerequisite for this is that as the right leg is planted the left leg is about level with it or has already overtaken it (L-17).

The torsion is aided by the action of the left arm which is constantly held back against the direction of the throw – the 'opposite pole' to the action of the right leg as it turns and drives in the throwing direction.

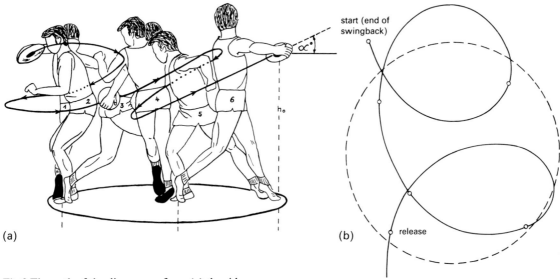

(a)

(b)

start (end of
swingback)

release

Fig 3 The path of the discus seen from (a) the side
(b) above

Path of the discus ———
Circle _ _ _

The duration of the transition phase should not exceed 10-12 per cent of the total time of the throwing action. The plant of the left leg (slightly bent and with the ankle fixed) should follow immediately (not more than 0.2sec) after that of the right leg, in order to ensure a quick transfer into the throwing phase.

The Throwing Phase
During the throwing phase the implement is accelerated to its ultimate speed through an angle of at least 270° (L-18 to 24). This demands that the shoulders are still directly above the right foot as the left foot comes to the ground. The throwing arm should still be clearly visible well behind the trunk and should be only very slightly below shoulder height.

The final speed of the implement results from an explosive rotation and extension around the fixed left side of the body. It begins with a dynamic turning-in of the still well bent right leg and is continued, together with a gradual extension of the right leg, in a definite successive action of trunk, shoulder and arm. The shoulder axis should meanwhile be kept as upright as possible. When the right knee (held at an optimal angle of about 130-140°) is pointing in the throwing direction and the pelvic axis is also at right angles to it, the throwing arm should still be pointing in the opposite direction, and just reaching the lowest point of the path of the implement (L-7 to 9; 19-20).

The inclination of the path of movement of the discus should now correspond to the desired direction of throw. The left leg now serves as a prop and the knee joint must therefore be braced. Its stretching forwards and upwards begins when the right knee points in the direction of the throw. The left arm, with a pulling movement, actively assists the unwinding of the upper body, and afterwards actively slows down the shoulder rotation, when the trunk and shoulder axis are parallel and at right-angles to the throwing direction (L-9 to 11).

Release of the implement should be at shoulder height and with full extension of the legs and without loss of contact with the ground, in order not to shorten the throwing radius (L-11).

The fast-moving body mass is checked by a quick change of leg and a strong bend of the support (right) leg and, thereby, a sinking of the centre of gravity.

CRITERIA FOR AN EFFICIENT DISCUS
TECHNIQUE
Ensure an optimum acceleration path (Fig 3) by:

a) A wide sweep of the implement in the direction of throw and the development of a strong torsion between hip and shoulder axis, as well as the throwing arm, which must be kept well up during the whole action right up to the final release.

Table 1   Structure of the Phases and Main Technical Points

		PRELIMINARY SWINGS	TURNS – START PHASE	
			Double Support	*Single Support*
	Beginning	– starting position	– turning-point of path of discus	– right foot leaves the ground
	End	– turning-point of path of discus	– right foot leaves the ground	– transfer weight to the left to start turn
	Function	– adoption of an optimal position for an extensive acceleration	– preliminary acceleration of the total system first with two-legged and then with one-leg support	
		– introduction of a strong 'twist' between hips, shoulder and arm	– powerful preparation for the turn (production of torque)	
Main Technical Points		– start position with an upright trunk and back to the direction of the throw	– lowering of the cg of body at the beginning of the turn, both legs well bent	
		– wide swing of the implement at shoulder height up to the line of both feet	– active turning into the direction of the throw of the left foot with the left leg bent at about 100° and bodyweight transferred to the left	
		– head and right hip only slightly turned to the rear	– a definite holding back of the shoulders (the left shoulder must not get ahead of the left knee). Looking at the throw from the right the discus must be visible behind the body	
		– great torsion between throwing arm, shoulder and hip axis	– slightly delayed lift of the right foot for the 'single-leg' start phase ('bandy legged' position) in order to operate stretch in the hip muscles	
			– a flat wide swing of the right leg in order to increase angular momentum	

b) An effort to attain an optimum radius of turn (distance between implement and the fulcrum of the left shoulder) through an extensive outward stretch of the throwing arm, especially during the phases of greatest acceleration (the beginning and release phases).

c) Favourable proportions of the course of acceleration during the individual phases of movement in relation to the possible effect upon the implement.

   (i) A long period of acceleration during the double-foot support phase (double-foot beginning phase and release phase).

(ii) Short path of the implement during the single-foot phase (transition phase) and also in the 'off-the-ground' phase.

d) ensure that the direction of movement is basically from left below to right above. Prerequisites for this are:

   (i) A strong bend of the legs in the starting phase (aim for 100–110°).

  (ii) A flat drive forwards for the 'jump' phase (aim for a flight angle of less than 40°).

  (iii) A well-bent right leg upon landing from the jump (angle at the knee of about 100°).

  (iv) A definite **rotation-extension** in the final

TURN PHASE	TRANSITION	RELEASE PHASE
– last push off left foot	– plant of right leg after turn	– plant of left leg (throwing position)
– plant of right leg after turn	– plant of left leg	– release of discus
– creation of torque for an effective throwing position	– dissipation of negative acceleration	– maximum final acceleration of the implement through a wide arc (270° optimum)
– achievement of a high rotational velocity by bringing the body segments as close as possible to the axis of rotation – in order to pass as quickly as possible through the phase of nil acceleration	– beginning of the second positive acceleration drive – longest possible maintenance of torque	
– drive off to the left when the thrower has turned his face in the direction of the throw	– plant of the right leg with a pronounced bend of the knee (about 100–110°) and with the foot turned in	– explosive turn and drive around a fixed left side with a definite sequence of leg, hips, trunk and arm and horizontal shoulders and pelvis
– quick drive off the ankle joint without straightening the knee		
– as the turn starts the throwing arm is at least at hip height and well behind the body	– instantaneous dynamic turning in of right leg	– extension of the right leg forward-upward
– a definite, dynamic downward plant of the right leg with the foot turned inwards – after take-off the free arm and the left leg are swiftly brought in as close as possible to the long axis of the body in order to decrease the amount of inertia and increase angular velocity	– conscious holding-back of throwing arm – the left arm points away from the direction of throw – plant of the left leg (locked knee joint) immediately after the landing of the right leg – the body's cg is above the bent right leg – the shoulder axis is definitely above the right leg	– checking action of the left leg until the right knee is pointing in the direction of throw, then extension upwards – pulling movement of the left arm assists the turn of the shoulders. The turning moment is checked when the hips and shoulder axis are parallel and at right angles to the direction of throw – the release is made at shoulder height with the shoulders level and without losing ground-contact from the legs

throwing phase.

e) Conformity of the turn-lift of the implement with the desired angle of release, especially during the second part of the turn (throwing movement).

f) Assurance of an optimal build-up of speed of action through:

  (i) Optimal relationship between the speed during the starting phase and the main phase of the movement, so that the effective use of the large muscle groups is ensured.

  (ii) Maintenance of a large radius of turn in the support phase in order to increase the angular velocity of the implement.

  (iii) A decrease of the moment of inertia of the body mass in the off-the-ground phase by bringing parts of the body in closer to the axis of rotation (long axis of the body) in order to increase angular velocity.

  (iv) Great acceleration during the throwing phase through an optimal transfer of momentum and coordination in the order leg, hip, shoulder, arm.

12 DISCUS
Dr Gudrun Lenz and Dr Paul Ward

Dr Paul Ward

USA
(Acknowledgements to the Athletics Congress of the USA)

Paul Ward, B.S., M.S., P.E.D., has coached and taught at five universities in the United States: California Western University, Portland State University, University of Wisconsin-Parkside, Indiana University and University of Kentucky. He has taught academic courses in physical education and his coaching responsibilities included American football, athletics, weightlifting and volleyball, in all of which sports he has competed successfully himself. He also played with the Detroit Lions in the National Football League.

A leading fitness expert, Dr Ward is recognised as one of the top biomechanics experts and coaches in the United States. Many of the weight-training machines and the weight equipment used in the United States today have been developed with his input and direction. Dr Ward is considered to be the father of circuit weight-training in the United States and has published scientific research documenting the physiological benefits of circuit weight-training and super-circuit weight-training.

Presently, Dr Ward works for the Health and Tennis Corporation of America, a company with the largest health club operation in the world (some 275 health clubs in 35 states). His position as Director of Education, Research and Development allows him to influence the educational and exercise programming of the membership.

Dr Ward is the Coordinator of the United States Olympic Committee Elite Athlete Project (Athletics-Throwers) and he works with the Athletics Congress of the USA Olympic Development Committees for men and women.

In the midst of all his many commitments, Dr Ward still finds the time to coach athletes himself - one of them is Lorna Griffin, the USA's best shot and discus thrower.

Discus

EVELYN JAHL (GDR) (Figs 4 and 5)

PRELIMINARY SWINGS AND STARTING POSITION (frames 1–3) Evelyn starts from an extensive backswing. The discus arm is not as high as other throwers but is well-torqued in a clockwise direction. The free arm (left) is extended and points opposite the discus. An important feature of the starting position is that the bodyweight is centred between the feet. This enables an easier movement into a heel–toe hammer turn of the left foot.

THE TRANSITION (frames 3–7) To start the turn, Evelyn unseats (displaces her centre of gravity toward the direction of the throw). This unseating is very dramatic (compare frame 1 with frame 6.) Very little weight is transferred to the left leg during this stage. Unlike other contemporary discus throwers, she uses a hammer-like heel–toe turn with the left foot. The left foot is turned approximately 180 degrees counter-clockwise before the right foot and leg are activated.

The left arm appears to be utilized to create some rotary momentum going into the turn. The right leg has been delayed in its action until the left foot is pointed in the direction of the throw. Although the body is supported by the left foot and leg, the centre of gravity is somewhat inside the left foot. This is a compensatory action for the subsequent rapid-moving right leg that will move in a wide arc until between 10 and 11 o'clock.

THE TURN (frames 7–11) The momentum for the turn is started by unseating in the direction of the throw coupled with a vigorous and fast movement of the right leg. The right leg moves at first in a wide arc to a position between 10 and 11 o'clock

at which it is forcefully pulled toward the middle of the circle. This action induces a great amount of torque between the hips and the upper-body/ discus unit. The discus is held away from the hip at all times in this style.

THE DRIVE FOOT LANDING (frames back 11–12, side 11–13) The exit from the back of the circle carries the thrower more than halfway across the circle. This is caused by the heel–toe turn of the left foot which naturally will displace the body further across the circle compared to a toe turn. The drive foot (right) lands at approximately 2 o'clock. The landing is on the ball of the foot which continues to move counter-clockwise as the bodyweight settles almost directly over the right foot. The discus is being held up and back of the rotating lower body. The left arm is rather passive until frames 12 (back) and 13 (side). The left arm position and action is not optimal but seems to be effective. The stretch on the anterior deltoids and chest muscles is less than optimal.

THE POWER POSITION (DELIVERY) (frames 13–14) Evelyn lands in a pre-torqued position with the discus well behind the hips and shoulders. The chest and anterior deltoids are put on stretch, but not optimally. The effective arm-pull on the discus is approximately 180 degrees. However, not enough frames are available to precisely define the arm-pull. The hip action of this thrower is around and up, although not much vertical displacement is noticed in this photo-sequence.

Fig 4 (*Overleaf*) Evelyn Jahl (GDR) in training for the 1981 World Cup (view from the rear of the circle)

Fig 4

1

2

5

6

9

10

13

14

At release the entire body has a backward leaning appearance which allows for a quite rigid and straight front leg with the entire foot remaining in contact with the ground. The back is hyperextended and rigid providing a solid base from which to whip the discus arm. The discus arm is extended and horizontal, maximizing the radius at release. The block of the left side seems to be very effective allowing for a good whipping action.

THE FINISH (frames 15–16) Evelyn's technique does not require a reverse. Apparently, most of the rotational and vertical forces have been transmitted to the discus or they have not been maximized in this technique; therefore, the thrower does not require a reverse to stabilize the body and prevent fouling. It is also possible that this thrower has been able to absorb the rotational forces effectively by twisting her body as shown in frame 16.

GENERAL OPINIONS Without making precise biomechanical measurements, it is difficult to make a valid judgment as to the efficiency of this technique. The heel-toe exit out of the back may be of value to some throwers who have a natural tendency to turn that way. My judgment is that when using the heel-toe technique there should be less unseating and a greater lowering of the centre of gravity in the exit out of the back.

Evelyn's left arm action at this power position could be optimized if the elbow would be extended vigorously in frames 11 to 13. In frames 13 and 14 the elbow should be flexed acutely and the left arm stopped to assist in the blocking of the left side.

LUIS DELIS (CUBA) (Fig 6)

PRELIMINARY SWINGS AND STARTING POSITION (frames 1–2) Luis has a backswing typical of most top-level throwers. The discus is held at shoulder level with the free arm diametrically opposite. The weight appears to be centred between both feet while the knees are bent to a semi-squat position.

THE TRANSITION (frames 3–7) The turning movement is initiated by swinging the free left arm horizontally backward followed by a lowering and shifting of the centre of gravity to the left rear. There is probably some unseating in the direction of the throw although it is difficult to determine

the extent from the photo-sequences. The left foot is turned approximately 90 degrees before the right foot is removed from the ground. The left arm appears to have transferred its momentum and is somewhat passive at this point (frames 6 and 7). The right leg is beginning to sweep around. The bodyweight seems to be more over the left leg and foot, although not completely; it appears to be slightly inside the left heel.

THE TURN (frames 7–16) As the thrower progresses through the turn, the left leg continues to bend so that there is significant lowering of the centre of gravity. The right leg has a moderately wide swing which contrasts to the wider Wilkins and Schmidt style. There is further displacement of the centre of gravity in the direction of the throw as the right leg races ahead of the shoulders and discus. Most of the separation between the hips and shoulders occurs at this time. There is significant upward movement of the centre of gravity as the thrower leaves the ground during the exit from the back. During the entire right-leg action the discus is held back and away from the right hip.

THE DRIVE-FOOT LANDING (frames 17–21) The drive from the back of the circle carries the thrower to the centre of the circle. The right foot lands on the ball with foot pointing at about 2 o'clock. There is immediate counter-clockwise movement of the right foot and leg. During this action there appears to be a compression of the legs into a semi-squat position. The left-arm action is rather passive until frame 20 when it begins to be swung vigorously backward putting the anterior deltoids and chest muscles on stretch. It is preferable that the left elbow be more extended at this point and then flexed and stopped in the blocking action. However, Luis may not be able to execute this action because the discus has already swept around counter-clockwise. This does not give time for the left arm to be extended and swung backwards in the delivery without interrupting the timing of the throw.

THE POWER POSITION (DELIVERY) (frames 22–25) When the front foot is grounded, the discus has already rotated counter-clockwise too much. The arm-pull is therefore shortened to about 135 degrees. It would seem more advantageous to have an arm-pull of between 180 and 225 if possible*. What appears to offset the short arm-pull is the long radius of the throwing arm coupled with a vigorous counter-clockwise hip rotation and a strong vertical force and block by the left leg.

Luis delivers the discus from a general backward lean of the trunk and body. Other top throwers exhibit this tendency, for example John Powell; while Wilkins, Schmidt and Plucknett have a vertical body orientation at release. Both feet remain in contact with the ground until the discus has been released indicating that the thrower has optimized applications of force. The strong left-side block seems to result in an effective whipping action of the discus arm.

THE REVERSE (frames 26–32) The rotary forces generated in the turn and power position have forced the thrower into a reverse to stabilize the body and prevent fouling. The arms and legs take up the angular momentum created in the throwing action. The thrower seems to effectively execute this phase of the throw.

GENERAL IMPRESSION The exit from the back is effective for Luis, although he could minimize the jumping up off the left leg. In my opinion, it would be more effective if he could ground the front leg earlier to give a longer arm-pull. The extension of the left arm at the elbow, properly timed with a horizontal backswing of the upper arm followed by a flexion of the elbow and strong blocking action of the whole left side in the power position and delivery phase, may be more effective. This may not be possible until the left foot is grounded early with the discus well back resulting in a long pull.

MARTINA OPITZ (GDR) (Fig 7)

PRELIMINARY SWINGS AND STARTING POSITION (frames 1–10) The preliminary swings basically set up the rhythm for the throw and place the athlete in an effective starting position. Martina starts with a shifting of her weight from left to right. During the backswing process there is an emphasis on squatting (frame 4). This procedure has no practical significance but reflects a stylistic variation that works well for this thrower. The discus arm is swept through a wide arc ending

*The problem with Delis is that his mobility is limited – F.D.

torqued in a clockwise (12 o'clock at back of circle) direction with the discus at shoulder height. The left (free) arm is straight and at shoulder height and directly opposite the discus. The bodyweight at the end of the backswing is predominantly on the right leg.

THE TRANSITION (frames 10–15) To start the turn Martina shifts her weight to the left side while squatting slightly. The movement of the upper body mass counter-clockwise assists the thrower in overcoming inertia at the start of the throw. Although it is difficult to perceive, there is a displacement of the bodyweight in the direction of throw (note frame 15). The left foot is turned approximately 115 degree counter-clockwise. The right leg has a delayed displacement from the ground until late in the weight transfer. This provides better control and balance in preparation for the exit from the back of the circle. Note that not all the body-weight is moved over the supporting left leg and foot. This is a compensation for the forthcoming rapid movement of the right leg in a wide arc to a position between 10 and 11 o'clock. The left arm is extended and held at shoulder height, but is relatively passive at this point.

THE TURN (frames 16–21) The momentum for the turn is started by the shifting of the weight from right to left and the slight displacement of the centre of gravity down and in the direction of the throw. The continued lowering and unseating displacement of the centre of gravity combined with the vigorous and fast movement of the right leg in an arc which is drastically shortened starting between 10 and 11 o'clock, coupled with a driving left leg, provides most of the motive force to the centre of the circle (frames 15–20). The left arm in this phase seems to be rather passive. The emphasis is on a stepping rotation to the middle of the circle.

The discus in the early part of this phase (frames 16–18) drops closer to the hip but quickly begins to move away from the hip as the turn progresses. The movement may appear to be predominantly

Fig 5 (*Overleaf*) Evelyn Jahl (GDR) in training (view from the side of the circle). Note the heel and toe turn
Fig 6 Luis Delis (Cuba) throwing 68m + in London, 1982
Fig 7 Martina Opitz (GDR) throwing 69.00m to gain 1st place in the 1983 European Cup

Fig 5

3

4

7

8

11

12

15

16

Fig 6

1

2

5

6

9

10

13

14

3

4

7

8

11

12

15

16

Fig 6

17

18

21

22

25

26

29

30

19

20

23

24

27

28

31

32

Fig 7

Fig 7

19

20

21

25

26

27

31

32

33

22

23

24

28

29

30

34

35

36

linear unless one views and appreciates the total action between frames 15 and 21. This larger view demonstrates dramatically the predominant rotational momentum.

THE DRIVE-FOOT LANDING (frames 21–26)   The exit from the back of the circle to the middle appears to carry the thrower halfway across the ring. There seems to be minimal elevation of the centre of gravity with the right foot coming down quickly at the centre. The drive foot (right) lands pointing at 3 o'clock. (Remember that the back of the circle is considered to be 12 o'clock.) The landing of the right foot is on the ball which continues to move counter-clockwise as the body mass settles almost directly over the right foot. Note that the discus is being held up and back of the rotating lower body. The left arm is rather passive until frame 24 when it begins to exert its influence in placing stretch on the anterior deltoids and chest muscles. This has an influence on keeping the discus back in a torqued position (frames 24–26). The discus arm is high and extended in the direction of the throw just before the left foot is grounded.

THE POWER POSITION (DELIVERY) (frames 27–32)   When the left (front) foot is grounded, it is the start of the power-producing movements. Martina has landed in a pre-torqued manner, ie the hips have moved ahead of the shoulders and discus. The chest and anterior deltoids have been put on stretch and subsequently will be put on maximum stretch resulting in maximum force production. The discus arm is well behind and will ultimately result in a pull of approximately 225 degrees. The most striking feature of this thrower's delivery is the vigorous around and upward action of the hips and the tremendous length of pull (whip) of the discus arm. This whip action is a reflection of the tremendous hip drive.

The discus path drops until 180 degrees opposite the landing area at which time it rises to maximize the radius at release being almost shoulder height (frames 31 and 32). The front-leg action is of extreme importance (frames 27–31). Its action is primarily responsible for stopping (blocking) the rotation of the hips, blocking the linear motions of the body, transferring these momenta to the upper body and ultimately to the discus. Additionally, the front leg, in this case the left leg, also is primarily responsible for the vertical lift of the centre of mass. The predominant amount of vertical force by the left leg is generated between frames 29 and 30. In 31 the upward force has been converted to rotary momentum which is applied to the discus. The left arm is synergistically stopped or blocked with the left side, transferring momentum to the discus. The release has been almost perfectly timed so that the front foot appears still in contact with the ground at release. Note that the trunk is vertical at release.

THE REVERSE (frames 32–36)   Martina has mastered the technique of maximizing torque and vertical lift so that the reverse is a consequence of the vertical and rotary forces that have been accumulated during the throw. This is demonstrated in frames 32–36. The feet have been switched and the upper body, arms and left leg have been extended and positioned so as to slow down the rotary motion and stabilize the thrower, which prevents fouling.

GENERAL IMPRESSION   Martina's technique represents a progressive step forward for European women's discus technique, primarily in the delivery and reverse stages. She has effectively summated all the forces at release so that she is forced to execute a reverse which has been typical of men throwers for a long time. The old technique of stopping, blocking and throwing minimizes or reduces the total forces at release that have been built up in the turn. The more progressive women throwers are adopting a more traditional and technically sound technique that produces a better utilization of the accumulated forces at release which usually produces, as a consequence, a reverse.

13 HAMMER

Jimmy Pedemonte

Italy
(Acknowledgements to the Federazione Italiana di Atletica Leggera)

Born in 1956 in Genoa, Jimmy Pedemonte began to be involved in sport as a shot putter, achieving Italian University Championship standard in 1978. With 8 years of coaching experience at the Genoa University Sports Centre, Jimmy Pedemonte was introduced to coaching hammer throwing by the former national coach, Professor Raffaello Palmarin, who he considers his master, and he acknowledges the help of Professor Renato Carnevali in enriching his coaching experience.

Pedemonte has almost completed his studies at the Higher Institute of Physical Education in Florence, while his many assignments with the Genoa University as throwers coach, include coaching at all levels from beginners to national level.

He has served as a consultant to a local roller-skating club which has developed two European champions, and as strength and conditioning coach for the University rugby team. He currently is the strength and conditioning coach for the 'Squali Genova' American football teams, and also serves as a consultant for the track and field departments of the Universities of Illinois and Purdue in the USA.

Pedemonte has written over 30 articles on the throwing events and on training methodologies, published since 1979 in magazines like *Track Technique, Modern Athlete and Coach, Athletics Weekly, Scholastic Coach, Nuova Atletica, Energia-Atal*, etc.

Hammer

During the last few years hammer throwing has experienced a radical transformation which has allowed an exceptional improvement in the level of performances. These changes, that may be found in the teaching methods, in the structure of training and in technical progress, have greatly modified the image of this event, changing it from a pure strength event (domain of the tall and very strong athletes) into an ability event where even athletes with an average frame have the possibility to emerge at international level.

At present coaches are looking for youngsters who have good coordination, optimal neuro-muscular capacities and an ability for great rotatory speed.

Bodyweight and strength, even if they are very important, are not enough to warrant the evolution of the young beginner towards international levels of performance.

RECENT METHODOLOGICAL AND TECHNICAL INNOVATIONS

The development of modern hammer-throwing technique has greatly influenced teaching methodology. Contrary to methods when one could presume that it was possible to reconstruct the motor stereotype year after year (eg building the athlete's technique with a standard implement, for 50m, then for 60m, then for 70m), at present we try early on to build with youngsters a dynamic stereotype which is very close to that needed to throw the 16lb (7.26kg) hammer to world record distances (eg building of the technique for 80m, with a 3kg hammer, then with a 4kg, 5kg, 6kg and 7kg). This is a consequence of the knowledge that once a technique has been stereotyped it's not pos-

sible to modify it significantly. Excellent practical results have been obtained through this system.

Owing to the obvious lack of strength in the growing phase, the young hammer thrower is not in a position to master the standard 16lb (7.26kg) implement with the necessary speed in order to throw it far. The standard hammer, whose weight is defined by IAAF specifications, does not allow the youngster to develop the specific speed, necessary for the dynamic structure of the movement, of top performances.

Therefore, the priority of modern youth training should be that of forming the dynamic structure (together with the mechanical structure) of the high-level performance, which is completely different to that which would be obtained through the use of unsuitable implements. This is only possible if light hammers are introduced at an early age. The evolution of the Soviet hammer thrower Igor Nikulin shown in Table 1 below, represents an actual model of this methodological innovation.[14]

The dynamic structure of world-class throwing is consolidated year after year, through the progress from a lighter hammer to an implement which is nearer and nearer to the standard one. Numerous elements have contributed to the technical progress of hammer throwing. Paradoxically nowadays the throwing fraternity rejects many aspects that only a few years ago were considered as being without question the basic elements of the throwing technique.

The fundamental trend of the modern throwing techniques lies in the increase of the radius of the path of the hammer in the turns. As everybody knows, the distance of flight of the projectile depends on the initial velocity (V_0), angle of release

Table 1
Distances Achieved by Igor Nikulin (USSR)

		Weight of the hammer				
Year	Age	3kg	4kg	5kg	6kg	7.26kg
1974	14	66.52	58.40	52.50	–	–
1975	15	75.20	67.60	58.00	54.36	49.92
1976	16	–	77.80	69.70	60.50	57.52
1977	17	–	84.40	78.48	73.46	62.18
1978	18	–	–	88.70	79.60	71.70
1979	19	–	–	95.32	82.86	75.20
1980	20	–	–	–	87.00	80.34
1982	22	–	–	–	–	83.54
1983	23	–	–	–	–	82.92
1984	24	–	–	–	–	82.56

(α_0) and height of release (H_0). In the majority of throwers the last two parameters are approximately identical. But an increase in the path of application of effort allows a considerable increase in release speed and consequently in the distance of the throw.[14]

The correlation between velocity of release and distance of the throw is shown in Table 2 below, where height and angle of release are constant.[16] In hammer throwing, unlike other forms of throwing, it is possible to increase the path of the hammer in the turns. According to research conducted by Soviet authors, an increase of the radius of turn by 26cm, at the expense of a certain amount of bending of the hip joint and inclination of the trunk, gives the athlete the possibility of increasing the length of the path by 6.50m, in a four-turns throw.[14] Logically the increase in the path gives the thrower the opportunity to impart a bigger release speed to the hammer.

In hammer throwing we have to remember that in each turn there are moments in which it is possible to actively influence the speed of the hammer, and other moments in which it is not possible to accelerate the implement. We refer to the double-support phases and to the single-support phases respectively.

Therefore it is important to increase the path of the hammer (radius of turn), but it is also imperative to prolong the phases when the hammer can be accelerated and to reduce the phases when the hammer decelerates. In other words, the acceleration of the hammer depends on the trajectory described by the hammer (space) and on the period of time during which we can actively influence the speed of the hammer ('active' space). However, we should not disregard the fact that in hammer throwing the acceleration is closely related to an exact distribution of the rotatory speed, which must reach its maximum value at the instant of release.[12] We want to point out the correlation existing between the precise distribution of speed and fluency of the turns. From the technical point of view this fluency is obtained through uninterrupted successive landing–turning actions of the right foot. From the proprioceptive point of view, the fluent throw is obtained by the natural sense for the rhythm from the athlete, which has to be encouraged and strengthened, both with beginners and with experienced throwers, using specific exercises (different changes of rhythm, turning with or without the hammer, throws at various intensities, etc).

In order to conclude on the rhythmic–dynamic aspect of the contemporary technique of hammer throwing, we want to point out the importance, especially for experienced athletes of international level, of starting with a quite high speed. The starting speed, however, should not upset the acceleration through the turns nor should it cause technical mistakes. Therefore it is a matter of optimizing individual abilities which will dictate the number of turns the thrower performs across the circle.

Because the acceleration must be carefully controlled and because it is difficult to perform the first turn on the ball of the left foot, those throwers who use the three turns technique start faster than the four turns exponents. For both techniques during the turns one should develop about 80–85 per cent of the speed of release.[18]

Table 2

Height of release, $H_0 = 2.0$m	Angle of release, $\alpha_0 = 44°$							
Velocity of release, V_0 (m/sec)	19	20	21	22	23	24	25	26
DISTANCE THROWN (METRES)	38.73	42.71	46.90	51.29	55.87	60.06	65.65	70.84

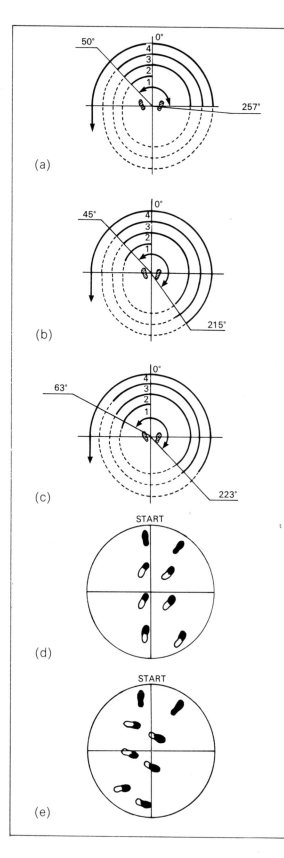

(a)

(b)

(c)

(d)

(e)

Fig 1 Samozvetov's classification: 1 late lift, late landing of right foot; 2 late lift, early landing of right foot (Sedykh); 3 early lift, late landing of right foot (Rudenkov); 4 early lift, early landing of right foot (Bondarchuk). The diagrams show acceleration paths and the degrees represent averages for all turns. (Note: concentric circles are shown for simplicity; in fact when viewed from above the hammerhead traces a spiral path.) (a) Rudenkov (b) Bondarchuk (c) Sedykh (d) Bondarchuk's footwork (e) Sedykh's footwork

Now we proceed to analyse how the need to prolong the double-support phases and to reduce the single-support phases has been put into practice.

The classification of the throwing techniques elaborated by Samozvetov is effective since it expresses the double- and single-support phases in azimuthal angles*; nevertheless it has to be updated because it considers the late lifting–early landing technique as not very popular and not very effective. But at present this method is popular and applied by almost all the top-level hammer throwers. In Fig 1 the technical variations according to Samozvetov's classification and the graphs corresponding to throwers of each group are shown.[15,6,20]

We have said that the acceleration of the hammer is related to its duration and direction. It depends on the passage from the double- to the single-support phase, and on the landing of the right foot at the end of the single-support phase.

The extension of the double-support phases logically finds its first application on the entry into the first turn.

While in the past the thrower shifted from the double- to the single-support phase after the low point of the hammer's orbit had passed in front of the right foot or, at most, approximately between the two feet, at present many of the top-level throwers enter into the first turn after the low point of the plane of rotation of the hammer has passed a point considerably moved to the left. The feet are turned about 90° to the left as the right foot lifts.

Only hammer throwers with excellent qualities of speed, timing and strength can utilize this system of entry with modified low point and delayed lifting. On the other hand, the present top throwers are better prepared with speed, coordination and strength, and we can assume that a greater

*Azimuthal angles are those observed from an overhead view of the hammer thrower – H.P.

240

Fig 2 Side view of the path of the hammerhead

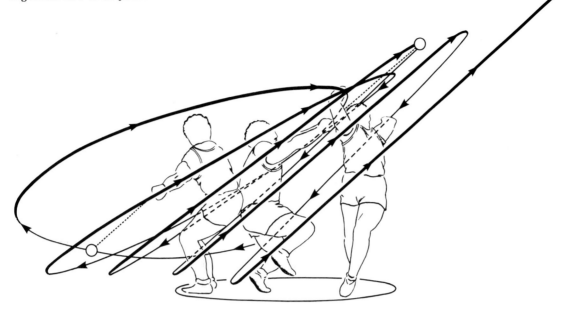

number of specialists should be able to use this system. Some authors see a direct correlation between the athlete's conditioning level, which has increased during the last few years, and the extension of the double-support phases.[5]

Another part of the technique of the hammer throw, the phase which precedes the entry into the first turn (ie the preliminary swings), has also experienced a transformation.

At present the orbit described by the hammerhead, especially that of the last swing, is flatter than in the past and this is also true, in certain cases, for the trajectory of the hammer during the first turn. As a rule of thumb, on the entry into the first turn (when both feet have turned 90 degrees) the hammerhead should be located at shoulder height or slightly lower. This depends on several factors, among them the starting position and the technique used for the swings. Another 'rule' suggests that the lighter the thrower, the more parallel the hammer should be on entry.[4]

The reasons for a flatter plane of the hammer path result from the wide radius already on the swings; and from the need to join in the most fluent way possible the plane of the orbit of the last swing with that of the first turn. The rotatory speed is improved with flat orbits as is the stability-balance of the turning system (thrower and hammer). The motivation for this change (displacement of the low point more to the left – delayed lifting – flat orbits) lies in the desire to bring, without forcing, the system thrower and hammer on to the common axis of rotation, which is ideally located vertically over the left foot (during the single-support phase), without any distortion of the circular trajectory of the hammer which were characteristics of the previous techniques (example: bending of the right arm).

The older techniques with low point on the right – early lifting – swings on steeply inclined orbits and held on the right side of the thrower usually resulted in a shortening of the radius, problems with the unstable balance of the whole system and a loss of rotatory speed.

However, it should be remembered that the starting plane of rotation described by the hammer will undergo a progressive modification in the course of the throwing action across the circle, so that during the final effort the hammer will be thrown at an optimum angle of release.

If we assume a constant height of release, the optimal angle of release increases as the speed increases.[16]

Release height, $H_0 = 2.0$m

Release speed, V_0(m/sec)	20	22	24	26
Optimum release angle, ($^\circ$)	43.6	43.9	44.05	44.2

In hammer throwing ($V_0 = 20$ to 26m/sec) the optimal angle of release should be taken about 44 degrees. In Fig 2 an actual example of progressive and correct steepening of the orbit is shown. It is traced from film of Yuri Sedykh's winning throw at the Montreal Olympics in 1976.

One could question if it is really necessary to keep both feet on the ground for such a long period of time. The answer is partially negative. The right foot should be lifted from the ground at the moment of the coincidence between the shoulder and hip axis, since to continue in the double-support phase now is meaningless as the thrower can no longer influence the hammer.

The risk of technical mistakes, in order to advance the hammer during the single-support phase, actually exists.

However, the objection to a late lifting of the right foot because it can result in a tendency to pull the left hip away from the axis of rotation with subsequent overturning and landing with too much of the bodyweight centred over the right foot, doesn't justify exclusion of this technical innovation, but it suggests an individualized approach, based on an estimate of benefits and drawbacks.

Nevertheless some advantage can still be gained by remaining on the double-support phase, even after the coincidence of the shoulder and hip axes, since this allows the use of the inertial forces developed by the hammer during the double-support phase.

The light pressing movement of the right foot is directed so as to continue the rotation of the left foot and it facilitates the uninterrupted sliding from the heel to the outer rim of the left foot and the passage of bodyweight on the left leg.

The conscious use of the inertial forces of the hammer, during the single-support phase, is another element of the contemporary technique of hammer throwing.[1]

During the single-support phase the hammer is the dominant element in the system thrower and implement.[2]

The thrower does not perform active movements with the legs and hips until the high point of the hammer path. On the other hand, the right leg starting from its lift-off moves actively until its landing. In the past we believed that the left leg and the pelvis played the main role in this phase. But the left leg and the pelvis cannot be active, being highly loaded isometrically by the bodyweight and inertial forces. It is impossible to in-

crease the velocity of the axis of the pelvis in relation to the velocity of the hammer during the single support phase, since that would require active or isotonic work of the muscles.[19] Therefore during this phase of the throwing action the role of greater activity is played by the right leg.

In order that the right leg can land and again accelerate the hammer, it is necessary to act on the heel of the supporting leg, to bring the corresponding knee forward and downward, beyond the point of support, and to obtain an ideal placement of the left foot and left hip at the end of the single-support phase. The active lowering on the left leg (or 'collapsing') should take place slightly before the landing of the right foot.[4] An early lowering reduces the tone of the trunk muscles and doesn't allow control of the hammer's movement, due to the lowering of the whole centre of gravity.[17] Furthermore it causes a withdrawal of the pelvis at the instant of landing. Advantages of correct lowering include absorption of centrifugal force, maintainance of the whole system on the rotation axis and an early landing of the right foot.

This technique needs systematic training, by 'dry' turns and by flexibility drills for the ankles. Lack of flexibility at the ankle joint results in a 'rigidity' of the left leg which causes the centre of gravity to fall on the right leg at the instant of landing. As we have already said, the right leg must be very active in reducing the single support phase.

According to Bondarchuk the right leg is the most important element in the contemporary hammer throw.[1]

There are different possibilities for reducing the time of the single-support phase. However, two are recognized and utilized in practice. One way is to keep the free leg very close to the supporting leg during the single-support phase, in a way similar to a figure skater as he keeps his arms close to his body.

It should also be remembered that the right knee, in order to prepare the right foot for an early landing, rises slightly from turn to turn, until it reaches approximately pelvis height. This action, besides preparing the right leg and right hip for an early landing also helps the trunk to counterbalance the centrifugal force.

In teaching and in the training of advanced athletes it is necessary to pay more attention to the active landing of the right foot instead of the lifting of the right knee.[9]

A second way to reduce the time in the single-support phase is to advance the landing of the right foot, before the thrower has his back completely to the intended direction of the throw. The shoulder and pelvis axes and the imaginary line connecting both feet no longer fall in the frontal plane. In other words, the 360-degree spin is not completed since the right foot is placed on the ground earlier, approximately inside a zone between 220 and 270 degrees, and in this way the thrower is able to accelerate the hammer at the very beginning of the double-support phase, without shortening the radius.

Thus the moving ahead of the hammer, which in the past was understood as an energetic torque between the shoulder and pelvis axis (that caused a significant bending of the 'isosceles triangle' – Sciukievic 1969 – represented by the shoulder axis, the arms and the hammerhead), at present is performed with the whole body, not just the arms.

THE FUNDAMENTAL ELEMENTS OF TECHNIQUE AND THE INDIVIDUAL VARIANTS

The technical foundation should take into account the fundamental elements of technique (ie those traits that really represent the 'framework' of the throwing action and that are generally applicable) and respect the characteristics of each single athlete, so that an individualized technique can be built.

Too often we as coaches have made the mistake of forcing all our athletes to throw in the same manner. The justification for this approach lies in taking the 'ideal' technical model from the style of renowned champions. In the majority of cases such a system only sets limits on natural motor expression.

Biomechanical research in the throwing events has confirmed the statement that a single way to throw an implement as far as possible (from a physical point of view we would say to reach the highest speed of release with optimal angle and release height) does not exist because of the great number of individual factors. The individual should only be moulded to those few elements which, because of their biomechanical and dynamic characteristics, appear to be basic and not capable of being set aside.

If, for instance, we refer to the Soviet 'school' of hammer throwing, it is easily demonstrated that while on the one hand every Russian thrower accomplishes certain fundamental elements of technique, on the other hand no two athletes throw in the same identical manner. In other words, in our opinion, the Soviet school is the school of basics and also of variants.

So as an example, in shot putting the movement can be performed in the orthodox straight-line shift (O'Brien) or in the rotatory method (Baryshnikov). Similarly, an identical speed of release can be obtained in different ways: either with the predominant use of the legs (Feuerbach) or with the predominant use of the trunk muscles (Beyer).[7] An analogy exists in discus throwing. There are two possibilities for creating the rotatory momentum at the beginning of the action: either through the action of the right leg (W. Schmidt) or through the trunk, supported by the fling of the left arm (Savinkova).

Techniques in the throwing events are based on movements that are not natural; in fact we build something which is extraneous to the usual motor experience of the individual. But in order that these necessary movements can be interpreted best it is necessary that they are modified by the thrower's motor-sensory system.

In other words, each athlete 'translates' according to his motor code the objective data represented by the fundamental elements of technique. We want to emphasize that one style is not better than another, but that one or another style becomes the best only when applied to the right athlete.

Consequently in teaching we must act according to the basic mechanics and dynamics and at the same time leave ample space to the personal interpretation of these basics. To disregard this hampers the complete evolution of the athlete toward high-level performances. Moreover, in this way it is possible to avoid unnecessary waste of time in learning microscopic details.

The important thing is that the underlying structure of the throwing action is consolidated; the remainder should be left to the sensibility of the individual.

We should also point out that sometimes technical details which could appear personal interpretations of the technique in reality are slight modifications made in order to correct a tendency for error. It is a contrivance which helps the athlete to perform the movement better. In other words, the individual variants play the double role of exploiting the personal interpretation of technique and of avoiding the tendency (different from individual to individual, in different parts of the throwing action) to make technical mistakes. These two roles unite in the main goal, which is doing what is right for the fundamental technical structure.

Therefore the problem is to discern the fundamental elements of hammer throwing technique, and to examine some of the possible individual interpretations relating to the different parts of the technique itself.

Since we have already discussed the basic dynamic elements (rhythm; acceleration; fluency) the following concentrates on the basic mechanical elements of the hammer throw.

The three most important elements are: the rotation axis, the radius and the feet/leg work. Faults in these elements compromise the result of the throw.

The correct advancing–turning movement around the axis presupposes that the axis itself is vertical.[8] This position needs an upright position of the head, and the hips are fixed to the spine ie they are pushed forward by tensing the gluteal muscles.

An exception can appear in the first turn (eg Sedykh) where one aims more for the radius of rotation. Otherwise, the vertical position of the rotation axis should not be upset by excessive bending movements. This is closely related to the shifting of bodyweight in the double- and single-support phases, since it leads to the displacing–advancing movement of the rotation axis, caused by pressure exerted with the right foot from the double- to the single-support phases and related to balance on the axis, in the single-support phases. As a rule of thumb, during the double-support phases the bodyweight should be equally distributed over the two feet, and then goes slightly to the left; during the single-support phase it is completely over the left foot. On landing bodyweight is slightly on the right foot.

If the athlete shifts his centre of gravity too much to the left during the double-support phase this will render him 'unarmed' against the centrifugal force and he will lose his rotatory balance. Similar consequences result from too much bodyweight on the right foot when landing.

In the course of the throwing action, as centrifugal force increases and the trajectory of the hammer steepens, the distribution of bodyweight tends to lean more and more to the left at the instant of the right foot landing. The balancing of centrifugal and centripetal force demands this.

We have discussed the rotation radius. Now we would just add that the position of the shoulders (forward relaxed) definitely contributes to the steady increase of the radius.

The upper body (shoulders, arms) should not interfere in the rotation. Forces developed by the whole body are applied to the hammer with the arms, which are the transmission and not the engine. The modern throwing technique (late lift – early landing) has greatly increased the active role of the right foot. The position of early landing in which both feet are pointed toward about 270°, demands that the thrower performs a prolonged turning action on the right ball (about 180°), certainly longer than the 'old' techniques. The landing on the ball is another fundamental feature of the right foot's role.

The action of the left foot demands the passage on the heel during the double-support phase, and on the outside rim of the foot and then on the inside edge of the ball during the single-support phase. This action has the double function of allowing the advancement of the rotation axis and of 'protecting' the thrower from the centrifugal force.

Both legs should remain bent until the release. During the single-support phase the left leg drops, while the right foot passes close to the left leg. The landing is determined by the flexion of the left leg and advancement through the action of the left ankle, by a slight opening of the angle between the right thigh and leg, and by the action of the right ankle to the landing.

During the double-support phase (at the coincidence of the axis of the pelvis with the axis of the shoulders) the feet have to turn to the left by a full 90° in each turn. The left leg should never completely straighten and the overall action of the feet should be fluent and 'noiseless' (ie no striking against the ground).

The individual technical variants always have advantages and disadvantages. So, for instance, the landing of the right foot on the heel (Dmitrienko, Tamm) certainly helps to 'fix' the hips in relation to the axis of rotation, but on the other hand is extremely difficult to learn and master. If the detail really helps the athlete to dominate the fundamental element (in this case the maintainance of the rotation axis) and the thrower has the capacity for learning it, one can proceed with or at least try to insert this variant into the general technical scheme.

Under this circumstance, the variant has the function of helping the fundamental element of technique.

Another example is that concerning the performance of the preliminary swings. There are two variants: the first with an active leading of the hammer through a circular movement of the trunk (rotation of the shoulder axis to the right) with reduced shifting of the hips; the second variant is characterized by greater opposing movements of the hips on the opposite side to the direction of the hammerhead and by the absence of any rotation of the shoulders to the right (Sedykh).[17] But then there are some athletes (Litvinov) who utilize both movements: rotation of the shoulders and wide shifts of the hips. Again, both variants present positive and negative aspects, but these are always relative to the capacities and sensibilities of the individual.

With the first variant, the rotation of the shoulder axis to the right allows the athlete to 'take contact' with the implement at the high point of its trajectory and permits the production of acceleration of the hammer during the descent, thanks to the shifting of the centre of gravity of the thrower from the right to the left foot. Nevertheless this system has the disadvantage that the bodyweight is displaced from one leg to the other. This can be a complication for some athletes, which is better avoided.

With the second variant, the problems of instability of the system thrower and hammer are avoided, but on the other hand it can happen that the athlete loses the contact with the hammer, tends to bring the implement to the left through a 'dragging' movement and doesn't succeed in moving correctly on the rotation axis, as a consequence. What's important is that the main element, in this case the placement of the hammerhead on a trajectory which permits the best transition possible from the second swing to the entry into the first turn, is accomplished in its aims.

The methods can differ, but should always be reasoned on the level of ability, capacity for assimilation and tendency to certain mistakes of each individual thrower.

Another example of a variant could be that concerning the position of the head through the whole throwing action. The importance of keeping the head upright and thence of avoiding a low chin or an exaggerated leading of the head, relative to the other bodyparts, into the action, must be emphasized. It is true that the head tends naturally to lead the movements of the body. Nevertheless good hammer throwing technique demands that this does not happen. The reason is that the 'dragging' of the head to the left involves the left shoulder in the same movement (thus causing a distortion of the triangle and the unbalancing of the system to the right) which must be avoided.

Furthermore, in order to keep the axis of rotation 'fixed' (the Russians call it 'statuesque pose') the shoulders and hips axes should remain on the same transversal plane.

A lowered position of the head favours the 'breaking' of the rotation axis at shoulder level, or even at the hip level. Nevertheless we think that training aimed at stabilizing the position of the head with the eyes focussed on the hammerhead in superfluous. In fact in practice we notice that hammer throwers either look at the hammerhead (eg Sedykh, Fig 3) or they look at the sky (eg Tamm, Fig 4) or they keep their heads very high, backward.

The important thing is that the head is not lowered and that it doesn't lead the movement too much, relative to the other bodyparts, with a typical 'chin on the left shoulder' position.

An individual approach can also be seen in the choice of the number of turns (three or four). This should be based on the evaluation of the physical capacities of the thrower (speed - coordination) but above all on his rhythmic-dynamic capacities.

Objective data which can give the coach clearer guidance on whether to change the number of turns from three or four does not exist. It is worth mentioning that, in our experience, the question concerning the number of turns is always about the introduction of the fourth turn and never about reducing from four to three.

Very often the introduction of the fourth turn is used by the idle thrower to solve technical and acceleration problems, through one more turn.[12] This hypothesis can be confirmed by statistical

Fig 3 Head positions: Sedykh focusses on the hammerhead

Fig 4 Head positions: Tamm focusses on the sky

data which indicate a small number of hammer throwers who begin their careers with four turns and a large number who pass from three to four turns.

We agree with the idea that the improvement of performances as a consequence of perfecting the movements that are repeated turn after turn should be pursued, rather than an increase in the number of turns. It is wrong to think that it is only possible to increase the rotation speed by increasing the space of acceleration of the hammer, by means of the addition of the fourth turn.[3]

In practice, first of all we have to evaluate how far it is possible to exploit the thrower's speed, which doesn't depend on the number of turns but on a rational rhythm developed across the circle. In this sense, the passage to four turns should not be considered as the solution of the rhythmical and accelerative problems, which are fundamentals in hammer throwing.[12]

As a consequence, the four-turn technique can only be recommended to those athletes who despite good rhythmical acceleration are not able to develop their maximal rotatory speed at the end of the third turn, and to those throwers who are short and light.

ANALYSIS OF THROWING SEQUENCES

Personally I agree with those experts who maintain that when looking at sequences one should not be too critical when analyzing them (considering the event as a succession of still positions). One certainly misses the rhythm of the throw and the overall view of the throwing technique, but on the other hand they do represent a precious visual aid for confirming the theoretical points treated in the previous pages. They also allow me to widen certain technical traits and to complete this chapter on the hammer throw. Therefore I shall avoid a pedantic analysis of each frame and rather give an overall opinion. I suggest that at first one should look at each sequence frame by frame and then look at them from the first to the last frame from a synthetical view, and also to compare certain positions of one sequence with the same of another sequence.

Yuri Sedykh (USSR) (Fig 5)
Hammer specialists watching Sedykh throwing at the Montreal Olympics in 1976 were conscious that a new era was beginning for the hammer throw. On each turn Sedykh turned 90 degrees to

the left and his early landing (250–270 degrees) was something no other hammer thrower in Montreal did. Even if this new technical approach was not as striking as was the Fosbury flop, it had, in my opinion, an analogous influence on the subsequent improvement in performances. By observing this sequence as a whole I would emphasize: the natural compensating opposition against the pull of the hammer (frames 12–17 and 21 - beginning of the double-support phase; frames 15–19 and 23 - end of the double-support phase); the progressive lowering of the centre of gravity during the single-support phase (frames 14–18 and 22), always performed with perfect balance, wide radius and knees together.

Sedykh is an athlete with a very subtle motor sensibility as the position of the head reveals (frames 17 and 21; 18 and 22; 19 and 23); his eyes always focussed on the hammerhead ensure a maximum radius and that the hammer is never dragged but follows its own circular orbit. Of particular importance is the activity of the right foot in its milling action, which because of the early landing turns for about 180 degrees (example: frames 15, 16, 17).

The three athletes shown in these sequences perform the preliminary swings in three different ways. Unlike Litvinov, Sedykh does not turn his shoulders to the right in the first swing, but there is a noticeable shifting of the hips (frames 5 vs 9). The change in the plane of rotation of the hammerhead (1 to 5) is due to the fact that Sedykh, during the second swing, brings the hammer more to the left with the arms almost straight (5) and then the elbows are higher (6–7) than in the first swing. The entry into the first turn (10–12) has always been a point of discussion because Sedykh performs it in a somewhat personalized way. During the last few years he has changed it by reducing his so-typical forward lean of the trunk and by shifting the low point somewhat back to the right. However, without oversimplifying this subject, I can argue that Sedykh's lean to the right (frames 11–12) (but without any drag of the left shoulder into the turn or pulling of the left hip away from the axis of rotation) is a natural consequence the extent of which is due to several factors. They are: the athlete's weight; the specific nature of Sedykh's technique; the radius of the hammer's rotation; and the fact that, because at this stage the hammer is accelerated by the displacement (leading) of the

hips and by the arms and trunk muscles (the legs are not much involved in providing energy to the hammer), the athlete has to control carefully the balance of the system thrower and hammer, avoiding too much bodyweight on the left foot which will prevent the exploitation of the inertial forces of the hammer and render him 'unarmed' against the centrifugal force.

In other words, because according to Newton's second law, during the first turn it is the hammer which makes the thrower turn and not the contrary, greater control on the hammer is therefore required at this stage. However, frame 12 is a crucial pose: even if at present, Sedykh's low point is slightly on the right (compared to its position a few years ago) the hammerhead, after 90 degrees of rotation of the feet still has a full 90 degrees of rising arc; furthermore the two feet on the ground after 90 degrees of rotation (frame 12) and the characteristic 220–270-degree position of the feet on landing (15, 19, 23) is something that, before Sedykh, was almost unknown.

Smoothness, wonderful rhythm and the ability to allow the hammer to follow its own path during the whole throw are the best overall characteristics of Sedykh's throwing style.

Zdzislaw Kwasny (Poland) (Fig 6)

Judging from this sequence, nobody could guess that this effort has been measured at 80.18m. This is a typical example where we can only deduce that, in spite of some technical deficiencies, Kwasny has exceeded the 80m barrier due to a correct accelerative rhythm and especially to a very powerful delivery, both of which can be seen in the frames.

The shifting of the hips from one foot to the other is noticeable in frames 1 and 6, and the rotation of the shoulders to the right (relative to the feet which are located approximately at the middle of the back edge of the circle) is evident (1 and 8). The movement is very wide and properly controlled. Width and control appear to be the dominant features of Kwasny's swings and entry into the first turn.

From the widest rotation of the shoulders to the right (frame 7) Kwasny begins the turn by bring-

Fig 5 (*Overleaf*) Yuri Sedykh (USSR)
Fig 6 Zdzislaw Kwasny (Pol) throwing 80.18m in the 1983 European Cup

247

Fig 5

Fig 5

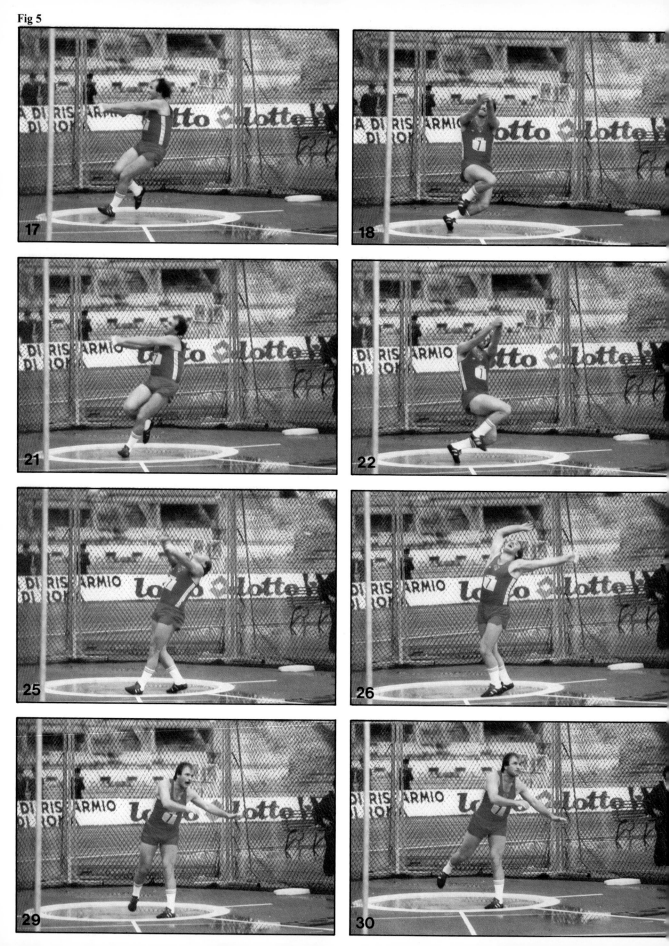

Fig 6

Fig 6

ing the centre of gravity to the left, and at this moment the arms and hammer are in a perfectly horizontal position.

The entry into the first turn (frames 8 to 11) is the most convincing phase of Kwasny's technique. The hammerhead follows a very wide path and it is properly under control, until the moment when the hammerhead is roughly between the two feet (11). But starting from the next frame (12) Kwasny begins to make some quite obvious mistakes.

The exaggerated lifting of the hammer (and of the right leg) (frames 12 to 13) has a negative effect on the speed of rotation of the hammer and furthermore causes difficulties in the movement of the system thrower and hammer around the vertical axis of rotation. However, Kwasny manages the second part of the single-support phase a little better, so that owing to a relatively reduced speed on the hammer he manages the turn in a quite satisfactory manner. But with the second turn things change. The overall sensation is that smoothness disappears: Kwasny 'fights' against the hammer. The action is much more 'forced', drags and jerks are now evident. In 16 Kwasny leans back more than necessary. In 17 we notice that the hammer is flatter (in 22 it is flatter still, ie the high point is going forward), but it is still too high to allow him a satisfactory advancement and landing.

Frames 18 and 19 show us a leading and landing technique that the new generation of Soviet hammer throwers had obliged us to forget. The torque between the shoulder and hip axes (19) is very evident (60 degrees?). The entry into the third turn is performed with a completely straightened left leg, the leading on the hammer begins here (note the shoulders and hips axes).

I consider Kwasny as a great compensator. One would expect a falling to the right when landing, as a consequence of the straight left leg, but this doesn't happen owing to a good action of the left leg (which bends) during the single-support phase (frames 22 and 23) and to a greater activity of the right leg, which compensates for the previous mistake. From a comparison of the single-support phases of the second and third turn (17 and 22) it appears that the hips are better positioned in the third turn, thanks to a better position of the hammer and of the right knee. Nevertheless the arms are bent and shoulders contracted (22 and 23).

Notice the short distance covered by the hammer and the large movement of the hips in 22 to 23.

Relatively speaking, in Kwasny's technique the final effort together with the initial phase are the best performed phases and certainly those which made most significant contribution to the distance thrown. In frame 24 Kwasny lands slightly earlier than in the other turns, keeping the hammer quite far back. During the real delivery (25 to 28) where he brings the bodyweight to the left, until it is equally distributed over the two feet, we are presented with a powerful working of the back muscles, while the radius is still wide and the left leg bent. Until the hammerhead reaches the low point, the left leg remains bent (26) and then it straightens (27). The hammer is released with an elastic fling of the arms, upward (27 and 28) and outward (29 and 30).

Certainly Kwasny represents an exception among the modern hammer throwers of world level, either because he throws with a three-turns technique, or because he belongs, according to Samozvetov's classification, to the 'late lift – late landing' group and finally because the orbit of his hammer doesn't progressively steepen from turn to turn, but remains about the same during the three turns, even if the high and low points go slightly to the left. Referring to the latter, it appears to be erratic and forced, but in order to give a more definitive opinion, more information should be gathered. The overall impression is that we are faced with a particularly powerful athlete, able to greatly improve his technique thanks to his good natural motor sensibility.

Sergei Litvinov (USSR) (Fig 7)
Litvinov, the former world record holder, is shown here throwing 81.52m in the 1983 European Cup.

PRELIMINARY SWINGS (frames 1 to 10) In my opinion this sequence gives an excellent model of the technique of the swings. The swings' tasks (progressive placement of the hammerhead on the most suitable orbit for the entry into the first turn; progressive acceleration in order to reach an optimal starting speed) are accomplished in an exemplary way and are clearly visible.

The first swing (1 to 5) is performed with great looseness, the hammer's orbit is more vertical than the second swing and kept on the right of the athlete. This is due to the position of the trunk (turned to the right) and of the elbows (1 and 9) and to the action of the arms. In frame 2 Litvinov nearly leans the right arm on the right side of the trunk (2 and 10).

At the beginning of the second swing the hammer is brought more to the left (6–7) and kept higher to the right, without the torque of the trunk which had characterized the first swing (2–3 vs 10–11). As a consequence the orbit is flatter and the low point is more to the left (4 vs 13), allowing a fluent blending of the orbits of the swings with that of the first turn. The flatter orbit of the second swing is due to the greater velocity imparted to the hammer; to the wider shifting of the centre of gravity; and to the position of the trunk and of the elbows. The fists are over the head (1 and 9), so the action is centred on the vertical axis of the thrower.

It is well-known that the countering of the hips is associated with a leading (accelerative) aspect. This is clearly noticeable in the sequence. During the first swing the countering-leading (hammer to the left, bodyweight on the right foot – frame 1; hammer to the right, bodyweight on the left foot – frame 5) is rather reduced, whilst in the second swing, performed more vigorously, it is more accentuated. Litvinov lifts and shifts his right foot to the right (6–8) (he widens his supporting base), thus creating the conditions for a wider lateral shifting and leading. The greater energy so provided to the hammer is clearly visible by comparing frames 1 and 9.

ENTRY INTO THE FIRST TURN (11 to 14) This phase is mostly the mechanical and dynamic consequence of the preliminary swings. At this stage by exploiting the inertial forces of the hammerhead it is the *hammer* which makes the *thrower* turn. Therefore it is a matter of allowing these forces to act.

This entry shows an exceptional control on the hammer (11 to 16); this is of course more difficult for a toe-heel exponent.

Frame 14 shows the level of ability of this champion: the prolonged double-support phase requires a very active right-leg action (15–16) so that the whole body, except the arms, is ahead of the hammer. Notice that in frame 15 Litvinov is on the outside edge of his left foot instead of on the ball. He will be on the outside edge of the left foot, as almost all top hammer throwers are, on all his turns. This will enable him to maintain greater stability while being in a very unstable position and to use the left heel-knee forward-downward action later (before landing).

THE TURNS (15 to 27) Notice that in the first turn, and partially in the second, Litvinov lands with the outside edge of the right foot (16 and 20) then while milling he works on the ball and, just before lifting off, on the inside edge of the ball. This aspect, and the particular position of the head on entering (14 and 15) are personal and should not be taught to youngsters.

Litvinov ends his first turn (frame 16) on the balls of the feet with the whole body in advance of the arms and hammer, pointing at about 270 degrees. The double-support phase is incredibly long (16 to 18), but immediately active. From the instant of landing to the low point position he increases speed on the hammer through the activity of the legs, back muscles (especially those on the left side) aided by the descent of the hammer. These forces are transmitted to the hammer through the arms.

Notice the difference between frames 18 and 19. While the first is the image of applying force to the hammer, the latter shows that the thrower undergoes the 'phase of inertia', and in the next frame (20) he is ready to apply force to the implement again.

On entry into the third turn, the low point is slightly more to the left (21) than the previous turns and the athlete has the ability to keep his left leg bent. Perfect balance and relaxed upper body are a must during the single-support phase. Litvinov shows this is frame 22. The new Soviet trend in hammer throwing can be seen in 23 and 24: these two key poses would have been considered as great mistakes only a few years ago. Notice the quick landing, the long arms, the position of the hammer on the right of the circle, the position of the hips and feet in 23 and the position of the hammer to the left in 24.

During the last turn we are presented with the greatest counteraction of the centrifugal force. But the progressive lowering of the centre of gravity (19–20, 22–23, 25–26) is always performed without

Fig 7 (*Overleaf*) Sergei Litvinov (USSR) throwing 81.52m in the 1983 European Cup for a new UK Allcomers record. Litvinov was 1983 world champion

Fig 7

Fig 7

any trouble for a perfect balance and very wide radius. Also notice that the left leg is never completely straightened (from frame 11 to the delivery) and the right foot always lands on the ball.

THE FINAL EFFORT (27 to 32) As soon as he lands Litvinov begins to bring the bodyweight to the left (notice the left foot and trunk-head position in 27) and with the movement of the hammer to the low point, gradually shifts it to the right side (frame 28) until it is equally distributed on both legs (29). We are convinced that until the low point the final effort should not differ from the previous turns (24 vs 28); in other words the delivery should be a continuation of the preceding turns and not some new movement. During the final effort, centrifugal force can reach values of 350-400kgms, while the weight of the thrower is usually around 100kg. Therefore it is the centrifugal force which commands and so it must be obeyed. Thus one could say that the less we notice the delivery, the better it has been performed. The sequence of different body segments during the delivery follows a pattern of back muscles and arms, then by acting on the active pivot (the left leg) the athlete should straighten his legs (29 to 31) until the release of the hammer.

References

1	A Bondarchuk	in *Ljogkaja Atletika* no. 1/1977 and no. 6/1980.
2	A Bondarchuk	'Sedykh's hammer technique' in *Circle* no. 13 March 1980.
3	A Bondarchuk	'Three or four turns?' in *Modern Athlete and Coach* (Australia), vol 17, no. 1 January 1979.
4	A Bondarchuk and O Dmitrusenko	Seminar on hammer throwing for specialized coaches, Tirrenia, Italy, 11–13 November 1982.
5	A Bondarchuk	'The hammer throw' from *A Trainer's Manual for Track and Field*, ed. LS Chomenkow Fizkulturi i sport, Moscow 1982 (courtesy of Kevin McGill).
6	J Dapena	Biomechanical analysis for hammer throw, USOC/The Athletics Congress, USA, July 1982.
7	O Grigalka	'Shot put techniques' in *Modern Athlete and Coach*, vol 19, no. 4 October 1981.
8	S Harmaty	'Hammer throw' in *Az Atletika Oktatasa*, Budapest 1975.
9	C Johnson	'Training drills for hammer throwers' in *Circle* no. 13 March 1980.
10	E Klement	'Some thoughts on the hammer throw' (report on a coaching tour) by Merv Kemp, Australia 1983.
11	R Palmarin	'General thoughts about Igor Nikulin's evolution' in *Circle* no. 17 March 1981.
12	R Palmarin	'Opinioni sulla tecnica a tre o quattro giri nel lancio del martello' ('Opinions on the three- or four-turns techniques in hammer throwing') in *Atletica Studi* (Italy) no. 3/1982.
13	J Pedemonte	'Advice to novice hammer throwers' in *Modern Athlete and Coach*, vol 19, no. 1 January 1982.
14	V Petrov	'Hammer throw technique and drills' in *Modern Athlete and Coach*, vol 20, no. 1 January 1982.
15	A Samozvetov	'The acceleration of hammer' in *The Throws* ed. Fred Wilt, Tafnews press, USA, 1974.
16	G Schmolinsky	*Track and Field in East Germany*, Sportverlag Berlin 1978.
17	E Sciukievic and M Krivonosov	'The hammer throw', Fizkulturi i sport, Moscow 1969.
18	P Tschiene	Seminar for track throwing coaches, Tirrenia, Italy, April 1977.
19	P Tschiene	'Technical reasons of progress in hammer throw' in *Hammer Notes* (USA), no. 6/1982.
20	J Goldhammer	in *Hammer Notes* (USA), no. 7/1983.

14 JAVELIN
Dr Jeno Koltai

Hungary
(Acknowledgements to the Magyar Atlétikai Szövetség)

Jenö Koltai took his physical education diploma in 1941 at the Hungarian College for Physical Education in Budapest and taught there from 1943 to his retirement in 1978. He was the head of the track and field department for most of that time and in 1975 he was appointed professor and first rector of the College, which was raised to the rank of university. In 1981 the title of doctor honoris causa was conferred on him.

His scientific research has included performance improvement through training and the translation of exercise theory into practice.

He worked as a coach from 1941 to 1972 while continuing his academic work. From 1949 he became more and more involved in the preparation of the Hungarian throwers and by the end of the fifties he was chief coach of the throwing group. He directed the 1968 Olympic preparation of the national track and field team. Among his personal pupils the most successful ones who won medals and placings in the Olympic Games and European Championships were Angela Ránkiné Németh, Gergely Kulcsár, Zsigmond Nagy and Miklós Németh.

Dr Jenö Koltai lectures extensively at home and abroad and he has published widely in journals, books and textbooks in the field of physical education and sport. His book *The Teaching of the Track and Field Events* was published in Italy in 1978. Jenö has been writer and consultant in four educational films, two of which received awards at the International Sports Film Festival.

As a coach and physical educator he took part continuously in the professional work of the Hungarian National Athletic Federation (MASZ), in the advanced education of the coaches as well as in their refresher courses. From 1965 to 1966 Dr Koltai was captain of MASZ and has been a member of the MASZ presidency and a member of the Hungarian Olympic Committee (MOB) since 1965. From 1973 to 1980 he was a member of the MOB presidency. He is still a member of the MOB, of the ITFCA presidency, of the Hungarian Physical Education and Sport Scientific Council (TSTT) and an honorary member in the MASZ presidency.

Dr Koltai's text was translated by Tibor Hortobágyi and Etele Kovacs, and the drawings were done by József Tihanyi.

Javelin

GENERAL INTRODUCTION

The javelin is thrown by both male and female throwers at all ages, ie Adolescents, Juniors and Seniors. Furthermore, it is one of the events in decathlon and heptathlon.

Details of the design of the runway and landing sector and exact specifications of the javelins used are given in the *IAAF Handbook*. Within the limitations of the rules, and by applying all relevant theory and practice, the thrower's aim is to throw the javelin as far as possible.

This is achieved by:

a) gaining optimum momentum in the run-up;
b) using this momentum to attain a proper release position which is preceded by an uninterrupted transition from running to the actual throw;
c) recruiting muscles used in an effective order to produce the highest release speed, to initiate the throw at an optimum angle and to provide a proper alignment and trajectory of the javelin.

Of all the throwing events in track and field, it is in the javelin throw where the highest initial release velocity is attained. That is why the javelin throw requires the fastest explosive movement from extensive stretching and pretension of the muscles (Fig 1). Moreover, it is also important to recruit and coordinate the muscles used in the correct order.

Observations of the physiques of javelin throwers reveal that short, medium and very tall athletes compete with success. Keeping in mind that long arms as well as wide shoulders positively influence the distance thrown, tall physique is suggested. Because the javelin is relatively light there is no point in building up very heavy athletes with extra bodyweight. Naturally, large body mass is not a drawback if the athlete is very fast, explosive and powerful and his flexibility is above average.

TECHNICAL DESCRIPTION

Technical execution of the javelin throw is a smooth movement from the first strides of the run-up to the final position after release. Only for the sake of the analysis is this continuous movement broken down into the following parts:

a) run-up and production of the momentum;
b) transition from run-up to throw – 'Arch-forming';
c) acceleration of the implement and release;
d) movements after release and reverse.

Run-up and Production of Momentum

Through the approach the athlete aims to gain optimum momentum which helps to attain a favourable throwing position and to make use of the strength of the muscles acting through to the release.

STARTING POSITION AT THE BEGINNING OF THE RUN-UP, HANDHOLD AND THE JAVELIN-CARRY
Before starting the run-up the athlete should assume a position to which he is accustomed, ie with one or other foot forward, or feet side-by-side.

The javelin should be grasped with the fingers of the throwing arm which can produce the strongest grip. The grip should be firm providing a stable support for the implement but not rigid, so that the javelin can be easily controlled; the fingers must not slip away from the grip during release.

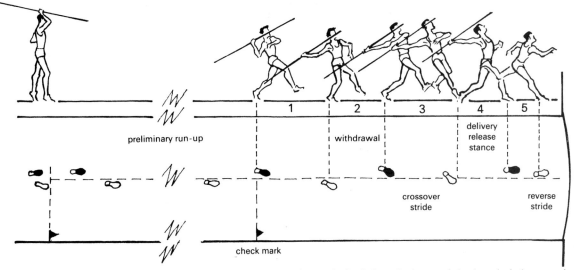

Fig 1 Definition of the various phases in javelin throwing

The javelin grip used by most good throwers is the one in which the middle finger coils around the body of the javelin and rests against the upper edge of the binding, opposite the thumb, which also rests against the 'ledge' of the binding. The index finger holds the body of the javelin on the side of the middle finger. The function of the index finger is to support and help the work of the middle finger and thumb during the release action.

The method of carrying the javelin also depends on individual preference. The carry during the run-up should not hinder the athlete's movements and it should provide the thrower with a position from which he is able to easily assume the final release position. It is suggested that the javelin should be carried with the hand positioned close to the temple and the tip of the javelin held and directed forward–inward.

The approach is actually divided into two parts: from the start of the run-up to the withdrawal of the javelin; and from the start of the withdrawal to the moment when the thrower arrives in the throwing position.

FIRST PART OF THE RUN-UP The athlete starts with some easy strides, generally from a standing position; speed of running should increase gradually. While running, the throwing arm and the javelin, in a form described above, should move to and fro according to the rhythm and pattern of the running. The other arm should also move freely and in harmony with the running action. (Note: in

the technical description a right-handed thrower is taken as the example.)

The total run-up length of top-level throwers is about 30m. Length and speed of the run-up vary from athlete to athlete. However, a run-up should be chosen which makes it possible for the thrower to attain the optimum velocity required for the release easily without any unnecessary expenditure of energy, so that the greatest possible throwing effort can be generated.

The conclusion is that the run-up should be suited to the entire throwing activity since too fast an approach will result in a hurried and inadequate release. On the other hand, too slow a run-up will not achieve the momentum needed for the release. Throwers at all levels of physical condition or technical skill should strive for the optimal run-up speed and length in competitions.

Length and speed of run-up are both influenced by external factors, such as surface of the track, its traction (or lack of it), direction of wind etc, and by the level of physical readiness of the athlete. Generally, most athletes use a check mark at the very beginning of the run-up. A run-up adjusted for prevailing conditions can be established during warm-up, which is started at this check

Fig 2 (*Overleaf*) Ferenc Paragi (Hungary), European record holder. The execution of the throw is excellent with legs, trunk and shoulders. But the tip of the javelin (frames 6–11) rises too high which is caused by the premature wrist extension as well as inaccurate directing of the javelin with the fingers

Fig 3 Tom Petranoff (USA), world record holder and silver medallist in the 1983 world championships

Fig 2

7

8

9

13

14

15

5

6

10

11

12

16

17

18

Fig 3

mark; the run-up should be characterized by its accuracy, rhythm, optimum speed and ease.

The first part of the run-up (started at the first check mark and finished at a second check mark where the implement is withdrawn) is covered usually in 12 strides and, rarely, 14 strides.

THE SECOND PART OF THE RUN-UP This is the preparation for the throw, the withdrawal of the javelin (see Fig 1). When this second check mark is reached by the left foot the body position is unaltered. As the right leg moves forward the trunk is rotated to the right and the right shoulder points to the rear. This gradual rotation of the trunk to the right is needed to withdraw the javelin continuously backward in a straight line. The javelin in the right hand should be pushed back over the shoulder very smoothly. (See Fig 4, frames 1–10.) The rotation of the trunk to the right results in a rotation to the right of the pelvic axis. That is why it is difficult to drive the right leg forward. Therefore, this right-leg stride should be maintained forcefully according to the normal running pattern; landing with this leg so that the foot is still pointing forward.

Withdrawal of the right shoulder is followed by a backward lean of the trunk. Attempts should be made to pass over the right leg with minimum braking effect. Following this, and while the left leg is pushed forward, the right arm and hand continue to move gradually backward. A proper withdrawal occurs if the javelin remains as close to the face as possible. (See Fig 4, frames 1 to 13 and Fig 5, frames 9 and 10.)

Contact of the left foot with the ground is in front of the line drawn vertically from the centre of gravity. That is why the momentum of the run-up slows down a little. Preparation for a favourable release position is preceded by this braking action. The slight backward lean of the trunk provides a gradual transition from the run-up to the throw. While performing this stride the supporting leg and the trunk are in line. The thrower must not allow the hips to be much ahead of the trunk. (See Fig 3, frame 11 and Fig 5, frame 10.)

When the athlete is rolling over the left leg, the line of the shoulders is rotated 90 degrees to the right. The pelvic axis should turn to the right as much as the torsion from the shoulder area demands; do not load the right leg with too much

extra work. (See Fig 3, frame 12; Fig 4, frame 10; and Fig 5, frame 11.)

The momentum gained in the approach will push the athlete forward and over the left leg. The next stride, ie the right-leg stride and the contact with the ground, is one of the most important stages of the javelin throw. The javelin, held in the right hand with palm upwards, should be level with the right shoulder, elbow and wrist relaxed. The shaft of the javelin almost touches the lower arm, its tip is located close to the face (the athlete just 'smells' the tip); the tip is pointing in the direction of the throw and is slightly higher than the level of the left shoulder. The left arm is almost extended and positioned ahead of the left side of the body so that the elbow, and to a small degree the palm too, are facing the direction of throw. This alignment of the arms helps the athlete to assume a position in which the left shoulder is situated higher than the right shoulder and the upper body leans backward.

As the right leg comes to the ground the athlete should strive to leave his body behind. Immediately after passing over the left leg, the forward movement of the right leg should be accelerated. This fast action coincides with the movement of the right shoulder and the javelin. The backward lean is due to this 'double' action.

This right-leg stride is a sort of bound – a slightly higher step than the others in order that more time can be devoted to the backward lean of the trunk. Care should be taken not to make this bounding stride too high. A very high right stride results in a longer airborne period and a greater shock on landing, excessively loading this leg. Moreover, the athlete must not 'jump' off from the left leg too early since this will result in a similar fault. The left leg should move forward with a slight delay, and this movement should be initiated with a powerful thrust at the ankle. (See Fig 2, frame 2 and Fig 4, frame 17.)

This thrusting forward of the body mass during this phase of the throw is of great significance since sufficient momentum will be produced to allow the thrower to pass over his right foot into the final release position.

As the right leg is swung forward, the shoulders are lined up pointing to the direction of the throw. Among top-level javelin throwers it will be observed that the torso is turned so that the upper left side of the shoulder can be seen from the direction of throw (Fig 2, frame 2 and Fig 3, frames 12 and 13). This over-rotated position has both advantages and disadvantages. If this rotation is exaggerated 'by the arm holding the javelin the muscles around the shoulders and the chest become stretched too early and the accurate direction of release of the javelin is hindered. On the other hand, this position has the advantage that the strong trunk musculature can be more effectively used. Rotation of the shoulder-line is accompanied by a rotation of the pelvic axis. To contribute to an effective release the rotation of the pelvic axis must not be greater than is needed to rotate the shoulders into the direction of the throw. (See Fig 2, frame 2 and Fig 3, frames 12 and 13.)

During the throw athletes usually look forward. There is no reason for turning the head back; it has no positive effect on the movement.

Upon landing the right leg should be ahead of the line drawn vertically from the centre of gravity to the ground; also the knee and the foot should be kept within the plane of the run-up. Speaking figuratively the thrower should 'cross' this plane by pushing his leg to the left. (In this context we can speak about a 'cross-step' pattern.) Once the right-leg stride is accomplished as described above, several demands could be met such as:

a) a firm balance is attained during this stride;
b) correct landing of the left leg becomes easier;
c) incorrect lateral movements of the centre of gravity during the throwing position and the release can be avoided;
d) while accelerating the javelin during the release, and by exerting force through the javelin, the centre of mass moves towards the plant (left) foot, and this braced front leg forms a firm support over which the body can pass.

It is very difficult to avoid the situation where the right foot turns to the right on landing, due to the rotation of the pelvis. The athlete should try, however, to restrict this rotation of the right foot to no more than 40–50 degrees. The right foot contacts the ground first with the outer edge of the sole and heel and then the total weight of the body presses the whole surface down to the ground. (See Fig 2, frames 5 and 6; Fig 3, frame 14; Fig 4, frames 21 to 23; and Fig 5, frames 13 and 14.)

When the right foot contacts the ground the trunk and the axis of the right leg form one line.

The right foot contacting the ground initiates the flow of momentum from the run-up in to the release movement. Before going into details of the release let us sum up the basic characteristics of the second part of the run-up, the withdrawal of the javelin, and the preparatory strides into the throwing position:

1 The majority of throwers who reach the check mark with the left foot use the so-called 'five-stride rhythm' $(3+1+1)$. Out of these five strides three are needed for the preparation, one stride is referred to as the throwing step and the final stride is the post-release step or reverse. There are, however, athletes who prefer a seven-stride rhythm; five strides seem to be sufficient to prepare and carry out the throw accurately, but the seven-stride rhythm makes it even easier and more flexible.

2 In this phase two basic tasks should be carried out:
a) use of momentum gained during run-up to properly pre-stretch the muscles contributing to the release in order to increase the force available for the acceleration of the javelin;
b) a favourable position should be assumed by the throwing arm to create the 'arch of the body' and to carry out the throw correctly.

Optimal momentum built up during the approach does not adversely affect the power of the release (as compared to throws done from a standing position), indeed a positive effect can even be observed.

It is commonly misunderstood that the body of the thrower should further accelerate during the preparatory strides if executed correctly. Logic contradicts this. This last preparatory stride (starting from the left leg and finishing on the right leg) differs from a normal running stride since the shoulder is turned away, the line of the hips is also rotated, the thrower is airborne, all of which points to a braking action. An even greater decrease in speed of the upper body or the right arm should occur, since this is the position in which the trunk of the thrower leans back the most with the landing leg far ahead of the vertical line of the centre of gravity. (See Fig 2, frames 5 and 6; Fig 3, frames 13 and 14; Fig 4, frames 17 to 21; and Fig 5, frames 12 and 13.)

Fig 4 (*Overleaf*) Maria Colon (Cuba), 1980 Olympic champion

Fig 4

Fig 4

17

18

21

22

25

26

29

30

19

20

23

24

27

28

31

32

Upon landing on the right foot, the athlete settles into a low position so that a smooth progression of the upper body and strike with the left foot on the ground can be achieved. Elevation of the trunk during this phase is an extremely bad fault since the hips will be high and this higher position hinders left-foot planting. An even greater load should be born by the left foot, which checks the total momentum of the run-up. During this settling movement on the right leg the thrower should drive forward with his right leg and rotate it in the direction of the throw. The heel of the right foot lifts up and rotates outwards. Pushing forward and at the same time rotating the right knee to the front causes the pelvis to begin its rotation to the left. (See Fig 2, frames 6 to 9; Fig 3, frames 15 and 16; Fig 4, frames 23 to 27; and Fig 5, frames 14 and 15.)

As soon as the athlete's momentum carries him over the right foot, the left foot should be planted on the ground as quickly as possible. The character of this striking movement is flat. As the left leg is planted the left arm is halfway to 'opening' entirely. The pectoral muscles on the left side are stretched so that the chest can rotate into the direction of the throw easily. Direction of motion of the left arm is to the left backward–downward. A similar series of movements is induced in response to this movement on the right side by means of which the right arm is helped to remain back with the javelin, and the back of the body is forced toward the midline. (See Fig 2, frames 11 and 12; Fig 3, frames 16 and 17; Fig 4, frames 27 and 28; and Fig 5, frames 15 and 16.)

Fig 6 (*Below*) Drawings from film of Paragi's world record throw of 96.72m in 1980

The movement of the right shoulder, ie continuously driving forward, makes it necessary to raise the javelin above the shoulder. This movement should be carried out so that the throwing arm remains as far to the rear as possible. When the line of the shoulders rotates to the left an unavoidable flexion occurs at the elbow joint; despite this, efforts should be made to delay the arm strike. This is necessary because a proper arch-position of the trunk can be produced only when the throwing arm and shoulders are kept well back. If the implement is voluntarily accelerated too early, the pre-tension produced in the muscles is lost.

The left foot should be placed on the ground about 30cm to the left of the line of the direction of the throw. The foot plant is executed in such a way that the heel and full sole of the shoe are pressed firmly to the ground and immediately start the braking action. First the ankle then the knee joint contribute to this action. Due to momentum, there will be a slight bend in the left knee and the muscles of the thigh will be eccentrically contracted owing to the very heavy load. This slight knee bend in response to the braking action cannot be considered as a mistake since soon after this the stretched position will help the further functioning of the muscles. Too much knee bend should, however, be avoided.

In practice it is obvious that those athletes whose left legs are extremely bent use a run-up exceeding their physical abilities. The ideal plant of the left foot occurs when the foot is pressed to the ground from a position in which it is turned slightly inwards, and the full support is attained by pressing first down the inner edge of the heel and sole followed by the full sole touching down. The ankle in this position can help to check the momentum; the action of the force through the

1 2 3 4

knee joint will be much more effective. The plant with the left foot carried out in this way results in a firm stance. It should, however, be noted that this sort of foot plant is very difficult to achieve since the rotation of the trunk should be started before this planting process takes place; moreover this rotation with the trunk to the left causes the left foot itself to move to the left. Execution of this movement is even more difficult for those whose anatomy does not favour it, ie if the left foot is turned outward naturally.

Proper execution of the left-foot plant is very important **since during the release it is the only factor contributing to the vertical component of the throw**. Further acceleration of the system body and javelin can be gained through the active work of the left foot. The braking effect of the left leg is very important in the acceleration of the right hip.

The length of the throwing stride should be calculated in relation to the individual's anatomical structure and to the individual's physical capacity. If the throwing stride is elongated – the thrower 'sits down' – the throw cannot be adequately supported by the left foot, and the athlete will not be able in the release phase to 'attack' the implement. On the other hand, too short a throwing stride results in an 'empty' left-foot action, ie no active support is provided by the left foot during the release. In practice it is observed that the length of the throwing stride among top-level javelin throwers is about 1.4–1.5m.

A complete **arched position** of the body is attained if the right foot, during the very last moments of its action on the ground, continues to assist the driving action of the right hip, and if the left foot blocks the left hip, which also produces

acceleration on the right side. The 'opening action' with the left arm should be continued, producing stretch in the pectoral muscles and contributing to the formation of the arched position. The opening out of the left arm, the pulling action of the left shoulder toward the left and downwards and the rotation of the trunk to the left all cause the right shoulder to turn rapidly towards the direction of throw. (See Fig 2, frames 12 and 13; Fig 3, frames 17 and 18; Fig 4, frames 28 and 29; and Fig 5, frames 16 and 17.)

As the left foot contacts the ground the head should be facing the direction of the throw, playing an important role in the formation of the arch. The chin should be high and the face turned upward. This alignment is a natural outcome of the arched position, resulting from the speedy drive forward of the chest. The shortening of the muscles on the back of the neck also positively influences this action. There is a coordinated action of the muscles involved since in the arched position the neck muscles pull back the head, the trapezius muscles pull back the shoulders, the rhomboid and scapula muscles pull together the scapuli and the deep back muscles extend the upper part of the spine. This muscular activity helps to stretch muscles located around the chest and the abdominal area, and provides a firm base for the action of those muscles concerned with the release.

At the end of the arching movement an even greater stretching is created around the right

Fig 5 (*Overleaf*) Sofia Sakarafa (Greece) set a world record of 74.20m in 1982

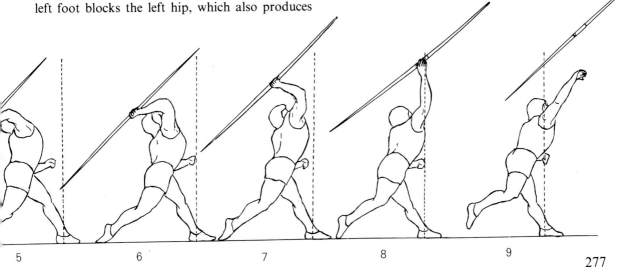

5   6   7   8   9

Fig 5

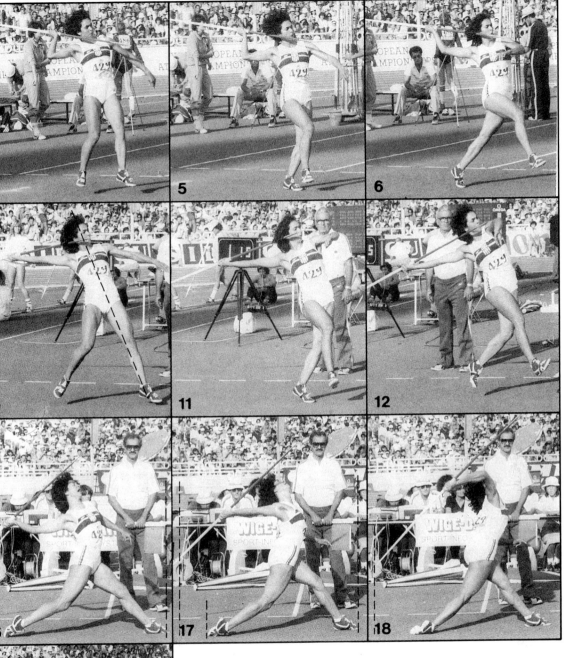

shoulder. This desired tension around the shoulder area is induced only when the right side of the body is driven very forcefully forward and the throwing arm stays well back. (See Fig 2, frame 14 and Fig 6, frame 4.)

The throwing arm should remain to the rear so that the right shoulder, the upper arm and the elbow move upward–forward, while the hand holding the javelin remains even further back and at a lower position. The greater the tension produced, the more the hand is left behind and the faster the throwing shoulder moves in the direction of throw. During this phase of the throw a very bad fault is to allow the throwing hand to bend backwards so that the tip of the javelin rises and moves away from the face. This should be avoided at all costs.

Acceleration of the Javelin and its Release

As soon as the greatest amount of tension is attained in the arched position, the actual throw (the release or arm strike) takes place. In this arched position the left leg finally executes a powerful lifting action. The large muscles of the leg, ie primarily the quadriceps femoris and the extensors of the ankle, recoil with an enormous quantity of potential energy resulting from the stretch given to them from absorbing the run-up momentum. The arm holding the javelin is still held well back to the rear, and in the shoulder and the elbow joints an overextended state occurs. Due to the anatomical structure of the shoulder joint, the arm cannot be fully extended in this position. It depends on the individual capabilities as to the degree the athlete is able to 'leave his arm behind' while throwing. However, the striking arm should not flex voluntarily too early since it will break the arching position and negatively influence the final acceleration of the implement.

From this it is not concluded that the arm strike (ie the throwing action with the arm) should be achieved with an entirely extended arm. Path analysis of the javelin shows that the implement in the effective phase of release moves along a very slightly curved path which is almost a straight line (Fig 7).

From a biomechanical point of view, the release with an extended arm can also be considered detrimental since the elbow extensors and the wrist flexors cannot be involved in the release, to accelerate the implement.

The release is initiated from the point when the 'arching position' of the body is the greatest so that all the muscles (ie the abdominal, chest, shoulder, upper-arm muscles) can act effectively. An active role is taken in the release by the left leg which lifts the body with its final extension. The muscles around the waist and the hips and the deep back muscles brake the forward movement of the waist and the hips, and the momentum of these body parts is transferred through the right arm to accelerate the implement.

Correct execution in this phase causes the javelin to move above the level of the throwing shoulder and in line with the path of the centre of gravity of the implement. The angle between the long axis of the javelin and the horizontal is about 30–35 degrees. The tip of the javelin should not be elevated over the head. It is important that the driving force on the javelin is along its long axis. The javelin can at any time deviate from the line; most frequently, even among top-level throwers, the direction of this deviation is upward and slightly to the right (Fig 2, frames 11 to 15). Elevation of the point of the javelin is due to the fact that the wrist of the thrower extends too soon, often as early as the beginning of the arch forming or just before the arm strike. This mistake can result in hitting the ground with the tail of the javelin. The wrist should be extended only when the hand is in line with the elbow, ie just after the initiation of the release.

To evaluate the production of the throwing force let us first look at the action of the left leg. The role it plays in the transformation of energy, braking the left hip and elevating the body have already been discussed. The left leg, however, has one more very important function: it must be a very firm supporting system, and the effectiveness of the throw is highly dependent on its activity.

Body parts over the hip, which is braked by the left leg, due to their inertia move further forward in the direction of the throw. The right side of the body moves at a higher speed compared to the left side of the body, since the right side is farther from the axis of rotation. This progression over the left leg is regulated by the hip musculature. It can be speeded up by the hip flexors and the abdominal muscles, while by contracting the hip extensors and the back muscles it can be decelerated. Since the acceleration of the javelin is carried out by the throwing arm, it will produce a braking

280

KEY
○ body's centre of gravity
--- the vertical line passes
   through the supporting leg,
   and the line to the right
   connects the supporting foot
   to the throwing fingers
×...× path of the javelin's
   centre of gravity during
   the release action and in
   the beginning of flight

Fig 7 (*Below*) Drawing of the release action, made from film of Fig 5
Fig 8 (*Right*) The moment of release in a throw by Paragi. The drawing was made from film which was shot from above and to the rear

KEY
◄----◄ path of the throwing shoulder
○——○ path of the throwing elbow
×...× path of the javelin's centre of gravity
●   ● path of the throwing fingers

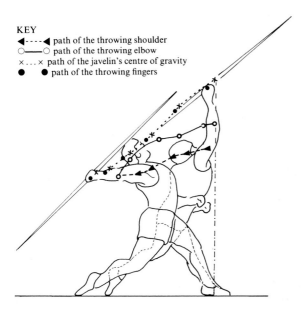

effect in the shoulder joint, and around the shoulder and chest area so that the effective function of the hip flexors and that of the abdominal muscles is required. (See Fig 2, frames 13 to 17; Fig 6, frames 3 to 8; and Fig 7.)

To create a position in which the left leg can function effectively, the behaviour of the legs and the body parts during the last strides should be such that while planting the centre of mass passes over the supporting left foot. The centre of gravity may deviate slightly to the left with little detriment to the throwing action, but deviation to the right is considered to be a mistake. The more to the right the planting takes place, the less effective is the left leg. The support with the left leg becomes labile and the momentum of the body is insufficient to supply the absent support. Similarly, if the support is too low, ie the planting knee is over-bent or it is not in contact with the ground, the muscles contributing to the acceleration of the javelin cannot have adequate support from the body parts.

The force production of the thrower is effective if: (a) the path of the centre of gravity of the thrower passes close to the vertical plane through the plant foot (Fig 8), and (b) the line drawn from

the left foot up to the right shoulder is almost vertical (Fig 8).

The acceleration of the javelin above the level of the hips is a very economic process, since first the bigger and slower muscles are recruited then smaller and smaller and faster and faster muscles with higher contraction speeds are switched on to give further thrust to the javelin. After recruiting the hip and the abdominal muscles, the order of muscle recruitment is: pectoral muscles, anterior part of the deltoids; triceps brachii, flexors of the palm and fingers.

This process has two other characteristics. Firstly, force produced in a joint will enhance subsequent force-production of other joints by lengthening them before contraction. Secondly, body parts moving in the direction of the throw while accelerating the implement provide the basis for

Fig 9 (*Overleaf*) Tina Lillak (Finland), world record holder at 74.76m and 1983 world champion. The left leg blocks too much too soon. A striking feature of her throwing is the way she lands on the right foot in the throwing position – the right foot and knee are turned outwards
Fig 10 Petra Felke (GDR) was 9th in the 1983 world championships. Felke set a new GDR record of 74.72m in 1984

Fig 9

Fig 10

Fig 10

the next part of the body being involved in this process. Though body parts functioning sooner will slow down, their speed even by the end of the release will remain high enough not to hinder the action of body parts with higher speed (Fig 7).

Thus the longest possible path of acceleration is provided, and the segment speeds amount to a total release speed of about 30m/s, a speed that cannot be produced by one muscle-group alone.

In addition to the acceleration of the javelin the athlete should direct it along a path which assures its optimum flight. In order to realise this:

a) the javelin should follow a straight line;
b) an effective acceleration of the hand should occur mainly in the final stage of the release, which should be exerted along the long axis of the implement;
c) the long axis of the javelin at the beginning of its flight should have a favourable attitude angle, and the long axis of the javelin should be along the line of the path of the centre of gravity.

There is a vertical component in the acceleration of the javelin. This vertical component is provided by the thrower applying a coordinated series of movements to the javelin. Gradual elevation of the right shoulder can be achieved by partly lowering the left shoulder and partly by the lifting work of the left leg. All this serves as a basis for the further vertical lift of the elbow and the wrist joints. (See Fig 2, frames 11 to 14 and Fig 7.)

When the javelin is accelerated by the upper arm the elbow also speeds up and lifts upward; actually it will be above the level of the hand holding the javelin. To this movement of the upper arm is added the action of the muscles around the elbow joint, which are stretched to their extreme. Finally the lower arm and the hand get involved in the movement which is similar to the lash of a whip. The lower arm speeds up the hand to a very high velocity over quite a long distance. This distance can be lengthened if the elbow is extended, ie attempts are made to keep it extended. The radius from the shoulder to the wrist, if it is increased gradually, will help the athlete to release the javelin along a straight line and a higher javelin speed will result from this same angular velocity. (See Fig 2, frames 13 to 17 and Fig 7.)

The final strike of the javelin during the release is carried out by the fingers. Although the palm is

moving at a considerable velocity, these small but very fast muscles are able to give some more momentum to the javelin. The striking, pushing activity done by the fingers is a very important part of the throw. The fingers coming off the javelin incorrectly in this last phase can produce a detrimental impulse on the javelin causing rotation around the short axis of the javelin, and too great a rotation can be produced around the long axis of the javelin. Correct execution of the action of the fingers occurs if the fingers are in a pronated position after the release. The palm should face upward then forward and, after releasing the javelin, outward.

Final acceleration of the javelin by the fingers and the hand is a phase of great significance in a successful throw. If the direction or application of force is not in line with the long axis of the javelin, the javelin will bend to an extent depending on the out-of-line forces and on the flexibility of the implement. Results can be quite easily observed when the javelin is airborne. Precession originates from the spin of the javelin around its long axis and from flexion of the implement. Flight of a spinning oscillating javelin is inefficient since the surface of the javelin is increased which results in greater air-drag.

Rotation around the short axis is also obviously detrimental. Several mistakes can be committed during the throw, the most significant of which have already been discussed, ie deviation of the point of the javelin from the line of the throw. This analysis can be made by viewing the thrower from the side. Essential mistakes can also be observed by seeing the throw from above and behind. Some top-level javelin throwers in preparing for the release rotate their trunk far to the right, almost with their backs to the direction of throw, and the musculature of the throwing arm, extended over the line of the shoulders, is stretched earlier than needed. Using stones, pebbles or small balls in training, this extreme backward movement of the throwing arm is quite natural during the

Fig 11 (*Overleaf*) Dainis Kula (USSR) throwing 91.88m in the 1983 GB v USSR match. Kula was 1980 Olympic champion. The unusual feature of Kula's throwing is the placing of his left foot in the delivery position. This foot swings away to the left in what is called 'in the bucket' in discus throwing. However, Kula compensates by leaning to the right and into the direction of the throw as his arm strikes. Purists would condemn this technique

Fig 11

1

2

5

6

9

10

13

14

3

4

7

8

11

12

15

16

Fig 11

17

18

21

22

25

26

29

30

19

20

23

24

27

28

31

32

so-called 'impulse step' when the right leg is swung forcefully forward.

More and more frequently javelin throwers are using small balls of varying weights during training. However, ball-throwing exercises do have a negative influence on the execution of the throw and detrimental movement patterns are learned. A ball or a pebble can be thrown farther by: flexing the wrist backward; initiating the throw from an over-extended position with respect to the throwing arm; and directing the ball or the pebble along a curved path. When throwing a ball or a small ball no problems emerge from the above but when throwing a javelin they are detrimental.

When directing the javelin on a curved path, the chance of throwing the javelin incorrectly increases mainly in the last phase of the throw when the fingers give their momentum to the implement. The distance between the centre of gravity of the latest javelins and the fingers (first, second and third) accelerating it almost equals the length of the grip, ie 13–15cm. The centre of gravity of the javelin is located in the part of the grip closest to the tip of the javelin but it is grasped by the fingers at the opposite end of the grip. That is why a rotation around the short axis and a flexion of the javelin occur when the final force on the javelin does not pass through the centre of gravity of the javelin (or the javelin directed along a curved path is not released at the moment when its long axis is in line with the tangent of the curve). Those who use a curved release have unreliable competition performances. In competition when the psychological stimulus is high and the thrower mobilizes energy reserves for an all-out effort, it is very difficult for the athlete to meet all the technical demands on him.

To improve technical execution, and to ensure consistent throwing, the following remarks should be made:

Extreme rotation of the trunk is acceptable but a curved path of the javelin in the acceleration phase of the arm-and-hand should be eliminated. It can be done only if the hand holding the javelin, the shoulder and the elbow joints are properly relaxed by the end of the 'impulse step'. In this case the distance between right shoulder and the body of the javelin should not exceed 5–12cm; the javelin is located very close to the face. This will have the result that:
(a) the musculature around the shoulder joint

should be sufficiently stretched during 'arch-forming';
(b) the point of the javelin should not go too much to the side of the head of the thrower so that the path along the straight line will be easier. Thus rotation of the javelin around the long axis can be minimized at the moment when the arm strike is initiated. (See Fig 3, frame 14; Fig 4, frame 21; and Fig 5, frame 13.)

The release angle in relation to the flight characteristics of modern javelins should be discussed. In the past decade javelin manufacturers have used wind-tunnels and computer techniques to reveal optimal flexibility, external shape and mass distribution characteristics of javelins. Implement specifications have to be kept in mind in the course of experimentation using javelins of varying designs. Scientific research has produced the almost perfect javelin as far as its aerodynamic profile is concerned. Improvement of javelin design plays a crucial role in the development of javelin performances. The latest types of javelin with very light points and improved flight characteristics in the second part of flight do not land flat but have an elongated landing phase. The longest throws have an angle of release of about 35 degrees. According to experience, measurements and computations, a headwind needs a smaller angle of release while a following wind requires a greater angle of release.

There are prerequisites for a favourable flight as follows:

a) When released, the javelin should meet the air with the smallest possible area since air-drag is a function of the square of speed. The long axis of the javelin therefore should be in line with the direction of force-development;
b) the angle of release depends on the speed of release and the direction of wind. It should be 30–35 degrees;
c) the less vibration, the farther the javelin flies;
d) it is suggested that less energy should be used for the so-called 'stabilizing' rotation around the long axis.

Post-release Position
Completing his release, the athlete whose right leg is slipping behind him should do a long step forward to brake the momentum of the body. Efforts have to be made to avoid a foul throw. It is therefore suggested that the centre of gravity should be

lowered as much as possible (Fig 3, frame 22).

If there is too much momentum remaining from the throw it means that the throw was not efficient. In theory it can be shown and verified that optimal conversion of the energy gained during the run-up to the javelin's speed is made if the body after release has no more momentum. In practice, however, one can observe that even the highest-ranked throwers need a distance of 1.5–2.0m from the planting leg to the throwing line to avoid fouling the throwing line.

Technical execution of the javelin throw is composed of different types of motion and it is necessary to carry out this series of movements at the maximum possible speed. Individual characteristics have a basic determining role in technical execution. It is therefore suggested that athletes do not try to copy the techniques blindly. Individual differences are quite clearly demonstrated even among the best javelin throwers. Naturally, the basic biomechanical principles must not be overlooked, but specific individual characteristics should also be taken into consideration in building individual technique.

15 WALKS
Julian Hopkins

England
(Acknowledgements to the British Amateur Athletic Board)

Julian Hopkins first became involved in coaching in 1969 whilst still competing at national level. A visit to the Lugano Trophy final of 1970 made a big impact on his coaching ideas and ambitions. He became the British National Event Coach in 1974 and held the position until he resigned in 1984. During this period he frequently travelled abroad with Great Britain teams and was team coach at the Lugano Trophy finals from 1975 to 1983. He coached and advised many international walkers in this period, including Steve Barry who broke several British records and won the 1982 Commonwealth 30km walk title.

Julian Hopkins has written many articles for *Athletics Coach* and, in 1976, wrote the (British Amateur Athletic Board) instructional booklet *Race Walking*. Since 1980 he has been campaigning for a radical change in the race walking rules. He has lectured at the Loughborough Summer School and on other aspects of the endurance events in the BAAB Coaches' Education Programme.

Walks

It is usual in athletic circles to group race walking with the endurance events, particularly those in the 10,000 to Marathon range. Whilst this is accurate physiologically it is rather misleading, for it fails to take into consideration the greater importance technique plays in successful performance at all levels of this skill. Although race walking exhibits many features of normal walking and is derived from it, considerable modifications are required to walk at speeds as high as 15km/hr. The physical requirements are also underlined when it is realized that to cover 20km at this speed necessitates taking some 200 steps, each about 125cm long, every minute for 1hr 20mins. The essential modifications occurred naturally as walking developed into an athletic discipline. The resulting technique is the natural way to walk quickly and it was only somewhat later that a 'definition of walking' appeared. The relevant IAAF rule is given here in full for future reference:

> Walking is progression by steps so taken that unbroken contact with the ground is maintained. At each step the advancing foot of the walker must make contact with the ground before the rear foot leaves the ground. During the period of each step in which a foot is on the ground the leg must be straightened i.e. not bent at the knee, at least for one moment and, in particular, the supporting leg must be straight in the vertically upright position.

As a walker failing to comply with this definition is liable to disqualification, the development of a sound technique assumes paramount importance Not only that, but basic speed is largely a function of technique whilst endurance is favourably affected by a walking action which is biomechanically efficient. Altogether it appears best to consider a walking race as a test of 'endurance of technique' and to place the walks in a category of their own labelled technique/endurance events. (Contrast this with the running events, in which there are no restrictions on technique.)

THE BASIC BIOMECHANICS OF NORMAL WALKING

A great deal of research has been carried out on the biomechanics of normal walking. The same cannot be said of race walking. However, as the latter is derived from normal walking much can be learnt from these studies. Indeed, the available information can form a framework for the understanding of athletic walking. Firstly, a simple hypothetical model of walking is considered.

'Compass' Gait

If the legs are considered to be rigid rods only able to flex and extend at the hip joints, then during walking the legs open and close like a pair of compasses. One leg swings at a time and there is a brief period of double support when both legs touch the ground. The body's centre of gravity rises and falls in a series of arcs of a circle of radius equal to the leg length. When the swinging leg passes the supporting leg the centre of gravity is at its greatest height. This means that the body has extra potential energy. As the swinging leg moves to full stride, the centre of gravity is lowered and the potential energy converted to kinetic energy.

This interchange of energies, similar to that occurring in a simple pendulum, plays an essential

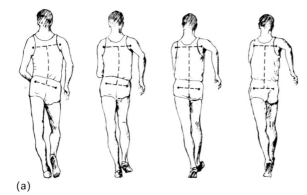

(a)

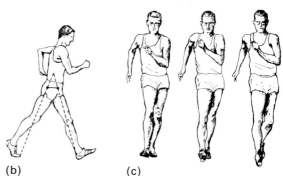

(b)   (c)

Fig 1 (a) These diagrams show the relationship between the shoulder axis and the pelvis during one step by a walker viewed from the rear. Note the decreasing lateral shift of the pelvis, pelvic tilt and spinal curvature up to the point of forward contact. (b) This shows how the pelvic rotation leads to greater step-length by increasing the effective leg-length. (c) These show the range of the arm action in the frontal plane and the placing of the feet on a straight line

role in normal walking. The conversion is not 100-per-cent efficient so the deficit has to be made good by energy from muscular action, principally functioning at the hip and ankle joints. This muscular output represents the energy cost of walking. Walking with this hypothetical gait would require a high energy output as large forces would be needed to alter the path of the centre of gravity abruptly where the arcs intersect. The 'wisdom of the body' modifies the gait to reduce the energy cost at a given speed.

Pelvic Rotation

The most significant modification is the rotation of the pelvis about the vertical axis of the body. Viewed from above, the pelvis rotates alternately to the left and to the right of the direction of travel. This has a number of effects. Firstly, the arcs described by the centre of gravity are flattened so less force is needed to alter the path of the centre of gravity. Secondly, the length of the legs is effectively increased. A given step-length can now be achieved with less hip-flexion and extension. Or, to put it another way, longer steps are possible with pelvic rotation.

Pelvic Tilt

The pelvis tilts downwards relative to the horizontal plane on the side of the swinging leg. Just be-

fore toe-off, the pelvis is suddenly lowered and, as it swings forward, gradually rises until heel-strike. This further reduces the vertical motion of the centre of gravity and lowers the energy cost of walking. Pelvic tilt forces the knee of the swinging leg to flex so the foot can clear the ground. The leg pendulum is shortened resulting in further energy-saving.

Flexion of the Supporting Leg

At heel-strike the leg is fully extended but almost immediately afterwards, starts to flex. This continues until the foot is flat on the ground. Knee flexion also reduces the vertical motion of the centre of gravity.

Plantar Flexion of the Supporting Ankle

To make the transition from double support to the swinging phase as smooth as possible, the ankle of the rear leg plantar flexes. This is a rotation of the ankle about a point near the front of the foot, as the heel is raised from the ground so that the toes move away from the lower leg. Coupled with increasing knee flexion of the supporting leg, plantar flexion further smoothes out the path of the body's centre of gravity.

Lateral Displacement of the Pelvis

In walking the centre of gravity also describes a wavy path in a horizontal plane as its position above the supporting leg alternates from one side to the other. This displacement requires a lateral shift of the pelvis. This is reduced somewhat by adduction at the hip joint and the advantageous angle between the long axes of the femur and tibia. The horizontal fluctuations of the centre of gravity are usually of about the same size as the vertical undulations.

THE BIOMECHANICS OF RACE WALKING

Race walking is in many respects a high-speed, more explosive version of normal walking. It bears the same relationship to slow walking as sprinting does to jogging. At the time, it is a more flowing rhythmical mode of progression. Having established the biomechanical elements of normal walking, it is now possible to list and explain the modifications necessary to enable walking to be carried out at far higher speeds.

1 There is no flexion of the supporting leg. This is, perhaps, the most obvious special feature of race walking. The rule requires that the supporting leg be fully extended when it is directly below the trunk. Consequently most walkers maintain full knee-extension of this leg from the instant of heel-contact to just before toe-off.

2 The degree of pelvic tilt is greatly increased. This is designed to minimize the rise of the body's centre of gravity as it passes over the fully extended supporting leg. The pelvic tilt now reaches its maximum when the swinging leg passes the supporting leg.

3 Pelvic rotation is considerably increased. This allows longer steps to be taken and further reduces the vertical motion of the centre of gravity. Step length can be as great as 125cm at 20km racing speeds, compared with less than 100cm during the fastest normal walking.,

4 A more powerful plantar flexion of the supporting ankle occurs. Increased speed indicates a greater demand for kinetic energy. In slow walking this comes from the potential energy put into the trunk by an almost vertical push from the rear foot. Obviously there is a limit to how much potential energy can be supplied in this manner. At higher speeds the necessary kinetic energy comes from the increasingly horizontal push of the rear foot via the ankle's plantar flexion. In slow walking the potential and kinetic energies of the body are almost exactly out of phase, ie when one is a maximum the other is a minimum and vice versa. This pendular interchange of energies can be as much as 65-per-cent efficient.

There is no such interchange of energies in race walking. In the latter, maximum kinetic energy occurs at the same time as maximum potential energy (as the considerable lifting of the heel in powerful plantar flexion also raises the centre of gravity). In essence the strong, predominantly horizontal, push from the stretched supporting leg is the most important feature of race-walking technique.

5 The tracks of the feet approach a single line. In normal walking the feet make two parallel tracks some centimetres apart. The majority of race walkers place their feet so that their inner borders fall along a single straight line, whilst elite walkers develop sufficient pelvic rotation to put one foot down directly in front of the other. This straight-line walking reduces the horizontal movement of the centre of gravity and thus the lateral shift of the pelvis. Attention is also paid to ensure that the foot is parallel to the direction of motion at toe-off and heel-contact. This maximizes both the effect of the drive from the rear foot and the length of the step.

6 The arm and shoulder movements are much more intense. These movements result from the rear-leg drive not acting directly through the centre of gravity. For example, right-leg drive propels the body forwards and pushes the right side of the trunk forwards and around to the left. If a walker does not use his arms, his trunk rotates alternately to the left and right of the direction of travel and the energy cost of walking rises considerably. The arm action takes up a great deal of this unwanted rotation, although it does not vanish completely from the trunk.

In marked contrast to slow walking, the arms are flexed to about a right angle throughout their swing. This reduces their moment of inertia about the shoulder joint and lowers the energy required to swing them at high frequency. As well as rotation about the trunk's vertical axis, the shoulder axis tilts downwards in the horizontal plane towards the supporting-leg side. This tilt is always opposite to that of the pelvis and appears, once again, to be an adjustment to maintain a more level path for the centre of gravity.

In summary, it can be said that the race walking technique allows the fastest speed of walking to be just about doubled (16km/hr as against 8km/hr for normal walking). The efficiency of the various mechanisms considered above is also illustrated by the vertical displacement of the centre of gravity in race walking being only 2–3cm, or about half of the value in normal walking.

Experiments reported in the scientific literature illustrate another interesting comparison. Walking at slow speeds is maintained by the consumption of chemical energy in the muscles leading to an efficiency $\left(\dfrac{\text{external work done}}{\text{energy consumption}} \right)$ of around 25 per cent. As the speed increases the efficiency increases, and this indicates that much of the work is done by the recoil of previously stretched muscles. In high-speed race walking the efficiency can be higher than 45 per cent. Similar mechanisms play an important part in the biomechanics of running, but it is a little surprising that they also play such a large part in race walking.

ANALYSIS OF RACE WALKING TECHNIQUE

In race walking the basic cyclical element is the single stride. This is the sequence of movements from heel-contact to the next heel-contact with the same foot. (It is not the same as a step, which is the sequence of movements from heel-contact to the next heel-contact with the opposite foot. Clearly step-length, as used earlier, is only half the length of a stride.)* To analyse the sequence of movements, it is necessary to sub divide the single stride into phases: rear swinging phase; front swinging phase; front supporting phase; and rear supporting phase.

An analysis will be made of the technique of the 1980 Olympic silver medallist Pyotr Potchenchuk (USSR), Fig 2. The stride considered starts in frame 2 and finishes in frame 17 and is that made by the walker's right leg.

Rear Swinging Phase (frames 2–5)
This phase starts as the rear foot leaves the ground at toe-off. It ends when the swinging foot is opposite the supporting foot, and ankle, hip, elbow and shoulder joints lie in a vertical line (frame 5).

The function of this phase is to provide recovery and relaxation for the leg muscles which have just contracted powerfully to provide the forward drive. This will allow a long forward swing of the leg. The pre-stretching of the leg muscles and strong plantar flexion of the ankle provide the energy for the forward swing. The knee flexes just sufficiently to allow the foot to swing forward low and straight.

*Note a similar problem of terminology in the long jump chapter—H.P.

At toe-off the pelvis has maximum backward rotation (frame 2). Note that throughout this sequence the degree of pelvic rotation can be gauged by noting the position of the stripes on the walker's shorts. As the leg swings forwards, the hip on that side sinks to reach its lowest position at the end of the phase (frame 5). So pelvic tilt is a maximum when pelvic rotation is at a minimum. The trunk is upright throughout this phase.

At toe-off the shoulder axis has its greatest contrarotation with respect to the pelvis. The arms have reached the highest point in their swings and the angle at the elbow is about 90 degrees. In frame 3 the arm action is reversing and shoulder-rotation decreasing. By frame 5 shoulder-rotation is a minimum and the arms have reached the lowest points of their swings with the elbow angle a little greater than 90 degrees.

Front Swinging Phase (frames 5–9)
This starts as the ankle of the swinging foot passes the ankle of the supporting foot and ends when the forward heel makes ground contact. The main task of this phase is to achieve an optimal step-length via an active forward swing of the leg.

The swinging leg has its greatest flexion at the start of the phase. In frames 5 and 6 knee flexion changes little as the thigh swings upwards just sufficiently to allow the lower leg to swing forward in a smooth natural fashion (7–9). Consequently, the foot swings straight forward in a low flat manner. The leg has just reached full extension at the instant the heel makes contact. There is no exaggerated extension of the step, for this would cause a lowering of the centre of gravity, a hard heel-contact and an unnecessary braking action. When the heel is placed down, the walker passes very briefly through a period of double support (9) as the rear foot has not yet been raised from the ground. This represents the continuous contact with the ground required by the definition of walking.

During this phase pelvic rotation increases throughout as it supports the forward-swing of the leg The hip joint on the swinging side rises from its lowest position throughout this phase. The arm on the swinging side is pulled strongly backwards and upwards, the elbow angle closing up a little by the end of the phase. The other arm swings forwards and round towards the mid-line of the trunk. By frame 9 the shoulder axis again has its greatest contrarotation with respect to the pelvis.

Front Supporting Phase (frames 10–12)

This starts with heel-contact (frame 10) and ends when the supporting leg is in the vertical position below the centre of gravity (12).

The function of this phase is to take up the body's weight, provide it with a stable support and create the correct tension in the leg muscle for the subsequent forward drive.

The heel is put down (frame 10) as softly as possible to reduce the inevitable deceleration of the body. At this instant the swinging leg becomes the supporting leg. Although it is extended, the knee is not locked as this would also tend to decelerate the body. The knee locks shortly after heel-contact which ensures that the supporting leg is completely straight in the vertical position (12) shortly after. Rolling the foot quickly onto the ground from the heel via the outer border of the foot (10–12) provides a more stable support for the bodyweight.

When heel-contact is made, pelvic rotation is at its greatest with the hip at its most advanced position (10). During this phase the hip rises to reach its highest point when the supporting leg is vertical (12). The arm action reverses again and the shoulder rotation about the body's longitudinal axis is at a maximum in frame 9 and decreases to zero at the end of the phase.

The trunk is in an upright position in 12 with the centre of gravity over the supporting leg so the body is in equilibrium. To achieve this the centre of gravity is shifted horizontally by a lateral displacement of the pelvis. This results in a lateral curvature of the spine which continues decreasingly up to shoulder level. This lateral displacement of the pelvis is kept to a minimum but it is just discernible in 12 and 13.

Rear Supporting Phase (frames 13–16)

This starts with the supporting leg vertical and ends when the rear foot leaves the ground.

The function of this phase is to produce an optimal drive to accerate the body forwards. It is the most important phase of the stride cycle, for only at this time can the walker actually accelerate his body and counteract the deceleration which must occur in the forward supporting phase.

After the vertical position has been reached, the knee joint remains fully extended as long as possible (13–15). The push-off occurs via the balls of the feet and finally the toes (15 and 16). There is a powerful plantar flexion of the ankle so that, before toe-of, the heel is raised high off the ground (16). The foot points exactly forwards through the push-off so that the effect of the forward drive is maximized.

As the rear leg drives the body forwards, the pelvis revolves strongly backwards around the body's longitudinal axis so that maximum pelvic rotation occurs at toe-off. The lateral displacement of the pelvis, and with it the lateral curvature of the spine, vanishes in this phase as the centre of gravity moves to a position directly over the mid-point between the feet. It is only during the period of acceleration that the trunk shows a small forward lean (13–15).

For comparative purposes it is interesting to look at the technique of another world-class Soviet walker, Vadim Tsvetkov, who is walking in second position in Fig 3. In comparison with Potchenchuk, the following points may be noted:

1 He shows a greater forward lean not only when his trunk is accelerating (frame 5) but also when it is decelerating (9). The forward lean of the head could be an influencing factor for, although it has only about 10 per cent of the body's weight, its great distance from the centre of gravity means that it has a considerable turning effect on the trunk.
2 The arm action is considerably higher but its range is somewhat smaller. It is the more acute angle at the elbow especially on the backswing (9) which gives the arm action its characteristics.
3 There is considerably less shoulder rotation (see 6 where it is at a maximum). It would appear that Tsvetkov's arm action absorbs more of the rotation transmitted to his upper body.

Fig 2 (*Overleaf*) 10km walk. Pyotr Potchenchuk (USSR) in action. He was 20km Olympic silver medallist in 1980
Fig 3 10km walk GB v USSR 1979. Vadim Tsvetkov (USSR) is in second place here but went on to win the race from his fellow Russians, Semyondi (No. 5) and Yevsukov (No. 3). Tsvetkov is a former holder of the world's best performance for 20km on the road
Fig 4 3000m walk. No. 1 is Roger Mills (GB), who was 3rd in the 1974 European 20km walk, and No. 2 is Steve Barry (GB) who won the Commonwealth Games 30km walk in 1982
Fig 5 Jose Marin (Spain) was 1982 European champion and 2nd in the 1983 World Championships both at 50km

Fig 2

1

2

3

7

8

9

13

14

15

4

5

6

10

11

12

16

17

18

Fig 2

19

20

21

25

26

27

31

32

33

22

23

24

28

29

30

34

35

36

Fig 3

1

2

5

6

9

10

13

14

3

4

7

8

11

12

15

16

Fig 4

3

4

7

8

11

12

15

16

Fig 4

19

20

23

24

27

28

31

32

Fig 5

4 During the rear supporting phase the leg hyper-extends, ie it goes beyond 180 degrees of extension at the knee joint. This can be seen in a number of frames (notably 5 and 8). Hyperextension occurs to a varying degree in many race walkers but is common among elite walkers (all three in this sequence, for example). It would appear to be a function of the laxity of ligaments and length of muscles at the rear of the knee joint. It is interesting to speculate that hyperextension might result in the following advantages:

a) A hyperextended supporting leg in the vertical position is effectively shorter than a leg extended to 180 degrees so helps to reduce the rise of the centre of gravity.

b) The trunk can move further ahead of the driving leg before the heel begins to rise appreciably (8). As the peak drive occurs about this point in the stride, the force is transferred more effectively to the trunk.

c) To a walking judge, hyperextension emphasizes that the walker has satisfied the criterion of straightening the supporting leg, especially in the vertical position.

The photosequence Fig 4 of British walkers Steve Barry (No. 2) and Roger Mills shows how differently two athletes may interpret a technique. The following points may be noted:

a) Their arm actions are in marked contrast, with Barry's similar to that of Tsvetkov, and Mills closer to that of Potchenchuk. Here it is the walker with the higher, more restricted action (Barry) who shows the greater range of shoulder rotation (compare Barry in frame 11 with Mills in 6). This highlights the considerable variation in arm and shoulder movements in race walking. These variations can be considered more ones of individual style than of technique.

b) Mills displays a particularly upright carriage even when his trunk is accelerating (compare Mills in frame 12 with Barry in 10). Generally, Barry has the more fluid upper-body movements.

c) Mills displays a remarkable range of ankle movement in frame 6. The considerable plantar flexion of the rear ankle allows a long step to be taken, but the dorsiflexion of the forward ankle appears excessive (compare with Barry in frame 11). It results in a locking of the forward knee before heel-contact, and the placing-down of such a rigid leg must cause unnecessary deceleration of the trunk. This contrasts markedly with Barry if the action of the latter's right leg is followed in frames 4–6. However, Mill's hyperextension of his supporting leg is so emphatic (starting in 7 and continuing to 11) that he is a very easy walker to judge for the straight-leg requirement.

The sequence (Fig 5) of Marin (Spain) illustrates an excellent arm action at the end of a 50km event held in hot conditions. It is interesting to note that this walker hyperextends his left leg (frames 1–3), but not his right leg (8–10). Such a difference in leg function, undoubtedly of anatomical origin, can cause problems for the walker. It did in fact cause a leg-straightening difficulty for this walker at one stage of his career.

THE ROLE OF CONTINUOUS CONTACT

It would be wrong to leave a discussion of race walking technique without some observations on the much-publicized problems of judging. Whilst leg straightening can be seen distinctly, continuous contact is not open to direct objective assessment as it lasts for only a fraction of the period of each step itself, only about 0.3sec. It is the photograph and the video replay which have brought about a serious dilemma for race walking. Time and time again walkers (including those regarded as the best technically) who have walked to the satisfaction of all present, have subsequently been shown to have failed to maintain continuous contact. Several studies have shown that walkers eventually fail to maintain contact at speeds greater than 13–14km/hr. (The actual speed depends on performance level and the degree of fatigue.) This implies that in events of 20km and below, there is a very high chance that a walker will not be maintaining contact throughout the race. At international level, this situation will also exist for the faster competitors during 50km events. Photographic studies at world level have shown a 20–40millisecond loss of contact (aerial phase) in a step of 300milliseconds duration. This was in a 20km event. The aerial phase lasted 20–30milliseconds during 50km walking. It should be borne in mind that a loss of contact has to be greater than about

60milliseconds before it becomes discernible to the eye.

All this evidence indicates that a loss of contact is inevitable, even with technically accomplished walkers, when today's racing speeds are achieved. (It is almost certain that this was true in the past but went unrecognized due to the lack of sufficiently good photographic techniques.) As walking speed increases (a) the absolute time of double support decreases and (b) the swinging phase becomes relatively longer than the supporting phase. Eventually, the two phases become equally long and double support vanishes.

At higher speeds, the swinging phase is longer than the supporting phase, ie there is an aerial phase in the stride. This is a perfectly natural progression. The walker does not alter his technique to achieve it nor does the onlooker detect any changes. Double support is an obvious feature of slow walking but it is not necessarily a feature of race walking – it depends on the walker's speed. It is hardly surprising that the relative length of the phases changes when racing speeds are 3 to 4 times faster than normal walking. It would be like expecting the relative length of the phases to be the same in jogging and sprinting!

In the author's opinion – one not supported by many at the time of writing – continuous contact is not a determining feature of race-walking technique and is not necessary in drawing a distinction between race walking and running. These two events each have a stride which is quite distinctive. In race walking the forward leg makes contact well in front of the centre of gravity and is fully extended from heel-contact to just before toe-off. In running ground-contact is made almost directly below the centre of gravity. The leg is considerably flexed at contact and through the 'vertical phase', and then extends to almost complete extension at toe-off. It can be argued that the straight supporting leg requirement alone provides the essential characteristics of the race walking stride. With this requirement it is not possible for the walker to flex his supporting leg under his trunk, as if compressing a spring, and then let it recoil to full extension like the runner. This is the essence of the runner's much faster mode of progression.

For too long, in the author's view, race walkers have been trying to fulfill an unrealistic criterion. Lack of contact has been regarded as a form of cheating, even if not deliberate, yet to achieve the speeds at which it occurs a walker must increase his power output throughout the race. This is the natural progression that is expected in an endurance event and a rule which effectively prevents this evolution cannot be correct for the event, and should be an urgent subject for debate by all concerned with race walking.

Index

Page numbers in *italic* refer to captions and illustrations